The Little Bastards

Jim Lindsay

Praise for

The Little Bastards

"Set in the 1950s, Lindsay's coming-of-age novel tours the physical, emotional, and, most importantly the vehicular landscapes of young narrator Sonny. Lindsay ruminates repeatedly on the fun and freedom of being a hot-rodding, blue-collar boy in the 50's, a nostalgia close to his heart. The prose is breezy, and will interest readers who lived through the era."

—Kirkus Reviews

"Jim Lindsay's coming of age story is richly evocative of the life and times of small-town kids during the 1950s. I quickly was immersed in Sonny's tale as he and his friends graduate from frantic bike rides around town while reading all about hot rods to actually working on and riding in their own, while listening all the while to the latest rock and roll music on the radio. The descriptions of the environment, the cool foggy days of western Oregon and the clubhouse hidden in blackberry thickest where the kids hang out, smoking cigarettes and listening to 45s are fabulous. Equally fascinating is the way Lindsay's narrator walks the reader through the intricacies of modifying cars and conveys the excitement of the drag races held on Otto's farm and the formalities of challenging racers. Add in the local high school girls who are just starting to appreciate these kids from the wrong side of town, and you've got the combination for a great story—and it rides beautifully."

—Readers' Favorites Book Reviews

"The quintessential coming-of-age tale of five boys in a mid-50s American small town, this is a Henry Gregor Felsen novel as might be told by J.D. Salinger. Not only is the story engaging and accurate but, thankfully for once, so is all of the hot rod and custom car terminology and action. Much like *American Graffiti* spread over five years instead of one night."

—Pat Ganahl, author and contributor

"*The Little Bastards* is a story about a group of boys growing up in the 50s. Lindsay, born in 1947 has a handle on those days. The plot is episodic. They smoke cigarettes, drink beer and drag race on public streets, all illegal activities, but their not real bad, just little bastards."

—Albert Drake, author

"This dose of nostalgia (not a good enough word) is a fun read, a visitation with a familiar past, even if not the immediate past of some of our younger trad hot rod and custom cousins. I think the protagonist in the book (is it actually Jim?) was cooler than I was (although I did wear motorcycle boots in elementary school.) It goes fast, doesn't labor over every drag race and every rise in the Levis; it moves and gets us to a point where we are able to leave the guy . . . well, you'll just have to read it and find out for yourself."

—Mark Morton, *Hop Up* magazine

Second Edition, 2014

ISBN: 1494356732
ISBN-13: 978-1494356736
Library of Congress Control Number: 2013922455

For my mother,
Genevieve

Preface

Thank you for opening this book. This novel is about growing up in the fifties. The decade didn't have a major war or hippies, but the boys and girls I have portrayed in this book were a product of the war and entered the fifties as children.

I made it all up, but it has good bones; it's the way it was. It was an era that experienced huge changes. I was there when our front door opened and two men wearing white coveralls carried in our new Motorola 21" and perched it in the middle of the living room. It was 1955 and we had a freezer and a real refrigerator and a Buick in our one-car garage.

It was exciting, and I was seeing the whole phenomenon over the handlebars of my Columbia bike with those big balloon tires that were good on gravel roads. These so-called improved roads surrounded our farm for several miles in all directions. My older brother, Bob, and his friends would take these corners sideways and drift through them in their jalopies.

Hot rod magazines were my link to the world of show cars and drag racing. I pored over these like they were important documents, not missing a word. When in Albany, a typical town of 10,000 souls, shopping with Mom or riding with Dad, I witnessed these older boys mimicking what I saw in those periodicals.

Hot rods and customs were driven by these creatures wearing bomber jackets and Elvis hair. The girls were there too, sitting close with lipstick and flirtation. They gathered at local service stations and would roar out with their pipes cackling. The police dogged them and wrote traffic tickets by the book full but couldn't slow the enthusiasm.

The fifties gradually faded out as Detroit was getting into the fest with their muscle cars. You didn't have to build them anymore, which took away the individualism of a self-made road rocket. The music survived a little while longer, until the Beatles got off the plane, relieving us from our innocence and simplicity.

I have told this story through the eyes of Sonny Mitchell, the fictional main character, who you may identify with. He and his friends mature from bicycles to cars with an air of cockiness and camaraderie; they walk with their shoulders back. At times, I became Sonny Mitchell as I rattled off this tale, and it about wore me out being a teenager in a sixty-some-year-old body.

I hope you love this book as much as I do. I can truthfully say, I loved writing it. There will be a sequel. So hang on and ride with Sonny Mitchell.

Chapter 1

Joe came pedaling into our yard, going like sixty, and did one of those laid down spin stops that throw gravel and grass everywhere. I know for a fact it was August 1954, because it was my fourteenth birthday, and I was out adjusting the new seat my folks had gotten me for my bike.

Joe was all fired up and panting like a madman.

"I was just down at the store turning in bottles when I heard a dispatch come over a cop's radio. There's a train wreck over at the golf course … and there's at least one fatality and maybe two more," Joe said.

He was having a tough time of it since he was breathing hard.

"We gotta get over there quick and see if we can get a look at him."

Lately, all of us had been talking about seeing a dead man, and being two of the youngest of our bunch, Joe and I hadn't seen one yet. He was hunched over holding on to the handlebars like he couldn't wait. His front wheel pointed towards the street as he looked over his shoulder at me. He was taller and could sit on his bike with both feet on the ground without teetering. His curly, red hair was all shiny with the sweat that was running down the sides of his cheeks onto his bare shoulders. I knew he was going whether I went along or not. I couldn't say no to an opportunity like that, so I jumped on and lit out after him.

"Why don't we take the trestle?" I shouted.

Joe yelled back over his shoulder, "The wreck is on the trestle." Not looking ahead, he damn near hit the neighbor's dog. Wobbling a bit, he recovered and poured on the gas for downtown.

We were on River Street, weaving in and out of traffic, going west towards the bridge that goes to North Willamette and the golf club. Joe looked like he was riding a shark. He had painted his bike flat black and had taken off the fenders. It was a Schwinn with a chrome spring up front that matched the wheels and absorbed the shock. I was on my green Columbia that I was running fenderless for the summer, with the handlebars upside down, and my tires pumped up tight as hell for fast riding.

Without warning, Joe cut to the right and disappeared into an alley between the creamery and Simpson's grain elevator. As I slowed to follow, I noticed a *Road Closed* sign ahead. In order to take the alternate route through the narrow alley, we had to jump the truck hoist. It was a cable and metal affair that was used to lift the front of the trucks so the grain would run into the pit. We had done this a thousand times in our years of haunting the place. This was our area.

Wap-wap went the tires as Joe crossed first. This ignited an explosion of a whole squadron of pigeons stationed under the roof, using it as their hangar while hiding from the heat of the sun. An instant later, as my tires *wapped*, I was met with a bird-shitting orgy falling like confetti on New Year's.

I followed Joe to the left, onto a trail that ran between the industrial buildings and the river, almost being consumed by the wild blackberry vines reaching for me. We were then a half-block north, parallel with River Street, heading toward downtown and the bridge, racing directly into the sun. It was hot like it gets in August and thc heat felt like sandpaper on my face. By staying on the trail, we flew right under the bridge, getting a moment of respite from the sun's glare. Under the structure, in the dirt, sat a couple of bums, one in an army coat upending a bottle wrapped in a brown bag. As I blew by, he dropped the glass from his lips and gave me a caveman stare as red juice ran from what teeth he had onto his beard. Joe then cut to the left and roared through a hot alley with garbage cans overflowing. It must have been the day before dump day, because it stank to high heaven and the flies were biting. We were swatting like we were on fire as we reached River Street again, and then we darted down the sidewalk back towards the bridge, scattering pedestrians as we weaved through them.

Joe took the corner of the bridge nearly lying flat, with his left hand out signaling a turn, which got him a long honk from a lady in a Nash wagon who damn near caught his rear tire. He would have gotten the middle finger too, but that was reserved for me, since I was right behind him and got the wrath of a man in a Dodge truck who had one hand on the horn and the other out the window. I beat the guy by a foot and shot him a satisfied look like I thought he needed the thrill.

We never used our seats all the way to the top of the old, steel bridge, and when we arced over, we let 'em loose and must have been doing 45, with the cool river breeze in our faces. Just about the time I got to liking how good it felt, I saw blue smoke coming off Joe's rear tire, so I started applying the coaster brake, easy, so I wouldn't get crossed up bad and have to ditch it. Tires were squealing and the horns went to blaring again as Joe swung out in front of the oncoming traffic to bail off. At the end of the bridge and to the right, there was a dirt trail that dropped thirty feet, straight down to the tee on the thirteenth hole of the golf course. As we plunged, we got air, and I'm sure we looked like bronco riders leaning back in the saddle trying to stay on.

The golf course wasn't exactly new territory for us, since we spent a lot of time over there looking for balls that we could turn in for money.

There were four golfers who must have been getting ready to tee off when they heard the two trains collide. They were just standing there looking away from us. Two on the right, two on the left, and we went barreling right between them going flat out. We went crashing through the brush between the thirteenth and sixth fairways, and Joe and his bike came out the other side looking all camouflaged. Other golfers were back to hacking away, and the balls were going everywhere. They were whizzing by with kind of a whistling noise that scared the shit out of me.

We were peddling and ducking as we crossed the eighth and eleventh fairways. We bolted out of the rough right onto the number ten green, where these three old duffers were standing around the pin. They were watching this guy, who was dressed like a leprechaun and had white, skinny legs, putt from off the green to the right just as I went zinging by the hole. I'm not joking you, his ball went right between my front and rear tires and damn near went in the hole. They were yelling and swinging their clubs at us.

"Get the hell out of the way, you little bastards!" one of them bellowed. Their curses and rants got dimmer as we pressed on.

After crossing the eighteenth, we slammed on the brakes, because the wreck was right in front of us. It was about twenty feet off the ground on top of the trestle; about half the caboose was just a bunch of splinters that had been crushed by the engine of the other train. Two ambulances and a hearse were backed up to the trestle, and there were tall ladders leaning on the rail where they had lowered the victims and the body.

We sat there looking over our handlebars trying to catch our breath. Two of the fellas had been loaded in ambulances and were moving out for the hospital. The other was already in the hearse with the door shut. There were cops all over the place, assessing what had happened with the railroad workers. Everyone seemed like they were in kind of a daze, including us.

It was a bad deal. One of the trains pulling log cars had stopped for some reason, while the other one came around the corner of the trestle. The engineer, who was on the blind side, rammed into the caboose, which had a brakeman and a couple of other workers inside. The poor guys saw what was about to happen, but couldn't jump because they were more than twenty-five feet above the ground. I got all this from overhearing a cop talking to a reporter from the local newspaper. After seeing all the destruction and people maimed and killed, I almost forgot why we had come all the way over there in such a hurry.

After retreating to our side of the river, we sprawled out on Joe's front lawn to recover. I was lying on my back in a nest of dandelions looking up into a big, red pool of glow that was the sun filtering through my eyelids. A ladybug crossed my chest, which must have seemed to her like a desert in the forest. It was summer and the yard was a utopia for little creatures in the overrun grass and weeds.

Since it was afternoon by then, Joe's mother, Sylvia Harden, was sitting on the porch nursing a glass of gin. She was preparing herself for another night tending bar at the Red Slipper, a dive leftover from the glory days of the war. She was laid back on an aluminum chair in her bathrobe, with her hair up in rollers. Having her feet propped up on the railing allowed her upper torso to be low enough she could reach the glass resting on the floor-boards of the porch. She wore a black mask over her eyes, the kind you see movie stars wear to bed; behind that mask was her world and she rarely came out of it.

Joe, who was backed up against a maple tree, said, "Sonny, I don't think we can call that a see today, because we didn't really see it since it was already in the car. It's a damn shame being's it's your birthday and all."

He sounded disappointed. I was looking right at the bottom of his Converses. The one on the left had a hole in it as big as a quarter and the one on the right had about a hundred knots in the strings. My eyes followed up his 501's to the knees, where the denim was just a memory, his bony hinges shiny and scarred. You could always see about two inches of his Penney's underwear above the jeans, and then it was freckles all the way up to those light blue eyes redheads have.

"I suppose you're right," I said. "The boys probably wouldn't go for it."

It was disappointing, since the summer was about over and so were the opportunities. It seemed anything worth remembering always happened in the summer-time.

Sylvia got up without saying a word and went back into the house, letting the screen door slam behind her. Joe didn't have much of a mother; she was more like a roommate who worked at night, never to be seen much. His dad had quit coming around, so Joe was pretty much left to fend for himself. He would have to get up on his own and make his breakfast if he wanted any at all. The rest of us would occasionally trade him out of his peanut butter and jelly sandwiches at school, thinking his diet could use a little variety. His real name was Joey, but we got to calling him Joe, because he was tough and we liked him for it.

Chapter 2

Since most of us lived down close to the river, we spent a lot of time there in the summer, because it was where the action was. The log trucks would enter a street right by Wilson's Mill, where my dad worked, and dump their loads into the river, which would make a wave almost reaching the other side. The logs were then rounded up by lumberjacks who actually rode them standing up, using long poles to steady themselves, and would make them into large rafts. Then a tugboat would push the whole deal down the Willamette River to Oregon City, where the logs were used to make paper.

This made a great playground for us, and in the evening, after everyone had gone home, we would haunt the place. We made about every kind of contraption that would float us. There was a calm place below the industrial buildings where we staged our flotilla, being pirates and waging wars. We had found each other at Lincoln Grade School so far back we couldn't remember when.

Turning into teenagers brought out our diverse personalities. Billy Wheeler was the oldest, nearing 16, and he was our leader, our Chief. He took the building of these boats seriously because of his mechanical instincts. Gary was into looks, not just his own, but his crafts had to look just right, and he wouldn't want to launch a new one until the one he was working on was varnished with a painted stripe or something. Johnny Smith was the youngest, but only by months, and would go along with about anything just to be included. Miles Fletcher, who was my age, was careful. He always had his eye on the shore and made sure he could make it back. He would caution us just to be met by playful jeers and insults. Joe Harden was our go-to man for raw materials. He had a way of coming up with supplies like nails and lumber. He could smell out a lonely hammer or a good inner tube like he had a schematic in his brain of a giant parts bin that included everything not tied down in our part of town.

I was a combination of all of them. I was one of the younger ones, but I could keep up. I was taller than Billy and as heavy as Joe and could take care of myself. In the summers, I got brown easy, not like Joe, who burned from top to bottom. I was just darker, with black hair and brown eyes.

We got to playing on the log rafts that were hundreds of feet long, jumping from one to another and in and out of the tugboats. There were signs all over the place saying to keep off, but that just added to the lure of it all. Playing on the logs was dangerous, because if you slipped off and fell between the logs, you might not find a place to get out, and then you'd drown like a rat.

The sawmills had this guy named Ernest who they hired to patrol the rafts to make sure none of the logs got stolen and to keep the kids off them when no one was around. We used to drive old Ernest crazy. He took the job seriously and stuck to his schedule religiously, making his patrols every hour on the hour, except when the fish were biting, and then he would work a hole right above where Deer Creek enters the river. He had this aluminum boat about fourteen feet long with a seven-and-a-half-horse Johnson on the back. He wore this red felt hat with carnival buttons all over it, along with suspenders over a flannel shirt every day of the year.

We could tell exactly where he was by just checking our watches, and we could depend on old Ernie to be right where he was supposed to be. It wasn't long before Ernest's name got shifted to Ernie, because we'd pin a nickname on about anyone sooner or later. Of course, we knew where all the trails were from the street down to the river, and we could just slip down there and make a pass across a raft or two and then beat it back up through the blackberries before he could catch us. I don't think he knew who we were, but he knew it was us, because he always called us little bastards.

One day, someone got this idea of sending a message over to Japan to the Japanese kids, about how we had gotten over the war and to tell them we didn't hold them responsible for it or anything. It had been ten years since it had ended and we felt like it was time to make amends.

From talking with Billy Wheeler, we decided about anything that went into the river ended up in Japan. Billy was pretty studious and knew all about rivers and oceans. Since it was summer and warm, we were spending time down at the river, so we decided to cut a few logs loose and make a little seaworthy ship to haul a token of our friendship to Japan.

It was a simple plan. We just waited until Ernest was clear up by the water plant. We lifted one of the ropes that held the logs together and liberated four nice little firs about twelve feet long. We tied them together with some rope that Joe borrowed from up at the cannery. Like I said, it was pretty warm, so we just bailed in after the logs and swam them down river, out of sight of Ernie, and tied them up in some brush under a bunch of willows.

After we made our little vessel seaworthy, we put together a nice little package for our counterparts in Japan. We spent a couple of hours cleaning up an empty fifteen-gallon grease bucket that still had a nice lid on it. Miles Fletcher got it out of his dad's service station, and with a liberal amount of gasoline, we washed the grease out of the can, getting most of it all over our Levi's and t-shirts. Of course we were puffing away on cigarettes, and it's a wonder we didn't torch ourselves. The bucket could be resealed airtight with the rubber gasket around the lid to keep everything nice and dry.

We filled our little barrel with things we thought would help those little Japanese get a shot of our western world culture. Some of the stuff, like the pair of Levi's and the white Penney's t-shirt, had seen better days, but the yo-yo was alright, and the roller skates hadn't been out of the Willamette Roller Rink long enough to hardly cool off. Meg and Denise Olsen, neighborhood girls who were older, ran with us like boys until they began to find out they were different. They sometimes would have relapses and spend time with us. This was one such time, and they dropped in a Bill Haley & His Comets 45 with "Rock Around the Clock" and "Shake, Rattle and Roll" on the backside. We didn't put in cap pistols or anything like that, because we figured they didn't want to be reminded of guns or war, but we did include a slingshot Billy had made with a jigsaw in his dad's garage.

The only thing that went in that you could eat was some hard candy, because we didn't know how long it would take to get there, and we thought anything else would probably spoil. Joe Harden's house was closest to the river, and we put the package together there so we could practically roll it down the bank to the craft. The sawmill gave up some metal strapping they use to tie lumber together, and along with a hammer and some nails, we secured the freight to the raft in a way we were convinced would make it to the island as sure as any ocean-going freighter could.

We planned the sendoff for Sunday, right after Ernie would quit for the night. There were several of us there, because it was a pretty big deal and none of us wanted to miss out on the event. Billy brought along a bottle of Olympia Beer he had liberated from their fridge in the garage; we figured we should christen the thing and make it official. We passed the bottle around so everyone could have a swig, and then Billy toasted it the *Little Bastard* with a little speech and tried to break the bottle over the logs. Of course, it didn't break and just went to the bottom like it was a bad omen or something. We untied the rope, jumped in, and swam it downstream to where the river got good and wide, and then we let it go.

The next day, we were fooling around down at the trestle, discussing the raft and how it was doing and how far it had gotten. All of the sudden, as we were looking downstream, we saw old Ernie's boat coming up the river kind of slow, coming against the current with the front of the boat riding up high in the water like he was towing something. Sure enough, it was the old fart and he was towing the raft. I don't have to tell you how goddamn mad we were. What made it even worse was that he had the grease bucket in the boat with him and he was rummaging around in it, pulling the stuff out.

Boy was I hot. We were all hot. There must have been about six of us up there watching this. We were kicking rocks and cussing old Ernie out like you can't imagine. We were talking revenge! We forgot all that forgiveness stuff with Japan in about a blink of an eye; we were out to get even. We swore and promised to get that old SOB if it took us the rest of the summer.

We came up with a plan that was pretty elaborate and going to take some good timing. I was going for sure, Billy and Joe volunteered, and we got Meg in on it for effect. Miles wouldn't go out on that trestle on a bet, and the rest were just going to have to watch from the sidelines, because there was only room for four where we were headed. We were familiar with the trestle and the train and when it crossed the river, and of course, we knew exactly when Ernest would come along in his boat and go under the trestle. We had been across the thing about a million times on our way to the golf course after balls. There wasn't a walkway across, so you had to time it so you wouldn't meet a train when you were out there in the middle or you might get run over, and it was way too high to jump. There were a couple of places you could step out of the way of the train—the train guys called them "refuge bays"—which we had used on occasion. Of course, old Ernie didn't know about any of this, and it so happens we would get a big kick out of tossing balls into Ernie's boat when he went under the trestle, which about made him shit his pants because he didn't know where they came from.

Here is what we did: We borrowed some burlap bags from Wilson's Mill and filled them with straw to make a couple of dummies. We bought some old clothes from the thrift shop, and when we got the dummies all dressed up, they looked pretty good. It didn't take a slide rule to figure out when the Old Southern Pacific and Ernest were going to rendezvous out at the trestle, one on top of it and the other going under. The first couple attempts we had to abort because the train wasn't on time. Finally, on Saturday afternoon, everything clicked.

The four of us were sitting up there enjoying the sun when old Ernie pulled out from between a couple of rafts and headed downriver towards the trestle, right on time. About then, we could hear the train tooting its horn when it was passing Second Street on its way to the trestle. Our hearts were starting to beat a little faster as the train approached the river, and old Ernie was heading our way with his usual all-business look about him. We were hiding out on one of the refuge bays with our dummies, waiting for the exact moment. When that train got about a hundred feet from us, we jumped up and started waving at old Ernie like we were just some poor kids in a tight spot and needed help. When he saw us, he sort of got halfway up from his seat and his pipe fell out of his mouth.

Man, you could see he was real worried, and he hit the throttle like he was coming to the rescue or something, even though there wasn't a damn thing he could do for us. Just at the last second, and I was getting real nervous, I'm here to tell you, we stepped back off the rail onto the refuge bay and threw the dummies over the side. The train went roaring by at the same time Ernie came under that trestle with the most horrific look on his face. Then he saw that something about those dummies floating in the water didn't look quite right. We were laughing our asses off at him when he looked up at us. The expression on his face turned to a disdainful look of hate, a look I don't care to ever see again.

The whole thing about killed Ernest. After that, we didn't hang around the river much anymore. I think that was about the last summer of my childhood.

Chapter 3

Our clubhouse was staked out in a gravel lot owned by the Rothschild Cannery; the lot was abandoned and hadn't been used for years. The building was covered with wild blackberry bushes, which grow rampant in western Oregon and crowd everything else out if not warred with. Over time, we whacked our way back to a corner protected by the overhang of a corrugated storage building full of crates and dying old remnants of food storage.

Being the littlest, Gary had been the reason we knew what was inside. He squeezed through a space a flounder couldn't fit through, between the locked chain doors, and plugged in an extension cord Billy had procured off a toaster. That day Gary became a "made man" in our association, catapulting us into the twentieth century with an electric light and power to run our radio and record player. We spent a lot of time there in late summer, after the berry and bean harvests were over, as we were sort of unemployed and waiting out the days until the dreaded school started up again.

One such afternoon, Gary was leaning back in his chair blowing smoke rings towards the ceiling of our hideaway. He had his feet perched up on the table, which was just a slab of plywood lying flat on two footlockers. The boxes contained the necessities we used on a daily basis: some poker chips, a bag of marbles, tobacco with rolling paper, a slingshot, and among other things, a city map and a Ouija board.

Facing Gary, at the opposite end of the table, sat Billy, in an overstuffed chair, with a rational look on his face, like he was reasoning out something. He was two years older and intelligent, our leader, or Chief, as we sometimes called him. To his left were Joe, Johnny, and me, buried in a couch that had seen better days.

Across from us, Miles sat on a Samsonite folding chair. Miles was, for lack of a better word, average. He wore glasses, was of medium build and height, with short brown hair. He had skin with the kind of pigment pimples craved; he usually had a crop of them and they flourished. But he was loyal and always ready to lift his end. At that moment, he was trying to keep a cigar he had confiscated from his dad's office at the Mobil Station going. Frank Fletcher owned the station where we pumped up our tires and fixed the tubes on our bikes. This is how we got to know Miles. First, because of the repair shop in the station, but then we became friends and bonded over like interests.

It was summer, warm but bearable in our surroundings. The shade of our roof was covered and walled in by the vines. We found early on we could transport about anything we could kipe or otherwise obtain back to our headquarters. We used two Radio Flyer wagons, one under the front of the object and one under the back, and down the sidewalk we would go. In fact, since we had become electrified with the power we borrowed from the old building, we were in the market for a fridge to go along with our radio and 45 rpm record player.

Out of the blue, Joe asked, "Why do you suppose old Ernest got to calling us little bastards?"

I guess this was a question for all of us and nobody in particular, because we all sat there pondering it for some time.

"I guess it was because he never could catch us," Miles said.

This brought out a couple of grunts and nods to the affirmative, but didn't get anything from Billy, who seemed to be in deep contemplation. He was sitting there rolling a cigarette back and forth on the top of his chair arm when he came out with, "My dad has a bastard file in the garage."

I knew that a file was used for smoothing or sharpening something, but like the rest of us, I hadn't heard of a bastard one.

"They're not as course as a course file and not quite smooth enough to be called a smooth one either," Billy went on. "They're just odd, like a bastard saw has an uncommon number of teeth, which makes them different too."

"Kind of like us," said Joe. "We aren't jocks and we aren't brainiacs. We're sort of in-between."

"Yeah," I said, "we don't fit in, like we don't fit the mold. I guess we are little bastards."

So that's what we called ourselves. The Little Bastards. Among ourselves at first, and then the word got out. And we became them.

We had been warned early on that summer that we might get a visit from a bunch of hoodlums from the far west side of town, and it wouldn't be friendly. White bread was eaten west and south of downtown, but west, along Deer Creek, was a slummy, downtrodden area called the Bottoms. The roads were either gravel or dirt, and the houses were built on any land that was a little higher than the floodplain. We had heard about this group of thugs, but hadn't had the pleasure of an encounter yet. We looked forward to it with anticipation and reluctance.

They called themselves the Hudson Raiders. Where that name came from, we didn't know, except there was a meatpacking plant in the Bottoms called Hudson's. Since the snitch had told us about the Raiders coming to our part of town, you can be sure we were on the lookout. Occasionally, we would see a stranger on a bike cruising about with no particular agenda that we could tell and we would make note of it. The informer, it turned out, must have been a double snitch, because somehow, the thugs found our hideout and came calling.

We had rendezvoused at the clubhouse that day and were just lollygagging around, smoking and listening to

45s. I reached a butt out of Johnny's pack on the table, spilling a couple more that went rolling. Joe pounced on one scooping it up and into his mouth.

"Jesus, Sonny!" Johnny said. "When are you guys going to buy your own?"

"When you run out, I guess," Billy said as he scarfed up a single before it cleared the table.

A few minutes had gone by since Gary had left and peddled back to his house for some cards in the interest of us having a game.

"Do you think they'll bring weapons?" Johnny asked.

"Shit, who knows?" said Billy. "From what I've heard, they don't need them they're so monster-like."

"Yeah, I've been told that they file their teeth before they go out on one of their raids," said Joe.

None of us would have made a scale hit barely more than triple digits, and we were all getting a little worried talking about the upcoming encounter with the Hudsons. We weren't sure if they were coming, but from the increasing reports of sightings, we felt we needed to be ready and had been going over some game plans and counter plans. From what we had heard of the Hudson Raiders and their reputation, the plan involved probably getting our asses kicked.

About then, Gary came hoofing up the trail that led to our hideout on a dead-ass run. "There's a whole pack of them coming!" he yelled.

He was out of breath from running. He bent over, putting his hands on his knees as we sprang to our feet. Before he could get out another syllable, we could hear bicycles piling up at our entrance to the street.

"Let's roll," Billy said as we headed for the gate.

Wanting to head them off before they entered our compound, the cigarettes we craved so much hit the air as we dug in, sprinting for the opening. Gravel was flying, but we hadn't gotten full out when we had to slam on the brakes. They were lined across our path just inside the hole. All six of them. The baddest looking gangster hoods I could ever imagine.

There just happened to be six of us, so naturally we lined up in a tidy sort of way and faced them, determined to protect our turf. As luck would have it, I was right in the middle with Joe to my left and Miles to my right. Billy and Johnny were to the right of Miles, and Gary was to the left of Joe. The two visitors in the middle across from Miles and me had to be brothers, because of their likeness. They were both about a half a head taller than me and a head taller than Miles. You could tell they had shaved their hair off for the summer a couple of months back, but the mousey brown coats hadn't seen care or soap since. They both were big and white with beady, small eyes and noses that looked as if their mother had mated with a Chester White boar with quality hams. These two were definitely the leaders, with the others almost cheerfully ready to go down for them.

I knew someone was going to jump; that's the way it always was. We were all sizing each other up, looking for the weakest link on both sides. Who was going to blink, and who was going to lunge? I was looking directly into those little eyes across from me, but could still see the eyes of the brother next to him. He was getting ready to go, and Miles was shaking, something I could feel because of our closeness. The big dope sprang and put his pudgy fist right between Miles' eyes, breaking his glasses neatly down the middle between the lenses. This knocked Miles back a step, and we all retreated the same to shore up the line. We were determined not to let them by. I knew Miles was way outmatched, and I made for the asshole that hit him, but Joe's right arm caught me in the chest to stop me. I guess Joe saw something I didn't, or he just wanted to see what Miles had in him. The big oaf paused, cocking his head a little like a puppy, curious, wondering what damage he had incurred. At this point, Miles stepped ahead just to be punched again, this time in the nose. Of course, blood came squirting out and Miles was crying, but somewhere inside of the kid something clicked, like a clock rolling him into pre-manhood. He gave out a war cry and went crashing into his opponent with both fists flailing and his eyes closed.

This sort of surprised the guy, and as he stepped back, he got tangled up in his shoe laces, falling down with Miles on top of him. Miles wouldn't let go and all the guy could do was get little punches in as they were rolling around in the gravel. Miles was holding his own until the asshole started kicking him in his balls with his knee. This really pissed our guy off, because all of a sudden, the oaf let out this ear-piercing scream. He was trying to get away from Miles, and Miles had his teeth sunk into this guy's shoulder, right in the meaty part where the nurses stab you with the needle. The big turd got his feet under him and ripped his arm away from Miles, leaving a hunk of meat hanging from Miles' mouth that was all red and dripping with blood. A look of shock came over the gang from the west as they gawked at Miles. In a flash, the look of shock became a look of fear as they ogled at part of their leader's arm hanging from Miles' mouth. They backed out, following their leader, not taking their eyes off what they reasoned could be a vampire by the looks of the blood running down Miles' chin.

As we were watching the escape of the bad guys, Miles was bent over horking up everything he had eaten in recent memory. As we recovered from the affair, we surrounded Miles, congratulating him and so on, still in disbelief of what had just happened. Billy pulled a shop rag from his back pocket and wiped Miles' face off and left it for him to blow his nose and rub the puke and blood off his shirt. The only victory that I could claim for myself was that I somehow had the wherewithal to grab Miles' glasses out of the rocks before they were trampled into crushed glass and plastic.

We decided we had better do something about fixing the specs for Miles because he obviously was having trouble seeing. Since we didn't trust Miles on a bike, we walked down to Fletcher's station on the corner. We swaggered with an air of cockiness bordering on conceited self-assurance. All the time we were poking at him and pushing him around with our admiration, and of course we were wallowing in self-appreciation for being part of it all.

Since we had the run of the place by then, we just moseyed into the shop area while Miles washed up in the men's room out behind. Billy, who was good with tools already, fired up the acetylene torch and carefully melted the plastic on the two broken ends of the eyeglasses and welded them back together. After holding the two parts together until they cooled, they became one again, never quite right, but Miles wore them like a trophy he surely deserved.

Chapter 4

I drank pop every chance I got and never turned down cookies or candy of any kind. There was always a big pitcher of Kool-Aid in the fridge and I poured enough of that liquefied sugar down my gullet to sink a ship. For this sin, a price was paid once a year, by my dad in money and me in pain, and my dear mother heard about it from both ends. During the other three hundred and sixty-some days I wasn't in the chair, I was worried about the next time I would be.

Old Dr. Gilmore had his office on the top floor of the old First National Bank building downtown, and that was intimidating enough with all the medieval villains and their beasts glaring down at us with scorn. When the dreadful day would arrive, I was dragged downtown by my mom, where we entered the bank, which was all marble and cold. The bankers in their white shirts and suspenders were partially cloaked behind a wall of the smoke given off by their cigars and pipes. They seemed to be in the land of money and power and couldn't give a shit about my predicament.

The elevator operator was this skinny old lady who had a mole on her nose, and her graying hair was put up in a bun held together by a big needle. She was mechanical in the way she pushed the buttons for up, down, and the floors. She'd been here since the beginning of time, knew just where we were headed, and wouldn't look you straight in the eye. It was like I was being led from death row and she was running the elevator that went up to the gallows. The office was down at the end of the hall and smelled like disinfectant mixed with something else; the first whiff of it put fear into your brain.

Dr. Gilmore's nurse, Lorraine, met us at the door, which was about ten feet tall with the snowy windows you couldn't see through. It had scary gold lettering on it that said *Dr. Gilmore, Dentist.*

"Hello, Sonny, how are you today?" Lorraine would say.

She had red hair and looked just like Lucille Ball dressed up in one of those white nurse's outfits. She was nice enough; it's just too bad she had to be in such an awful business. I'd guess I'd been in there about a hundred times and had about a thousand cavities filled. What really pissed me off was when I was going in while some kid was coming out with his mom falling all over herself congratulating him for another six months without a cavity. It would make me want to drive his pearly whites back about an inch towards his tonsils.

Early on, Old Dr. Gilmore decided I was allergic to Novocain, so I always had to take it cold turkey. On the fateful day he decided that, I was sitting there in the chair staring at the syringes he kept in this gallon jar right in front of you, where you had to look at them. They were in pink liquid like where they kept brains in the science room over at Lincoln. Old Gilmore pulled one out and shook it dry and then drew a full load out of this kind of tube-looking bottle. Then Lorraine crammed about six pieces of cotton in my mouth to soak up the blood and carnage. Everything started getting a little blurry for me as Dr. Gilmore was tilting his head back trying to get my mouth lined up through the appropriate lenses in his trifocals. When I felt that needle, which had to have been ten inches long, enter my gum, I was close to fainting, and I'm sure I was as white as Lorraine's uniform. He didn't just push the thing in either. He surged and drove it like he was pounding a pile driver, and then he pushed down on the plunger like he was forcing cold grease into a wheel bearing.

After he pulled the thing out, he slapped it down on the tray and wiped his forehead with the front of his apron and said, "Son of a bitch, I think the kid is sick."

Well, no shit, who wouldn't be a little ill after going through all that? So after that episode, he would grab the drill and go right to work, sans Novocain. He was afraid to use the new, modern version of the drill, because it was fast, and he thought it might get away from him.

He used the old drill, run by an electric motor, that looked like it came over on the Mayflower. It had these belts that went around a bunch of pulleys and was suspended by this little crane affair so he could pull it up and down and in and out. I guessed it was probably built right after the Civil War and he probably got it at some surplus store.

He would grind away until the thing got hot and then Lorraine would hose out my mouth and I would spit the water and blood into this ceramic bowl beside the chair. Dr. Gilmore and Lorraine would talk in code, sometimes leading up to something extra painful, and then chat away about a whole bunch of nonsense that didn't have a thing to do with my mouth. This made me feel a little left out. While I was there dying, they would go on like they hadn't a care in the world and life was grand.

"How was your golf game Saturday?" she would ask the doctor.

Dr. Gilmore would answer, "Oh, I just shot an almost par and beat the pants right off old Lawyer Johnson, and boy was he pissed."

All the time this was going on, Lorraine was chewing gum like a dog in a meat market, and Dr. Gilmore was whistling, which made my cavity hurt like hell. With the pain, gum chewing, and golf games, I began trying to put the whole thing out of my mind by sort of going out of my body and dreaming I was somewhere else.

I remember one time, I dreamt I was in the Marines and we were dumped on Omaha Beach. I was running out of the water and up onto the sand with my rifle, yelling like hell, when I took a bullet right in the mouth. I went end over end, landing flat on my back looking up in the sky, with my mouth hurting and throbbing like mad. Luckily, this nurse came crawling up beside me and assessed my situation and told me that she would get the doctor.

Pretty soon, a Navy corpsman crawled up on the other side of me, looked down into my face, and yelled, "Open wide!"

At that point, I wondered why such a young sailor would be wearing glasses of that caliber, but everything was kind of dreamy so I let it go.

Then the nurse started handing him tools back and forth while she was chewing gum like mad and yelling because it was noisy as hell with the cannons going off and bombs dropping. The corpsman was in there digging around trying to get the bullet out with this pry-bar-looking thing while explaining to the nurse how he had to miss a putt on the seventh green to keep from being demoted. He went on to say that he had sandbagged most of the game so the old admiral would come out ahead. My eyeballs were going back and forth like I was watching a tennis game, trying to keep track of his golfing and her gossiping.

I'm here to tell you it was a good day in my life when Old Dr. Gilmore hung the drill up for good. I'd still be going to him if he was down there; my mom and dad would never change once they got to doing business with someone. They were Mr. and Mrs. Loyal.

Anyway, one day as we were stepping out of the elevator, which was an elation in itself, stepping in was a kid about my age heading up to see the orthodontist across the hall from my dentist. We sized each other up like a couple of kids will do. I didn't think much about it at the time, except I remember his Buddy Holly glasses and his mouth full of wire, which was pretty uncommon on our side of town. Out on the street was this bicycle like I'd never seen cabled up to a parking meter. It was about as red as Christmas candy and so new you could smell the paint. This bike not only had a rear rack, but a headlight, a horn, and a radio right smack in the tank. It said *Radio Bike* on the side in letters that made it look like it was flying.

I knew I'd seen this guy before. There was a story in the paper bragging about how he had won some recital or some bullshit thing. The article had pictures of him plastered all over it, wearing a suit and bowtie and playing the piano. He had been coming past our house too. I'd be standing there with my hands gripping the handlebars of our lawnmower and he'd come whizzing by with his hands on a pair of bars with red, white, and blue ribbons streaming out behind them. Almost every Saturday, he would come along on that bike, about the same time, with flowers on his rear rack while I was out toiling in the yard.

Not long after we had converged at the elevator, the guy came limping along in front of our house with his pant leg caught in the chain and with the usual bouquet strapped on the rear rack. I kinda felt sorry for him; he looked like he had been in those straights for quite some time, so I thought I'd better help the guy. Plus, I was curious about the flowers. I suppose you know what it is like to get your pant leg caught in the chain; most people do. It's a bad deal, because there isn't much you can do for yourself without ending up in a heap on top of your bike.

The chain is on the right side, and when you get stuck, you can barely touch the ground with your right toe, if you're lucky, and if you lean over to the right to get your foot on the ground, you will go right on over with the bike on top of you. You can't get off the left side because you are tied down to the right side by your pant leg.

So here was this kid poking along careful like, straddling his bike, hopping with his left foot, trying not to go over and end up on his ass. I didn't want to go barging out to help him right off since he wasn't really asking, so I just stood there with my arms folded as he stopped right in front of me. He peered at me over his black, horn-rimmed glasses and let out a mouthful of obscenities like I had never heard before, and I'd heard about every word there is down at Wilson's Mill. Suddenly, there seemed more to this guy than I'd thought. Amongst all the profanities was a plea for help, or more of a demand for help. I knelt down and started working the pant leg around the sprocket while he slowly rolled the bike ahead. It was an unusually bad case, since the bike still had its fancy chrome chain guard on it.

He told me he had turned the corner onto Second Street and just missed this old, yellow tomcat that came running out between a couple of cars. Then the Dalmatian chasing the cat slammed right into the side of his bike, and that's what ran his pant leg into the chain. The poor SOB had been hopping along for several blocks before he got to my house. I tried hard to liberate his nice, white cords from the chain without tearing them, but they had gotten grease and oil on them and were probably done for good anyway. He said he was going to be in deep shit, because it was the third pair of white cords he had ruined that summer. I was thinking this guy must be pretty well-off, since I only had one pair in my life and the only time I wore them was to church or weddings.

After we got his pant leg out of the chain, we just stood around there exchanging pleasantries, and I'll have to admit I began to sort of like him. He had this infectious smile and his eyes would sort of light up when he would come out with something to say. He was about my size, with dark hair like mine. Along with the glasses, he was tall and skinny, which added to the Buddy Holly resemblance. I told him my name was Sonny and that I lived in Willamette with my folks and that my sister was older and had already moved out and married this Air Force guy. He introduced himself as Archibald and said his folks owned the Lawrence Funeral Parlor and that's why he came by every Saturday with flowers on his back rack.

Of course, I asked him right out if they really had dead people in the parlor.

"Hell, yes," he said, "all the time and sometimes more than one."

"What's it like having a stiff right there in the house at night?" I asked.

Archie replied, "You get used to it, even after dark; it ain't no big deal after a while."

We shot the breeze for a bit since Archie didn't seem to be in any hurry and all I had waiting for me was the lawn mower. I told him about the time when Joe and I went flying over the bridge on our bikes to see a dead man but didn't get there in time. This seemed funny to him since he was so used to having them around.

I could tell that he was forming a little trust for me after I told him what a great guy Joe was and about all my other friends who went to Lincoln and how we almost killed old Ernest. I didn't ask, but after a while, he came out with the offer that Joe and I were welcome to come down and see a dead man, but we would have to make arrangements so it wouldn't be during a funeral or anything. I was waiting for that and I accepted right away, while thinking how good this was going to be for Joe and me, the ones who hadn't seen a stiff yet, and it wouldn't hurt my stature with the older kids in our outfit.

We were a pretty tight group, growing up around the same neighborhood and going to Lincoln School. We weren't against bringing in someone else, even from the other side of town, if they had what it took. We hadn't discussed what it meant to have what it takes, but we agreed to decide on a per-case basis. We didn't have any sacred bylaws written in blood or anything, but by then, we were definitely a group, the Little Bastards.

That's how I got to know Archie, and I guess it just goes to show you that you can't always judge a book by its cover. When I first saw him riding that bike towards me looking like he had a poker up his ass, I never dreamed we would become good friends. He gradually became one of us. I guess we kinda helped him get the poker out.

Chapter 5

One afternoon in late October, Archie came riding up on his bike. I was out in the yard raking up the last of the maple leaves that hadn't dropped into the bed of the pickup. It was one of those days that starts out with heavy fog, and if you're lucky, it burns off sunny and doesn't go straight to clouds. This was one of the good ones, clear and cold enough to make your nose run.

Archie announced it was his last Saturday to pick up flowers because of the impending weather. He said one of the undertakers from down at the parlor would be taking over the picking up and delivering with one of the hearses.

I could tell by the way he was acting he had something else on his mind. It was like he knew something I didn't but couldn't wait to spit it out. He leaned over his handlebars and gave me one of those looks of his, like he did when he got excited. It was kind of like when you hit the button on the floorboard of a car; his eyes went from dim to bright.

"We just got a new one down at the house that you and Joe might like taking a look at," he said.

"So," I said, "you're finally making good on your promise."

I tried not to act overexcited. I switched to my defensive, don't-give-a-shit mode. I didn't want him to know that I would get on my knees and crawl all the way to the mortuary to see a body. Archie had made the offer a month before, and I'd practically forgotten about the promise. Come to find out, Archie wasn't holding out; he was just waiting for something kind of special to share with us.

"We got wicked Annie Jo Molly's cadaver down in the basement thawing out," he said.

My don't-give-a-shit attitude went right out the window. Annie Jo had been all over the news lately, including national TV. According to the accounts, she had gotten tired of her husband, Walt, coming home drunk and beating the shit out of her. One such night, she was waiting with a butcher knife, and when he started in, she stabbed him fourteen times, which just happened to be the number of years they had been married. After he was good and dead, she took his army issue .45 from his side of the dresser in the bedroom and swallowed the barrel, which resulted in the back of her head being blown off. It happened on a night when their two children were spending the night at some friend's house, so it was suspected Annie had planned the whole thing.

Archie filled me in on some more of the facts of the case that hadn't been available to the public. He had overheard the cops talking about murder when they dropped off her remains at the parlor. According to that account, Annie's parents were well-to-do and lived in Boston. They had a distrust for the local, small-town sheriff and his investigation, so they had their daughter's remains sent off to a body farm near Seattle for an extensive autopsy to find the real cause of death.

At this point, Archie gave out a little chuckle, showing his braces, which sparkled when he talked, and said, "It doesn't take a scientist to figure out that blowing off the back of her skull might have had something to do with it."

Anyway, the body farm had frozen her so she could be shipped back to Willamette to be embalmed and laid to rest. Evidently, she had left a note with her wishes to be buried out west and not to be returned to Boston.

Archie and I sealed the deal and set the date for the next evening, which he promised would give Annie enough time to warm up. He said Joe and I could stay overnight, which was still common for us. We were always staying at one another's homes and knew each other's families well; however, this would be the first night at Archie's. As fate would have it, all this happened on October 30, and the next evening was Halloween.

As soon as his shadow disappeared around the first corner, I was on my bike saddle, slapping leather for Joe's house. Like I said, it was clear and cold, except for the smoke from the fires of burning leaves and woodstoves. I could feel the warmth of the sweet-smelling fog engulfing me as I pumped for Joe's. My mouth was half open with the smile I had thinking about the good fortune brought about from Annie's demise. Warm saliva and tears caused by the wind slid across my frozen cheeks and turned to icicles when reaching my neck. I could hardly wait to enlighten old Joe.

We'd all been talking lately on how we were getting bummed out about Halloween. It had been our favorite time of year with the candy and pranks and so on. I guess it was our age that was causing the boredom with it. We just couldn't seem to scare ourselves good anymore. I was thinking that spending Halloween night in a mortuary with an infamous dead female murderer might bring back the splendor. I caught Joe out in the sun in front of the house oiling his chain. He was so engrossed in the lubricating that he didn't look up. He had his bike balanced upside down on the seat and handlebars while he pumped oil from this little Singer oil can, dribbling a drop on every link. His thumb was making this *klit-klatting* noise as he was working the bottom of the can. It sounded like a cricket chirping during mating season.

"You gotta take care of your equipment," Joe said as I rolled up close, not leaving the seat.

"Yeah," I got out. "I see you got your fenders on." I was panting like hell.

"They don't look so bitchin', but they sure come in handy rain time." *Klit-klat.* He was totally engrossed in his bike. He seemed completely disinterested in me being there. *Klit-klat.*

I dropped the bomb, "Archie has a body for us to look at."

Klit, he stopped midway through the action and a tear drop of oil probably hung in midair waiting for a response.

"What?" he said as his eyes moved from his bike to eyeballing me in a millisecond.

I caught him off guard and all of a sudden had his full attention. He set the can down, *klat*. He had been carefully rolling the chain around with the pedal and this came to a stop too.

"No shit," he said.

"Yeah, he just left my house on his bike." I said.

"So out with it, what's the deal?" he said.

Joe stood there in silence as I recalled to him the visit from Archie and the details of the frozen stiff in the basement and who it was. Of course I made it sound as morbid as I could. I saved the part about the stay over until the last, for good effect and all.

"Let me get this straight," he said. "We're going to spend Halloween night in a mortuary with a stiff?"

By then, I couldn't hold back and I was grinning like a pig in shit. Joe let out a whoop and then gave me a couple of hits in the shoulder and started shaking my hand. I got loose of him and he began spinning around, knocking over the bike and stepping on the oiler.

"Goddamn," he said. "We're going to spend Halloween night in a funeral home full of caskets and dead shit. Can you beat that?"

It was a done deal for Joe, since his mom didn't give a hoot where he was on Halloween or any other night. For me, it was different; I had to get permission from my folks to spend the night out. They'd never turned me down yet, but this was such an important night, I was a little apprehensive.

I broke the news about the stay over to them at the table over supper that night, but unlike the discussion with Joe, I made it sound far less morbid. There wasn't really any way I could make it sound different than what it was. Halloween in a mortuary.

Dad thought I was crazy as hell, but to my surprise, Mom said, "Sonny, I wish I could have done something like that when I was young and adventurous." She had a slight smile on her face, recollecting something about her youth, I was guessing. My dad's eyes were rolling like he was annoyed, but in a fond way, as he was looking at her with his chin in the palm of his hand.

I was in. They let me do it. They always seemed to let me have plenty of rope.

I telephoned Archie to confirm our stay over after I had hooked up with Joe and gotten permission from the folks. It was dark where our telephone hung. The hallway between the bedrooms and the bathroom was poorly lit and like a tunnel after the sun went down. I dialed the number he gave me; it was the first time I had called him. The phone at the other end began to ring a slow, drawn out roll, different and slightly eerie.

A low, masculine voice that had to have been Boris Karloff's answered with, "Funeral home."

After recovering, I asked if I could please speak with Archie.

The voice said, "I will fetch Master Archibald."

The next words that came were a total contrast. An utterance from a fourteen-year-old teenager. It was calming to hear some badinage from a peer after the formal straight talk from the Karloff guy.

"Who in the hell was that?" I asked.

"Oh, that was just Uncle Cesar. He grabs the phone when no one can beat him to it," Archie said nonchalantly. "He came from the old country and is a little hard to understand, so we don't encourage him to do the answering."

I told Archie we were on for the following evening, and he said to come after dinner, about seven.

"Great!" I said. "Do you think it'll be thawed out by then?"

This made me feel foolish since Archie had guaranteed it the day before.

"She'll be ready," he said.

Halloween came and was just like the previous day in that it started out foggy and cold, but then it burnt off to a sunny day. It was freezing-ass cold in the shade, but not bad in the rays. There was more leaf smoke and raking going on, as people were trying to beat the rain that was sure to come and stay.

Joe showed up at my house at about 6:30, since I lived west of him and the funeral parlor was west of me. After bantering back and forth about who was going to get scared and quit and who wasn't, we finally headed out. I threw my leg over my bike and pedaled out after Joe. He was wearing his bomber jacket over his white t-shirt, which you could see flapping above his Levi's. You could tell he was heading for a sleep over because of the toothbrush sticking out of his back pocket.

The streets were crawling with little ghosts and goblins dragging bags of candy behind them. As we pumped west, the masquerade party grew. The bigger the houses, the bigger the prize. In our part of town, you were lucky to get a green apple, but over west, you could score real candy bars. Our foray into the night seemed to take forever, because Joe would hop the curbs when he would see a gaggle of miniature ghosts, just to scatter them. He caught a single in the middle of the block who couldn't decide which way to leap as Joe was bearing down on him. The kid was decked out in this store-bought Lone Ranger outfit, including the silver pistols and mask. He was a pudgy little fella, about as wide as tall, and he was getting ready to take a bite off the end of this giant Big Hunk. He had his mouth wide open, and you could tell his salivary glands were pumping juice with his anticipation of the shot of sugar he was expecting. The Ranger was frozen as Joe steered by. Looking like a polo player taking the near side, Joe reached out as if swinging his mallet and liberated the treat from the fat little hand.

It seemed odd to me that when we reached the block the mortuary occupied, we ran out of trick-or-treaters. It was like it was off-limits. Suddenly, we had the whole street to ourselves. The street lights were on, but they seemed dimmed by the mist rolling in, in preparation for the following morning. It was like a London fog, damp and cold. The building stood out because it was made of stone and was mostly covered with ivy. It was going on winter, so most of the leaves were gone, leaving the limbs to crawl upward like blood vessels on an eyeball. The place was intimidating, to say the least, with its three stories and tile roof. The shutters were battened down like a fortress expecting a visit.

As we dropped our bikes, Joe said, "Are you sure you want to do this?" I noticed his voice cracked a little.

"Hell, yes," I said, trying to sound confident. "We came here to get the shit scared out of us and I think we're going to get our money's worth."

The arched doorway was vaguely lit by a lamp that could have come off a pirate ship. The two mammoth doors were set in a couple of feet, so when you reached to slam the door knocker, you were committed. Joe put what was left of the Big Hunk in his pocket before making our announcement. The knocker was this giant brass lion with a ring in his mouth. He grabbed the ring and gave it a clang that was scary loud. We stood there looking at each other, wondering if we should knock again or not, then the door on the left began to open.

The first thing I saw moving, except for the door, was a white glove, which I followed up to a long black sleeve. The man welcomed us in the same voice I had heard on the phone. He could have been Count Dracula himself. He was at least six-foot six barefoot. He had the suit with tails and the whole deal. His hair was jet black and his face was white, like he'd never seen the sun. He bowed as he invited us in. Upon entering the foyer, we were welcomed by a woman who was holding out a basket full of Halloween candy. She could have been the Count's twin sister, because she was a spitting image of him right down to the tall collar and red lips.

She said, in a soothing voice, that they had been expecting us and that they were happy to have guests since they were still waiting for their first little trick-or-treaters. I looked over at Joe, who was rolling his eyes with a "can you blame them" look. We were standing in a room as big as a house, with a chandelier overhead and a spiral staircase that came out of a wooden door as big as the back of a truck van. The whole place was decorated in circus colors, all gold and red, with carpet you could lose your shoe in.

We each numbly accepted a piece of candy that, I swear, was crawling around in the bowl. I was chasing this rubbery, wormy thing around my mouth when Uncle Cesar pulled on this red velvet rope hanging from the ceiling. This must have rung a bell somewhere, because all of a sudden, a door burst open with Archie and his mom and dad entering the lobby.

Archie introduced everyone around, including the welcoming committee. "Don't mind Uncle Cesar and Aunt Ana; they like to dress up for Halloween."

To that, Joe shot me an "I'm not so sure about that" look. We were then ushered into what looked like the private family quarters, where we met Archie's two older brothers, Hank and Thomas, who were home from college for the weekend.

Archie's dad was a normal father-looking guy who smoked a pipe, was tall, and had physical similarities to his older brother, Cesar, without the scary garb. He asked about our interest in cadavers as we were sipping the hot cider that was doled out to us. I answered in a way I would in science class and tried not to say it like it was purely morbid pre-adult curiosity, which it was.

About this time, the older brothers apologized for having to leave, but they were late for a party with a bunch of their friends from town. Archie's dad went on about dead bodies, calling them corpus delictis, and a bunch of other garble that came from a book I hope I never have to read. He volunteered Archie, who seemed more than willing, to show us the embalming room.

As we were descending the stone steps into the subterranean vault below the building, Archie said that his parents had high hopes of him carrying on the family business, which meant he would have to go to embalming school for a couple of years at a mortuary somewhere.

When we reached the cement floor, we walked to the end of a hallway and entered a room through a door that shut behind us, by itself it seemed. Archie flicked on a light, showing Annie Jo Molly lying face up under a sheet on a white marble table. It was a large room, with caskets stacked around on carts. Annie's table was in the center, drawing your eyes to it.

Her toenails still had red nail polish painted on them as they pointed up toward the huge light suspended from the concrete ceiling. The light was used only for operating on the cadaver and was off at the time. Her face was pinkish white, like a marble cue ball after polishing, and she had red circles around her closed eyes. Her hair was blonde and had been combed like it had never been messed up through the ordeal. You could see the threads of the sewing done to reattach the back of her head. It was easy to tell that she had been pretty. It was a wonder how someone could bring harm to a person so innocent and helpless looking.

Archie went on to explain the whole process with the embalming and washing and so on. He showed us one of the main veins where they were going to suck out the blood and pump in the formaldehyde, which he said would make her full-looking again and bring back some of her color.

"Right now, she's naturally dead, deader than a hammer," he said. "But when we get through with her, she'll look a little better."

He told us about rigor mortis as he offered up her arm. We both shook our heads and I said no thanks to that.

"You have to rub it out of 'em," he said.

As he was explaining away, I kept thinking the light was getting dimmer. I mentioned this, which just seemed to annoy Archie, who was really getting into the lecture by then. I couldn't help feeling the clammy silence in the room as he paused between his words. Old Joe was wondering about the diminishing light too, as he moved a little closer to my side.

"Jesus, Archie," I said, "it's getting damn near dark in here."

Archie raised his head slowly, tilting it slightly as if to say, "What the hell you talking about?"

Before either of us got out an answer, we heard this noise like a trunk that had been in the attic for forty years trying to open.

"Son of a bitch," Joe said, his voice about two octaves higher than normal, "that casket moved."

By the time I figured which box he was talking about, whatever it was doing had stopped. "You're nuts, Joe," I said.

"No, I ain't; that thing moved," he said.

"You guys are going looney?" Archie said.

About then we saw it give. The lid on the gold casket closest to us lifted. We both bolted for the door and Joe grabbed the knob. He turned around and looked at me with a face whiter than Molly's. He was holding the door knob in his hand. "We're locked in," he said.

We were standing there almost with our arms around each other looking at Archie, who was crouching over the corpse like Frankenstein tuning up his monster. The gold casket lid and the lid of the casket next to it opened at same time, both by bare, pink arms. We were about to shit our pants. Two faces appeared like jack-in-the-boxes.

One was Hank's and the other was Thomas', both laughing their asses off. Archie was in on it too.

Chapter 6

As we got a little older, the subject changed from frogs and marbles to model trains and airplanes, keeping us occupied until the serious stuff started. It was then, of course, girls and driving. All we could talk and think about were cars and driving and driving and cars. When I reached fourteen, Billy was getting close to having his license, and we were all counting the days, because we expected him to haul our asses around to places that passed the limits of bicycles. We already knew where all the cool hangouts were, but they were off-limits because of our transportation disability.

My dad had this maroon '50 Chevy pickup that was about five years old and had a little moss and mold on it, because he always parked on the street under the maple tree. He drove it to work at the mill every day, which was just down the street and over a couple of blocks to Water Street. Dad was the millwright who kept the machines running in Willamette, as well as in the company's other warehouses located in neighboring areas. I'd go down there on my bike sometimes after school to see Dad. Sometimes I would catch Jim Wilson, the owner, out on the dock next to the pop machine bullshitting with Dad. If things were going good that day, old Jim would cough up a nickel and buy me a Coke. This wasn't exactly free, though, because I would have to endure an interrogation on how school was going and the girlfriend situation and so on. Mr. Wilson was smooth and made you feel like an adult by just talking to you like he was interested in what you had to say. I liked him for it.

One Friday evening, Dad asked me if I wanted to go pheasant hunting. The following day was Saturday, opening day of pheasant season, the one Saturday of the year Dad took the entire day off. Dad never asked me to do much with just him, except maybe to go to the dump, which we did about once a month. We used thirty-gallon 2,4-d barrels Dad got from the farmers down at the mill. We chiseled the tops out and torched our garbage in them until they were filled with cans and glass that wouldn't burn.

Saturday was dump day. We would go after lunch, because in those days, he worked Saturday mornings. He would come home around noon and Mom would have a nice lunch ready for us. She went all out on Saturday because Dad carried his lunch bucket during the week with sandwiches, coffee, and a couple of oatmeal cookies. Every day was the same, though maybe a switcheroo on the sandwiches; it was wholesome, but I knew he looked forward to Saturday. I cherished the days we went to the dump together. Partly, I guess, just being alone with Dad and partly riding in the pickup. I watched as he drove it, shifting and throttling. I became pretty familiar with how the machine worked.

I'd seen plenty of pheasant hunters up and down the river and over the trestle in North Willamette. They carried these over and under and side-by-side shotguns and wore tan-colored, bullet-laden vests with red shirts and hats. They were your typical Elmer Fudd types. My dad wore the same garb he wore every day except for weddings and funerals. Khaki shirt and pants, lace up work shoes, and a baseball cap. I think he got used to wearing that stuff in the service and just kept right on with it.

I was real fired up about going hunting Friday evening, but the next morning, when Dad shook me awake while it was still dark, the whole romance of the thing seemed to just slip away in the fog of deep morning sleep.

Spooky, our little black cocker spaniel, was a veteran hunter and was going nuts with the smell of gun oil and the anticipation of another successful hunt. As we walked out the back door by the kitchen, I picked up the sack lunches Mom had set out for us. Dad was carrying the .22 single shot that always leaned up in the hallway by the telephone. At the time, I couldn't imagine why that dog thought it was neat to get up in the middle of the night, climb into a cold pickup, and leave town to chase around after a little innocent bird. I was fast asleep before we turned the first corner.

My dad grew up in the Depression. He was a natural survivor, and I think his hunting techniques reflected it.

He was after meat. I woke up when the Chevy hit the gravel, with the rocks clattering under the fenders. I didn't know exactly where we were since all the roads looked about the same, with borrow pits and ditches backed up by large, overgrown fencerows. It was perfect cover, with all the wild roses and blackberries for game birds to take shelter in after foraging in the fields. Dad pulled up and shut off the motor in a way that I knew meant I was going to hear him say something important.

"Well," he said, "this is how we are going to do it. You are going to do the driving and I'm going to do the shooting."

Spooky's ears popped up like she understood the part about who was going to drive and she glanced at me with a look of apprehension. Dad got out with the .22, walked around the front of the pickup, and opened the door.

"Scoot over," he said, "you can't drive from over here."

I plucked old Spooky up and plopped her down as I slipped under her and behind the wheel. I already knew a little more about driving than Dad was aware of, since I had taken the old truck around the block a couple of times.

The first time I drove a car, I was about twelve and my parents had gone to church. Since I had been sick that week, they thought I should stay home and rest. The church was just around the corner and up a couple of blocks, so we usually walked unless it was raining. Well, that day was nice and sunny, so they walked, and as soon as they got around the corner, I started feeling better. Right away, I was outside kicking a ball around the front yard, and pretty soon it bounced under the pickup. As I was leaning over fishing the ball out from under the running board, I noticed the keys were in the ignition.

We never locked anything around our place, including the house, except for the bathroom, which you could lock from the inside with this old skeleton key. Something was different that day, because I felt this urge pulling me into the truck like it was time to make a step forward. I got in and moved the seat forward a little and was just looking around when I noticed that Dad had left a half a pack of Chesterfields pinned between the sun visor and the roof. Well, being as some of us were already having a smoke once in a while, I lit one up with the matches that were lying on top of the ashtray.

While I was puffing away, I got to thinking maybe it would be nice to hear the motor running while I was enjoying my cigarette, so I pushed down on the starter. Chevy's had a pretty handy starter right next to the throttle, so you could apply a little gas while pushing on the pedal with your foot. I got it started and I was revving on it a little while, flicking my ashes out the window, when I heard these two voices at the same time.

"What's ya doing, Sonny, going for a drive?"

Damn, I was thinking, this is like my worst nightmare. It was Meg and Denise Olsen. I considered them peers since they had gone to the same grade school and shared some pretty hairy experiences with me and my other friends. You can imagine how embarrassing it was getting caught red-handed playing like I was an adult, which all of a sudden, I felt I was not. Before I could say boo, they were both in the pickup, jumping up and down, teasing the hell out of me. It was the usual dare deal, and of course, I couldn't back down, so it looked like we were going for a ride. In about twenty minutes, my folks were due to walk into the yard, so I decided to get a move on.

Man, those girls were really wired up, wiggling and giggling and prodding me along. I was in a tight spot. The Olsens were the prettiest girls on our side of town and getting prettier every day, if you know what I mean. With the changes they had gone through, they had become way out of my league. I'd watched my dad drive enough times and knew about how the clutch and the gear shift worked; I just had never gotten the chance to get the feel of it. So I put in the clutch, pulled the gear shift back where low was supposed to be on a column shift, and let out the clutch. It just jerked a couple of times and killed the motor.

I thought the girls were going to laugh themselves sick. I had accidently gotten the thing in high gear instead of low. It's hard to think when you're in the company of two girls who look like teenage movie stars but are acting like children. They could have wet their pants they were laughing so hard.

The second time, I pulled up on the shifter and dropped her into low with a lot of throttle to save me from killing the engine and having to endure the torture again. We launched. The back tires were parked on wet maple leaves and they got to spinning real good before we hit dry pavement, making a Broderick Crawford moment like on the TV show *Highway Patrol.* Crawford always did a wheel-squealing, tire-burning exit from gravel to pavement when he was after the latest bad guy. That's just how it was. I was burning rubber, and those girls really shut up then, because for a moment, they thought I knew what I was doing.

Anyway, I got us around the block without hitting anything and parked right back where we had been under the tree. All of a sudden, my ass was on fire! My cigarette had fallen down between my legs when we took that heroic leap. My Levi's were smoking and I was getting hot. I jumped out and started dancing around like a madman, which really got the girls going again. I excused myself and headed for the house, where I went straight to the bathroom and wet down my jeans before my underpants caught fire. With all of this, I still had the presence of mind to wash out my mouth with Listerine, because I didn't want my mom to smell smoke on my breath.

Dad said to start up the pickup, drive along at about 20, keeping my eyes peeled for pheasants, and if I saw one, to just keep on rolling along and come to a gradual stop, and then back up nice and steady and he'd plink it right out the window. He didn't go through the routine of how to start the motor or any of the rest of it, because that was how he was. He just expected me to be bright and get on with it, and I've always been thankful for it. I've always cringed when I saw some dad micromanaging his boy at some baseball game or something, telling the kid how to do every little thing. Then the old man goes ape shit congratulating him if he almost did something right. It just makes you want to puke.

That is how we did our hunting. We would just mosey along until we saw a Chiny or two along the road and we would start whispering back and forth about the best way to harvest the little bugger, and old Spooky would pick up on it and bury her head between her paws like she didn't trust herself to be quiet. As soon as Dad would squeeze the trigger, Spooky would about hit the ceiling and bolt out the same window where Dad made the shot. About half the time, he would be shooting out my window right over my lap. Dad never talked about what he did in the war, but somewhere, he sure learned how to shoot.

One time, we came upon a little group of pheasants, and he leveled the barrel and squeezed off one and just grazed the side of this rooster's head, and for some reason, that rooster flew straight up about a hundred feet and then just fell out of the sky. As Spooky was coming back with the rooster in her mouth, she hesitated and dropped it while trying to pick up another bird.

We sat there and watched this in total ignorance of what had happened. We figured the bullet must have glanced off the rooster's head and rammed right into the neck of the bird behind it, which happened to be a hen. My faithful dog gathered them up and brought them to us one at a time. Sure enough, the rooster began to wake up from the glancing blow, but then left this world in the jaws of a cocker spaniel. It was illegal as hell to be caught with a female pheasant. Being the way Dad was, there was no way that he was going to let that hen go to waste, so he put the hen into a brown paper bag and slipped it under the seat.

That was the one damn time we had to get stopped by a policeman, when we had the hen hidden behind the three roosters that were on the floor. We didn't have any idea why we were getting pulled over at the time, and it was a little tense for me, but old Dad was cool as can be. He just rolled down the window, handed his driver's license to the officer, and asked him what the problem was. It turned out to be just a burned out taillight. Dad said he could probably fix it on Monday when the parts store opened up.

Nothing was said until my dad pulled the truck up to the curb under the tree and shut it off. He sat there and didn't open the door, so I knew something was coming.

"Sonny, that little bird needed to be saved," he said, "but it was breaking the law, you know."

I nodded. "Yes."

"For the whole deal to work, people have to obey the laws," he continued.

"Yes, sir." I nodded again.

"It's up to your conscience to determine how you deal with certain situations, savvy?"

"Yes, sir."

He reached out and gave me a little bump on the shoulder, to sort of ram the point in.

Chapter 7

We made it through our freshman year and were even invited back to be sophomores. We felt this was a remarkable event, since none of us were scholarly, except Billy. He was going to be a senior, and was naturally intelligent, so he didn't have to try so hard. It wasn't because we weren't ambitious or anything; it just wasn't our deal. We were the hardworking types who liked achievements. We had different goals than acing a world history test about why Queen Somebody was banging a prince or something.

In fact, most of us were getting summer jobs and some of us were working after school. We began to want things and things cost money. Billy got a '40 Ford, and the first time I sat in that car, I could hardly think about anything else. Billy was kind of my mentor and he was a great role model. I had a habit of copying his moves as we were growing up. I wanted to have one of those cars like his, and I was determined to earn enough money so I could get one by the time I got my license. A driver's license was about the most important piece of paper anyone could ever own. It was like your own Declaration of Independence.

Miles Fletcher was working for his dad at the Mobil Station. Johnny Smith was in the lube bay down at his dad's Ford garage anytime he wasn't at school. Billy had done about everything from working on farms to boxing groceries at the Central Market. Joe just had a way, it seemed, to always turn something into a buck. For him, it was sometimes a means for survival.

I started working after school down at Wilson's Mill, sweeping the floor and eventually being hired on the summer I turned 15. It wasn't all about money. It was a step toward manhood when you carried your own lunch bucket and worked alongside other men, pulling your part of the load. There was something about the way Jim Wilson, the owner, handed me that first check that made me proud. He made me feel like he appreciated my effort; I think I grew a couple of inches that day.

Down at Wilson's, the summer help was always laid off after the last truckload of seed was dumped in August, and then the regular crew started the year-round routine of cleaning and bagging and so forth. When I was laid off that summer, I had a few weeks until school was to start, so I started looking to make a few more bucks to add to my stash. I had quite a bit of money saved up, which I had invested down at the First National Bank on First Street. I made money picking strawberries and beans in the summers before I got on at the seed mill and I saved darned near all of it. I had my bank book in the top drawer of my desk at home and I liked looking at the numbers as they added up with the interest. I knew I was going to need some serious money, because just buying the coupe would be big, but the cost of the speed equipment and dropped axle would choke a horse. I sure as hell wasn't going to be driving around town in a stock '40. Hell, I'd look like Grandma McDuck or something.

The day I got laid off from the mill, I was moping around down at the Fletcher Mobil Station. Billy and Archie were there changing the oil in Billy's coupe when they told me about a farmer out on Fisher Lane who needed a tractor driver for the rest of the summer. According to the boys, the man lived in a cul-de-sac off Broadway, right there in Willamette, and his last name was Crawford.

I didn't waste a lot of time getting over there on my bike. It was in West Side in a new development I hadn't been to before. After weaving in and out of this street and that, I came across a modern house with Crawford on the mailbox. It was about 6:30 in the evening and the garage doors were closed, so I didn't know if anyone was around. I was a little nervous since I had never officially applied for employment before. Down at Wilson's, I was a shoo-in because of my dad.

I mustered up the courage to ring the doorbell, and a slim, blonde lady opened the door with a smile. She was wearing slacks and a sweater and looked as if she took weekly visits to the beauty salon the way her hair and nails were kept. She wasn't your typical farm wife. I introduced myself and asked if she was affiliated with a farm out on Fisher Lane that was looking for a tractor driver.

She told me her name was Eleanor and she was glad to meet me. Yes, her husband and his brother owned the farm; she wasn't aware they were looking for help, but she didn't doubt it. I told her that I'd gotten laid off down at Wilson's Mill that day along with the other summer help. She got this kind of knowing look on her face and said, "I know old Jim down there, and if you can work for him, I'm sure you're just the kind of young man Rex is looking for."

Eleanor went on to say, "You should show up at 6:30 tomorrow morning, when Rex leaves for the farm."

I set my alarm for 6:00 and was out the door ten minutes later with my lunch, on my bike, pumping west. That was the earliest I'd ever slammed the screen door, besides last year's pheasant hunting. I hadn't been across town at that time of day before and I was amazed at the activity going on. I had never seen so many cats in my life. I always wondered how the garbage got picked up downtown, and I practically smacked into the truck when he was coming out of an alley next to Penney's. There were a couple of guys waiting for the tavern by the theater on First Street to open and an old woman plodding along pulling a Radio Flyer full of empties.

I swung around the corner by the hospital and turned west. I peddled by the cemetery, noticing that nothing seemed to ever change there. Thankfully, I was a couple of minutes early, because this guy who looked like Porter Wagoner came out of the Crawford home just as I was piling off my bike in his driveway. He had a gait about him showing he was enthusiastic and in a hurry. Expecting an interview, I was prepared with all the right answers.

He sort of sized me up as he reached for the door handle and then said, "Get in, kid."

I guess that was the interview, because there wasn't another syllable spoken all the way out to the farm, and Rex Crawford was laid back in the seat, shifting gears and smoking. He had this concentrated look on his face like he was planning out the day, or maybe his life. He was wearing a white cap called a duster, popular with guys who worked in the seed and grain mills, along with a golf shirt, Levi's, and white shoes. He looked like he should have been part of the Rat Pack rather than part of a farm. I wondered why Rex lived in town and not out on the farm, and I got to thinking maybe it was because it was handier for Eleanor, who probably had friends she liked to play bridge with or something.

As we were bombing along, I noticed the pickup had a burnt grass smell, like when our burn barrels would set the lawn on fire late in summer. I'd say we had gone about ten miles out south of town when we hit the gravel and I began to see where the smell originated. Most of the fields were black, and some of the undergrowth in the fencerows had been burnt, along with fence posts and a few telephone poles. In American history class, we had read about Sherman's March to the Sea, and the way things looked, I got to wondering if the old general had passed south of Willamette recently.

Rex took a hard left turn and bounced through one of the gates into a field that looked like all the rest, except there was a row of tractors lined up like a wagon train. The biggest pickup I had ever seen was servicing the tractors and that's where Rex left me off, again without saying a word. There was this kid who looked like he hadn't seen a haircut in a while leaning out of the back of the truck holding a diesel hose with its snout in one of the tractor's tanks. He invited me to start pumping and smiled, showing a silver front tooth. I think that was the new kid's job, because after a couple of tanks, I noticed that I was the only one sweating much. The truck was like one of those support vehicles they used along highway projects and it had enough stuff in it to keep an army going. It was loaded to the nuts with an air compressor, a big tool box, and all kinds of lube supplies, like oil and grease buckets.

As we were moving along fueling, an older fella about Rex's age was moving along slowly, kind of crouching like a monkey, checking the tractors and pumping a grease gun as he went. He introduced himself to me as Rex's brother, Albert, and said he was glad to have me along. I thought this guy was totally different from his brother. Albert was stout and looked like a farmer, wearing the normal khaki outfit with the hat and everything, and had his truck all decked out with essentials. Then there was his brother, Rex, and all he had in his pickup bed was a bag of golf clubs.

I noticed everyone was getting on tractors and warming them up, when Albert waved me over to one that was orange and said *Case* on the side of it. He fired it up while he was explaining all about it, and of course, he had to raise his voice over the noise and all. He went into great detail, telling me all about how it had power steering and that the motor was a 50 horsepower diesel. I could tell he was proud as hell of it. The tractor ahead of me was the first in line, and when it started out, Albert began explaining a little faster, since the tractor behind me was getting ready to move and, of course, mine was right in his way. The green one ahead of me, according to Albert, was pulling a disk that turns the soil over, and I was pulling a harrow that was just an angle iron affair with big teeth in it to sort of smooth the soil down. The other tractors were pulling lighter harrows and rollers behind them that made a soil bed ready for seeding. Hank, an old veteran of the farm I was told, was bringing up the rear, about two fields and a day and a half behind, with the grain drill, planting the seed and fertilizing at the same time.

By this time, Albert was practically yelling at me to go in third gear, and if I fell behind, to put it in fourth, and stay ahead of the guy behind me about two rounds and behind the guy up in front by a round or two. It seemed kind of funny to me that nobody ever asked me if I knew how to drive a tractor all this time, and it sort of reminded me of my first pheasant hunting trip with my dad. I slipped it into third and eased out on the clutch so I wouldn't kill the thing like I did with Meg and Denise that time in Dad's pickup, and took off smooth as hell. I kept my eye on the temperature and oil pressure gauges like I was told, and after a couple of turns, I looked back and I was harrowing dirt. I'll have to admit, there was a little horsing around out there since there wasn't anyone around to watch us. We were just four high-school-aged boys driving about a million dollars' worth of equipment around a big, borderless racing venue.

Noon rolled around and I got the feeling we weren't stopping for lunch. The kid who was driving the tractor behind me, and gaining on me all morning, passed by me as he was eating his baloney sandwich. He was covered with sweat and dirt; all I could see were his eyes and his mouth devouring his fare. We settled down to the grind after the sandwiches and cookies were gone. It was warming up, and it was hard to keep from dozing off, since we were all digesting, and that never changing buzz of the motors didn't help much.

Out of nowhere, Rex's pickup fender appeared right next to my left front wheel and he was waving me to stop. There were already two kids in back and one in front with Rex. I stopped the tractor and I could tell we were in a hurry, so I leapt over the side of the bed and we took off like we were late for a wedding. It was like hitting a switch; everyone went from being bored to death to being excited as hell, and of course, I didn't have a clue what was going on. The kids introduced themselves all around over the noise of the wind and the roar of Rex's Chevy. We were hanging on for dear life, since we weren't slowing down for ditches and everyone was getting a little air.

Come to find out, the wind had changed, making it a good day to burn the last field, since it was next to the railroad tracks. I was informed the burning was used to remove some of the straw and weeds and other pests of the breathing kind. According to one of the boys who had worked for the Crawford's a year or two, the fire liked to get out of control on that field and would burn up half the county, including the railroad property. That got everyone fired up. I could tell they liked burning fields, and the kid who was doing the talking was grinning like a skunk eating onions.

After going a couple of miles down the road, we wheeled into a field, bouncing over the plowed fire break, and pulled up beside a couple of tractors with water wagons. Old Albert was there in a cut-down farm truck with a tank on the back that looked like Fletcher's gas delivery rig. Everyone but me had the routine down, and as some of the boys mounted the tractors and wagons, one jumped up on the back of Albert's fire engine.

Rex looked at me and said, "Slam your ass on the tailgate, city boy."

Albert jumped down off the running board and lit up a Winston, and Rex had a Pall Mall going. They stood there puffing away, trying to see which way the wind was blowing by where their cigarette smoke was headed. Once they decided that the wind was in the direction they wanted, out came the matches, and then everyone really got wired up; even old Rex looked like he was in for a good time. The trick was to light the straw along the inside of the plowed firebreak on the downwind side of the field and let it burn out a ways against the wind till you had fifty or a hundred feet of burnt area, and then circle it.

The guys on the tractors would go along in front of the lighting and wet down areas where the firebreak was broken by some windblown straw or something. I found out what my job was soon enough when Rex handed me a pitchfork and said just sit here on the tailgate and scoop up a pile of straw, and when it got to burning real good, he would take off in the Chevy. I was supposed to drag the fork with the tongs downward, applying pressure that would pick up new straw and the burning straw would fall off. That is exactly what happened. Everything went along according to plan, with Albert patrolling up and down the fire line through the smoke. I don't think he could see where he was going half the time, because every once in a while, he would come roaring out from behind the wall of smoke with tears streaming down his face. The smoke was burning his eyes, but he was grinning, with both hands on the wheel and a cigarette sticking out of his mouth; it was like he couldn't get enough of it.

We waited around for a little while, letting the fire burn out against the wind. Everything was looking pretty safe when Rex said, "What the hell, let's circle it."

It was about all I could do to grip the fork with one hand and hang on to the pickup with the other while we were hitting ditches and weaving in and out down the fencerow.

When we made it around to where we started, old Rex was in escape mode, and all I heard was, "Hang on, kid!"

We bounced our way out onto the road away from the smoke, and as I looked back, it was like Hiroshima when the bomb ignited. There was this big mushroom cloud. The wind picked up, and there were these whirlwinds, hundreds of feet high, carrying straw as high as you could see. About that time, Albert came crashing through the fencerow out into the road, like a tank during the war in Europe. He cranked the steering wheel and headed our way, looking like General Patton in his khaki garb. He seemed to be in a distressed way as he came roaring up the road at us with limbs and brush all over him and his truck.

When he pulled up beside us, he was yelling over the noise of the pump engine that was running full-bore. He was waving his hands toward the fire as he was shouting.

"One of them damned whirlwinds dropped some hot straw over in Sammy Smith's field!" Sammy Smith was the neighbor bordering the field we had set fire. Albert's cigarette was bouncing up and down and he was excited as hell. "It's burning, and if the wind catches it, it's gonna go crazy and we're going to be in some real shit over this."

"I'll go use old Rosie's phone and call Henderson and get him out here. I think we're going to need some help before this is over," Rex yelled back.

Gravel was flying everywhere as he had the wheel cranked all the way over with his foot on the throttle. Every time he would shift gears, we would drift a little sideways, and then he leveled out at about 60, which seemed to be his limit on gravel. We came up to Rosie's place, a well-kept, two-story farmhouse painted white with a large covered porch. We slid to a stop and Rex jumped out and made for the door. His whole demeanor seemed to change when he knocked, and he was holding the duster in his other hand. A small, elderly woman opened the screen door. She was wearing a cotton dress and had her hair up in a bun. She smiled when she recognized

Rex, but then got a concerned look on her face when she was told of our predicament. I was too far away to hear what was said, but I could tell he thanked her after using her phone, and as soon as she shut the door, he was back to his old self, going off the end of the porch without using the step.

On the way back to the field, Rex seemed like he wanted to talk a little and explained how he had called Ralph Henderson, the fire chief at Porterville, which was the closest town with a fire department. According to Rex, Ralph also owned the local garage in the little town and fixed and serviced the locals' vehicles.

"When Henderson gets the call, he'll roll out from under whatever he's working on and head for the phone, cussing all the way about what the hell's up now," Rex explained. "If it's the red phone, he'll answer politely, because he likes being the fire chief. So after receiving the summons from some kind of fire or wreck, Ralph will jump into anything that will run, like a customer's car, and haul ass over to the fire hall, which is only a couple blocks from his shop, and blow the whistle. Then he'll start up the red Ford, the newest engine, and from there he'll come roaring out with the siren and lights going. About the time he gets the siren full tilt and the gumball whirling good, he'll slam on the breaks in front of Charlie's Market and run in and put a case of Hamm's on the department account. This will give the volunteers working close to the hall time to run and jump on the fire truck as Ralph is pulling out with lights flashing and the siren on kill.

When we got back to the field, the guys on the water wagons were going along putting out fires on fence posts and telephone poles. Albert had cut a hole in the fence so Ralph could get the Ford into Sammy's place and was there squirting out what he could with his truck. After we heard the siren coming from a distance, the truck showed up with the big gumball light rotating, making it look official and all. I could tell these guys knew what they were doing, because it didn't take old Ralph long to size up the situation and go right after it. With one volunteer running the front hose and one on the back hose, they had it under control in no time. Ralph had a satisfied look on his face when he came back, chugging through the ash and embers, making for the gate. Rex and Albert were right there to thank them, while the mill rat riding shotgun handed each of them a Hamm's from the cab, and then they were on their way. There was other field burning going on, so the fire department didn't hang around and bullshit long, because they needed to get back and fill up in case they got another call.

By the time we got all the posts and power poles extinguished, we were out of water. Albert and the boys manning the wagons headed back to the farm to fill up and get back to farming.

Rex and I were leaving the field in his pickup when he looked in the rearview mirror and said, "Son of a bitch, Sammy's field is on fire again!"

Chapter 8

I spun around in the seat and saw a spiral of smoke coming up in the field we had just come from, and it was growing fast. The wind had switched to the north and Rex said that would run the fire right into the railroad track. He said he was going to have to call Henderson again, and Ralph would be extra pissed this time, since he hated going out to the same fire twice. "We're going to the home place where I can use the phone to call the fire department," Rex said. "While we're there, I want you to run into the shop and get a case of beer out of the fridge."

We were doing the usual 60 until he started backing off the throttle and the motor started knocking. He pulled up the driveway past Albert and the boys who were filling their tanks with water from the well house. The shop was located past the well, next to the old house where Rex and Albert's mother lived. This is where Vic, the farm mechanic, was standing looking out at the smoke we had just come from.

"Son of a bitch, Vic," Rex said, "there's something wrong with this thing."

As I got out, I wondered how a pickup this new could sound like it was worn out already.

Vic opened the hood, pulled out the dip stick, and said, "Rex, there ain't no oil in it."

"Well, by God, there was oil in it when I bought it!" Rex said. Vic dumped about a gallon of 50 weight in the motor, which seemed to quiet it down a little. I ran to the fridge, and then we were off, back to the fire with the beer in the bed of the truck.

Rex took a left turn and circled around, crossing the railroad tracks below the fire to see how far it had spread. Sure enough, the fire was in the railroad property, burning like hell.

We were back in the field gate when Henderson returned for his second time. Rex had me hand the volunteers the beer, and old Ralph wasn't smiling much as he headed across the field toward the tracks.

Rex was in his thinking mode again. You could tell by the way he was attacking the cigarettes and the bottle of beer at the same time. I was standing there on the other side of the pickup box with my own cigarette, and of course, Rex had given me a Hamm's too, like he thought that would help me come up with a solution to the problem at hand. He knew he and Albert were in deep, because it wasn't the first time the Crawford farm had burnt up some of Southern Pacific Railroad property, and those ties weren't cheap. He decided to drive across the burnt field to the railroad tracks since the fire department from Franklin, a small town east of the farm, along with a couple of trucks from Willamette, were already there. Along with the engine from Porterville, it was quite a commotion, with all the flashing lights and crackling voices over the static of two-way radios.

We had gotten out of the pickup and were leaning up against it when, through the smoke, I could see a truck come up the tracks. It was painted silver, with blue and red stripes, the Southern Pacific logo, on the side and a spinning light of its own. These two official-looking guys, who the railroad men called brass hats, got out, wearing their yellow hardhats and white uniforms. They came tiptoeing through the smoldering grass and debris, trying not to get their shoes dirty. One was a little taller than average and the other was overly short, wearing glasses, and carrying a fancy leather notebook.

Old Rex remained leaning back on the fender of the Chevy, with his arms crossed, and braced himself for the ass chewing he was about to receive. It was not long coming either, as the tall one started right in by saying, "God damn you, Rex, you've really done it good this time, and you won't be getting away scot-free like last time."

The tall guy went on and on about all the ways the Crawfords would be punished, and each time he would make a point, the short guy would stomp his foot and write something down in the book. The tall guy was getting closer and closer and was almost thumping Rex's chest.

Right about then, I had to rub the sweat out of my eyes because I was looking at something I could hardly believe. A big, streamlined locomotive came chugging right up the tracks behind the silver rig these agents had just gotten out of. The huge machine made their little truck look insignificant, to say the least. Behind the locomotive was this fancy train car followed up by a caboose. Rex told me later that in the old days it was common for rich folk to ride around in their own coaches, especially big shots from the railroad hierarchy. As this was happening, the big guy's finger just kept pumping like a piston towards Rex's chest, but his head was jerked around backwards and his jaw had dropped clear to his belt. These guys were more surprised than we were. They didn't know whether to shit or go blind.

The silver train came to a stop, and a tall, distinguished guy dressed in hunting garb and wearing a big floppy hat with one side of the brim tied up emerged. He stepped over the fence, followed by these two guys who looked like butlers. The guy walked with the authority of General MacArthur but looked just like Teddy Roosevelt. He started out by announcing that he was Harold Henry Harriman from the Southern Pacific Railroad in Omaha and he was interested in meeting the owner of this property on which he was standing.

If old Rex was stunned like everyone else, including me, he didn't show it. "That would be me, Rex Crawford," he said as he stuck out his hand.

Mr. Harriman took his hand and gave it a shake, while they both looked each other squarely in the eyes.

This brought the big brass hat back to his senses, and he started in about how it was Rex's fire and he would see to it that the Crawfords would pay dearly for it this time for sure. I could tell these brass hats were trying to make some points, since they knew Harriman was a big shot in the company.

Mr. Harriman turned on him with a wrath like I'd never seen.

"My grandfather was known as a robber baron. We in the family and company have been trying to live that down for three generations. I'll have you know it is not company policy to be treating our neighbors in the way I've just witnessed," he said. He then told them to kindly wait quietly while he finished his business with Mr. Crawford and then they would be dismissed.

Boy, were the tables turned, the ass chewers became the ass chewed. One of the butlers politely broke in and explained the reason for their visit. "Mr. Harriman is a sporting man and has hunted game all over the world, but has never bagged a Chinese pheasant like you have here in Oregon."

"Hell, that's easy," said Rex, who was relieved the subject had changed. "When we start burning in the fall, the Chinies fly right up there to Rock Butte or over to the bluff."

He pointed over at some hills that puff up right in the middle of the valley.

Rex went on, "I'll get a couple of gunny sacks from the warehouse in the morning and you'll have them full by noon."

"Oh bully," Harriman said, excited like. He even sounded like old Roosevelt.

Albert's two water wagons came by a little late. They had to wait at the home place until the tanks were full, so they missed out on the action. The other kids came riding by, taking in the spectacle with eyes as big as saucers. I gave them a little salute with my beer, and I could tell they were envious as hell. When Albert came by, he and Rex exchanged looks, but you couldn't tell what they were thinking, though they both looked relieved. I jumped up on the back of one of the wagons as it was headed towards the track to put out railroad ties.

As I was riding along looking back, I could see old Harriman had one hand over Rex's shoulder and the other wrapped around a Hamm's while looking toward Rock Butte. The only thing the two agents had in their hands were their hats, and they were looking down at the charred earth.

I got a ride back to town that night with Albert, because he had to make a late-night parts run for a stalled tractor so he was going that way anyway. He had me fill him in about the dude in the private railcar. While we were discussing the events of the day, I couldn't help noticing how much different he was than his brother. I hardly ever saw the two of them look at each other, let alone speak. I'd known other brothers, but they were always hanging out together and were good friends. I've always wished I could have had one. When I told him how the tables turned on those local railroad agents he was laughing so hard I was afraid he was going to fall out of the truck.

The next morning, I was back at Rex's house, waiting when he came out. I was surprised since he almost had a smile on his face and he even called me by my name. He was talkative on the way out and I just let him go since I was a little sleepy anyway. He told me how important it was that we get done with the planting before school started, because then they would lose the summer help and the year-round guys liked to go deer hunting about then.

I asked, "Speaking of hunting, how's old Harriman going to get his pheasants?"

"I just turned that over to Albert since that's more down his alley," he answered. Rex's eyes sort of bugged out when he would make a point and they were really bugging out as he slammed his fist on the dash and said, "Old Albert will get him so many birds he'll be eating pheasant under glass all the way back to Omaha."

Every day was about the same. We started up the tractors at seven in the morning and shut down at seven at night. I kept my hours in this John Deere planner book, and it was pretty simple since every day was 12 hours and we worked 6 days a week. Of course, I never asked how much I was getting paid, but I knew it was adding up fast.

After the three weeks were about up, Rex paid me the morning of my last day. He asked me how many hours I had worked. I pulled out the planner and handed it over to him. He handed it back and said he wasn't going to add it up for me. I told him that counting the rest of that day I'd worked 12 hours a day for 18 days.

He said, "That's two hundred and sixteen hours. How's a dollar and a quarter sound?"

"Great." I answered. It was twenty-five cents an hour more than I expected.

"That comes to about two hundred seventy and we don't need to take out any taxes this time because you're short-term help."

I thought this was getting better all the time.

He stopped the Chevy, leaned ahead, pulled his checkbook out of his back pocket, and laid his cigarette in the ashtray. He wrote the check out right there on his knee and tore it off without writing down the transaction.

His eyes got that bugged-out look again when he handed me the check and said, "How about an even three hundred and you can come back and work for us any old time you want?"

As I shook his hand and thanked him, I could hardly get the grin off my face.

That day, we were in the last field, right by the railroad tracks we almost burnt up, and it was starting to spit rain. It wasn't bothering anything because the ground was so dry and the machinery was still working fine. Old Hank had caught up with the seeding and was right in the field with us, so we all finished about the same time. As we were leaving the field, the sky got dark and it started pouring. The disks and harrows had these hydraulic affairs built right on to them so we could just lift them and drive the tractors right down the road with the tires slinging mud from the field. We got drenched on the way back to the farm. The water and dirt were running down our faces, leaving our eyes gleaming and teeth shining like a tribe I'd seen in the *National Geographic*.

It was still raining like hell when we got to the warehouse, where Hank drove his tractor and the seeder under cover while all the rest of us parked our rigs outside. I jumped in the backseat of the silver-toothed boy's car to get a ride back to Willamette. Everyone was headed to town to cash their checks. I glanced out the side window as we passed the shop where the big pickup was parked. Rex and Albert were sitting on the tailgate in the rain. Rex had his arm over Albert's shoulder and they were laughing, sharing a bottle of Hamm's.

Chapter 9

I should have been a little leery of Archie's party invitation after the Halloween episode. "The Halloween Classic" is what we called it ever after. He pulled off a coup on us that has been unrivaled since.

Archie was our connection to West Side, which was pretty exciting in the fact that we never felt welcome over in that part of town because of our status and the natural social barrier that had existed for years, dividing the city. The imaginary line ran north and south, down the middle of Peterson Street, dividing the town into east and west.

If we managed to cross the line unescorted by a parent or a townie, we would receive wrath of some kind, including jeers and sometimes even a cascade of rocks. Of course, this just made the lure and temptation greater. All the main stores were over on the west, and that is where we would go with our moms for shopping and other services. During these excursions, we would get a glimpse of kids from the other side and little sneers, if we were even acknowledged.

By the time of the invitation, we were in our freshman year, and the students from the other side who had been sort of a blur before began to come into focus. Especially the female ones. It was the forbidden fruit deal. The more we couldn't have them, the more it was getting under our skin. From the rumors we heard and the occasional flirt we received, we began to think these girls were way ahead of the ones over on our side. We could hardly keep up with them, but that didn't hamper our obsession, the phenomenon of the West Side rich girl.

So Archie had the keys to West Side. His family was well-heeled and in the upper crust, and he was respected as well. He got invited to the parties and was included in the events. However, as time went on, he spent more and more time with us, which was good in that he offered another flavor to our little band.

The invite included Gary Brown, Johnny Smith, and me. We had been running together since the initiation of the Little Bastards and we were right in the core of the thing. We all agreed to take Archie up on his offer, and in fact, we were giddy about it. The talk had been switching to girls a lot, since we were getting to the age where things were brewing inside us. The juices were beginning to flow. Right off the bat, it was competitive, like everything was with us. No one would admit that they hadn't a clue. All we really knew was what we had read in the rags we lifted any chance we could. Some of the older guys down at the mill offered up their wisdom and advice occasionally, even if not asked. The whole conglomeration that was running amuck in our brain matter was about to explode.

The party was to be the following Saturday night at a two-story house on a street they called Mortgage Row, which was a community of lawyers, doctors, and the like. It was owned by Clifford A. Clouse, an architect in town. He and his wife, Helen, would be going to the Elks Club Valentine's Day party for the evening, hence their daughter, Cindy, was throwing a party, also with the Valentine's theme. According to Archie, the dress code was to be something red and white, and some hearts would be nice.

When Archie gave us this information at school, Gary said, "Yeah, like that's going to happen."

By the look on Archie's face, I could tell he was beginning to wonder if he was doing the right thing by dropping the three of us right in the middle of his little nest of angels. The dress code for us would be bomber jackets over J.C. Penney's t-shirts, Levi's, and engineer boots.

"I can't wait until they ask to see my hearts," said Johnny. "They'll be all over my undies and I'll just have to drop my drawers to show 'em."

"Uh-huh," I rolled my eyes. "That'll be the day."

Come Saturday night, we met up at my house and lit out for Archie's, taking the back streets and keeping quiet. Once we got with Archie, we were back to our don't-give-a-shit mode, beating ourselves into a frenzy with the anticipation of the event.

I noticed when we arrived that there weren't any bikes other than ours, which we slammed down on the manicured front lawn. The house was one of the new split-levels with big windows and a three-car garage. One door was open, revealing the back of a Cadillac and a riding lawnmower. *This is definitely high-end*, I thought to myself.

Archie rang the bell next to a pair of large, wooden doors lit up by a porch light that was supposed to look like a torch. One of the doors was opened by a girl sporting a white dress with red hearts all over it. Clearly, this dress was going to be worn once and then tossed. She had her hair all done up with curls like she was going to the prom or something and had been tuning up all day for sure.

She invited us through a foyer as large as our living room. This opened up to a massive chamber where the party was happening. It was to be an affair with lots of color and gaiety. There were a couple of guys in sweaters and slacks drinking Cokes by the window. When they looked up from their conversation about the upcoming baseball season, they shot us a look of apprehension. After sizing us up with a little scorn, they fell right back into who was going to pitch and so on. The girls were crowded around the hi-fi, spinning 45s around their index fingers. I noticed right off this event wasn't chaperoned, which strengthened my theory about the west being out ahead of us, socially speaking.

When the door behind closed, all eyes fell on us. Seven teenage girls were all looking us up and down to the tune of "Only You" by The Platters. They were eyeing us like we were from some other planet. Since the boys weren't interested, Archie made an attempt to introduce us to the girls. They were weaving and giggling so much he couldn't track them long enough to make it stick. One parted the crowd and came at me, latching onto my arm.

Sylvia Hunsminger was her name, and before she got done wrangling me around, she had rubbed her chest all over my young body. She was better at it than most fourteen-year-olds should be. She had a hold on me and would turn me around showing me to her friends like I was a new toy. Each time she would spin me, she would wipe the front of me with her knockers. I couldn't have said "shit" if my mouth was full of it. She was tall, about two inches short of me, and had matured way faster than was safe.

She was the Marilyn Monroe type, with an hour glass body, blonde hair, and full lips that were as red as our hostess's hearts. She had blues eyes that never seemed to leave me. She looked eighteen and acted like it too.

Archie came to the rescue by practically wedging between us to make a formal introduction. This act unhooked her momentarily while he rattled off my résumé. I already knew something about her because we had encountered her the summer before at the Willamette Country Club swimming pool. Gary and Johnny were in on that too, and I was hoping she didn't recognize us and trusting the boys not to spill the beans.

The previous summer, one of our enterprises was searching out golf balls on the course and turning them in for cash. We had a hideaway between the fifth and sixth holes where we took refuge, watching for drunken golfers who were always losing their balls, and we would be right there to pounce. On a good day, we could round up a pretty good sack full and cash it in for enough for some smokes and a pop or two.

On the way to the greens keeper's shack, where we would cash in the balls, we had to pass the swimming pool, and we could hear the rich kids splashing around in the water. It had a high fence, so we couldn't see in to ogle at the girls or anything. It was torture. Walking by on a hot day in our jeans and boots, hearing those little jackoffs having all that fun, was punishment. If we happened to be close when the spring went off on the diving board, we were in for a free shower and that's all we got.

One day, when Gary made the ball delivery by himself, he noticed the door to the locker room was unlocked. He slipped in to find the room was filled with swimming gear, fins, and snorkels. He was going on about this down at our hideaway one afternoon, which gave me an idea.

"Do you think that we could get in there and get our hands on the gear?" I asked.

"Hell yeah," he said. "It's wide open and for the taking."

"I'm not talking about lifting the stuff," I said thoughtfully. "What if we got in with our suits on and put on the goggles and all. Do you think we could get into the pool sort of incognito like?"

"That might work." Gary was tracking. "They'd never know who we were with all that shit on."

"Yeah, maybe," I said. "The hard part would be to act like little shithead rich kids."

We agreed it was worth a try and shook hands all around. The gig was on.

The following day, we met up at my house and pedaled for the golf course. It was a warm afternoon and we had our trunks on under our jeans. We swung out to the hideaway, dropped our Levi's, and headed for the clubhouse in just our swim trunks. We dumped our bikes behind the garbage cans and nonchalantly waltzed by the lone vehicle in the pool parking lot, which was a Vespa motor scooter. The scooter was owned by the lifeguard, Miss Susan Miller, the high school girls' P.E. teacher, who worked the pool in the summer. She was famous for being a Nazi-like drill instructor and didn't put up with any shit from anyone.

Gary checked the door, and sure enough, it was unlocked. He motioned for us to follow him in. The room was all cement and smelled like a chlorinated dirty clothes hamper. We helped ourselves to goggles and fins and Johnny grabbed a loose snorkel as we departed. A door at the end of the room, past the girls and boys bathrooms, led to the pool. I pushed it open with authority, looking like I had done it a hundred times before. It was total mayhem in and around the pool, so we went unnoticed as we threw ourselves in at the shallow end and began splashing around like the other idiots. With the goggles on we looked like everyone else, so we just concentrated on having a good old time.

The Nazi woman was perched on her throne halfway up one side of the pool, but she was mostly interested in this true detective magazine she was reading. On the other side, in the shade of the fence, a lady we took for someone's mother was sitting at a poolside table smoking Kool cigarettes, which she lit with a stack of wooden matches. Johnny commented that he wouldn't mind trying one of the mentholated weeds sometime.

I had pulled myself up on the edge of our end of the pool to let the sun warm me up when I noticed someone at the opposite end doing the same. She was a platinum blonde with eyes as blue as the pool. She was young but had the body and look of a much older female. I knew her name from school, Sylvia Hunsminger, and her feet were dangling in the water and she was leaning back on her hands, which made her chest stick out about like my eyeballs were popping out.

I poked Gary when he came gurgling by with the snorkel in his mouth. He stood up and took a look, giving out a long low whistle of wonder. There was so much going on, she wasn't going to notice a couple of creeps like us watching, so we just got an eyeful.

Johnny came kicking along on his back and saddled up next to us. He was jabbering on about something until he noticed we weren't really there, so he followed our eyes to the target and let out, "Oh my God."

About this time, the water goddess slipped into the pool to cool off. She dropped in careful not to wet her hair or those lovely red lips. After a minute of her cooling off and us cooling our pipes, she popped back up on the edge. This, of course, made her white two-piece all wet and she shivered in the slight breeze that was floating across the pool. The sudden cold snap that hit her skin made her nipples stick out like first grade pencils.

She was way ahead in physical maturity, but her ladylikeness hadn't caught up. She was wiggling her knees back and forth like she was fanning a fire, which naturally just drew our eyes right to her crotch. We were flailing around trying to look busy but just couldn't keep our eyes off the target. The comments were flying back and forth under our breath, weighing and judging like it was a meat auction.

Gary made the observation that he thought he could see a pubic hair. To this, Johnny came to attention and was intensely looking for the same.

"I can definitely see one," I said.

"Yeah, for sure," Gary said.

This was getting to Johnny, because he just couldn't make one out no matter how much he stared. We were having a little fun with him now that we got him going. Johnny was a little younger and a model of naivety. He was the only one of us on the pudgy side, not because of his eating habits, just a natural state. He seemed to be engrossed with the concept of seeing a female pubic hair, which made our job egging him on easy.

"I'm going in for a closer look-see," he said as he was strapping on the snorkel. He stuck it in his mouth, lowered the goggles, and pushed off like a frogman leaving a sub. He swam in a zigzag formation to throw off any detection, all the time working his way north. About halfway across, he seemed to lose his bearings and started drifting. Maybe it was fogged up goggles or maybe the crowded conditions, but anyway, he crashed head on into the cement wall right between Sylvia's legs. As he jerked his head up, he tore off the goggles just in time to look straight at Miss Hunsminger's article. She let out a scream. Not a sophisticated, eighteen-year-old beauty queen scream, but a thirteen-year-old little girl's scream of terror.

This started things moving. Miss Miller, eighty pounds over average, threw the magazine over her shoulder as she leaped off her elevated chair. She headed for the scene in a fast waddle, not giving Johnny enough time to make an escape. I'm not sure if he had recovered from the shock of it all, but before he could move, Susan came down on him with one of her monster feet on his head and submerged him underwater. I think she would have drowned him if he hadn't wiggled loose and came up coughing and spitting. She then reached down with those enormous, elephantine arms and pulled him straight out of the pool by his ears.

By this time, we had evacuated, and I was holding the metal gate open for Johnny's exit. He was hopping along pulling off the fins on the run. As he removed them, he flicked them into the pool, along with the goggles and snorkel, in kind of a last ditch "up yours." He could out move old Susan without the fins and such, and by the time they made a lap around the pool, he was up to speed and she just couldn't waddle that fast, but she kept yelling, "I'm going to catch you, you little perverted son of a bitch!"

The lady at the table had gotten up and gone for something and missed out on all the excitement, but she had left her Kools, along with the matches. Where Johnny got the wherewithal, I don't know, but when he was going by her table on the last lap around the pool, he reached down and scooped up the pack and a couple of matches.

As soon as Johnny made it through the gate, I slammed it shut, and we made for the bikes. We were tearing out of the lot when Johnny made the assertion that she wasn't coming after us. He wheeled over to the Vespa and jammed a matchstick into the air valve on the rear tire, which started hissing air.

"When she jumps her fat ass on this little thing, she's gonna really be pissed." He grinned.

A few minutes later, we could be found back at the hideaway smoking Kools and reflecting.

Anyway, that was my first encounter with Sylvia, and it was looking like the second was going to be equally as interesting. Once Archie dropped the intervention, she was all over me again. Gary and Johnny couldn't hardly believe what they were seeing. I couldn't so much see it as I was feeling it. The other girls seemed to be used to her and the way she went after it. They seemed a little amused, probably more with me and the way I was trying to handle the frisking.

Cindy came over to the hi-fi and the girls went after dance partners, and of course, there was no saying no to Miss Hunsminger. Luckily, I had done a little dancing down at the Elks where I took some lessons. I actually kind of liked dancing, but I got such a ribbing from the boys that I gave it up. Everyone was doing the bop and so was I. Of course, every time I would give Sylvia a spin she would come by like we were crammed into an elevator with a dozen other people. She would give a rub or bury my head into her hair or brush up against my cheek on each flyby.

This was taking effect on me. I was being aroused to the point that I was constantly trying to find a new place for my dick. It got hard as an icicle and I was afraid it was going to shatter at any moment. Once it got bad enough, I went to the bathroom between songs to readjust my setup in my underwear and jeans. The bathroom was at the end of a long hallway with a floor made of oak, which made it slippery, and we were all in our stocking feet. When I came out, Sylvia was about to come in, but instead, she grabbed me and slid me around a little with an embrace and then planted those red lips on mine. I'd really never had much of a kiss before, except from Great-grandma down at the nursing home, which I avoided like the plague. This was different, wet and soft and big. I was trying to do my part, mostly just doing what she was doing back. She parted my lips with her tongue, and in it came, moving around in there in search of the same. It sent a surge up my legs and then to my cranium and back to my loins like lightning strikes. It had the energy of a hotwire fence but felt good instead of real bad.

A new song came on that she said she just had to dance to. It was "Earth Angel," and we slow danced around the room, locked together like train cars going over a cliff. Nothing else seemed to matter. We were flying out there and we weren't worried about hitting the bottom.

Well, the bottom arrived with headlights appearing in the driveway. The music got quieter and the lights brighter. Archie came up and said, "Let's blast, this party's over."

About then, Sylvia pulled my arms from around her waist and raised them up and held them on her breasts for a millisecond and said, "Feel these?"

"Yes," I croaked.

"Well, you can't have them," she said. She gave me a look like she'd just bit into a sour apple, spun around, and disappeared. The party was over.

As we were slipping out the door to the sound of "Black Denim Trousers and Motorcycle Boots" by The Cheers, something was starting to go from real good to real bad. My balls started aching like only they can. It was like I took a direct hit from a bowling ball while doing the splits. The more I tried to walk, the worse it got. They were like two big red pears hanging between my legs, so tender and sore I could hardly move. I was walking like a little kid with his diaper full of shit. There was no way I could get on my bike. Gary and Johnny headed out to beat their curfew, but good old Archie walked along with me pushing the bikes. We had all sorts of causes and reasons with good and bad outcomes for my balls, but we really didn't have a clue.

Going west, we came to a Shell Station just closing up. Archie knew the fella, who I recognized as the only black man in town. When there is only one, you can't help noticing. We stopped there under the lights to give my balls a rest, and old Jake came up to see if anything was wrong.

"Hi, Jake," Archie said, "Sonny here's balls are aching like mad and he can hardly get along."

"Well," Jake said, "what's you all been up to tonight?"

Archie did the talking, because my voice was too high to make much of a noise.

"We've been dancing with some rich girls over on Mortgage Row," he said.

"That's it," said Jake, very matter of fact.

"That's what?" I managed.

Jake looked at me half-sad and half-envious, "Sonny, you got yourself lover's nuts. Blue balls, they call 'em. It's from having all this activity with a female but not getting on with the final event," Jake explained. "I'll take you guys home. Give me them bikes and I'll throw them in the back of my truck here and we'll be off."

I carefully got in among the shifter and brake, odds and ends that all of a sudden looked like weapons after my cojones. Everything was suspect.

We dropped Archie off and then old Jake whistled and talked all the way to my house, where he helped me with the bike and assured me that everything would be alright come morning. I told him thanks. He said the same with a wink and he was gone.

I shuffled into the house, thankful that everyone was asleep, and slipped between the sheets with a tortured smile on my face.

Chapter 10

During my early years of high school, I kept having this reoccurring dream that it was my first day of classes and I was wearing these black brogues with cleats on the soles. I had three cleats on the right front, one small one on the left front, and on the heels I had big horseshoe cleats that encompassed the whole back of the shoe. Anyway, I got a hall pass from the teacher and headed for my locker to get the homework I had forgotten. I began to sort of skate like the speed skaters you see on TV in the Olympics, bent over and my arms going back and forth and all.

The high school was pretty new and it had long, wide halls lined with light brown lockers and classroom doors. The floors were all shiny and had that waxy schoolhouse smell. There was no one around, so I got going faster and faster, fantasizing I was on the home stretch up somewhere in the Alps with all these movie people taking pictures and beautiful women watching. Then I came to this corner and began to realize I was in trouble. I was leaning into it, trying to keep my feet under me and dragging one foot sideways, but I just couldn't get it under control.

Halfway through the corner, I saw three girls standing by a locker with a mirror on the inside of the door, and they looked as if they were trying on each other's lipsticks. When they saw me, their eyes got as big as saucers and they froze. They looked like three grade school kids watching *War of the Worlds* through doe eyes and from the front row. I knew I was in trouble, so I aimed for the locker right between the girls and slammed into it with a sound anyone who ever went to school remembers. Of course, the girls let out a scream and their books flew all over the floor, and I was in a spin like a freestyle skater, bouncing off the locker doors with my feet tangled up in Science 101 and the Basics of Math.

I let out a meek, "Sorry."

I couldn't see any reason to stick around and face the wrath, so I pushed on. That's when I heard a masculine voice behind me coming around the corner saying, "Hey there, youngster, I want to have a talk with you."

Glancing over my shoulder, I could see it was my worst nightmare. Now, doesn't it seem odd that I was thinking *nightmare* inside of a nightmare? But that is the way it was each time it reoccurred. It was Ashley Klink, who was the vice principal at the school, and he was the law. He was in charge of discipline and he took it seriously.

He was taller than everyone else, had a big, balding head, and part of one of his front teeth had been broken off. He had a nervous way of nodding all the time, like he approved of the way he carried out his job. The story was, he had been in a prison camp in Germany during the war. After that and other experiences, he liked things kind of orderly. I had heard about how he would break up fights in the hallways and drag both parties back to his office by their collars, while smiling and greeting students on his way. I had some of my own encounters with old Klink later on, singularly and a few times when he invited all of us Little Bastards to the conference room next to his office. His voice would come over the intercom, and of course, he didn't give us the respect of calling us the Little Bastards, but would read off all our names, and we would leave our respective rooms and head down for another ass chewing session.

I could hear Mr. Klink starting to run, which was not hard, because he was heavy and his shoes were big. So, of course, I'm just churning away trying to get traction with those cleats not hooking up. The faster I got going, the closer he got, and I could feel his breath on the back of my neck, and I knew that any second he was going to reach for my collar and pull my feet right off the ground. The very second that it was going to happen, the bell would always ring and 48 doors would fly open with 1,200 students hitting the hallways at the same time. I was saved again as I glided into the mob and never looked back.

Since Willamette High was such a big school with so many students, it was unusual to end up with a class with some of your friends, especially those who were a grade or two in front of or behind you. However, that is what happened. Billy had been down to see his counselor at the end of his junior year and discovered that he hadn't taken biology, which was required to qualify for graduation. Usually, biology is taken your sophomore year, and if not then, your junior year.

As luck would have it, Seymour Pugsley, the biology teacher, got five of us Little Bastards all at once in his last class of the day. I don't know how old he was, but not more than mid-twenties, and he was weird. He was skinny and tall enough you could see almost all of his white socks, because he had his belt pulled way up above his bellybutton. Seymour had a narrow face with a pointed nose and black hair that was always parted just right but usually seemed to need a trim. I don't know how anyone could stand up or sit down so straight. He almost made me a little posture conscious. I stood up straight, but when it came to sitting, especially in a school chair, it just wasn't right for a guy to perch there on the edge of the seat looking like old Archie did that first time I saw him on his bike.

I'll have to admit we had a little fun with Mr. Pugsley, pulling the usual stunts we were good at. He seemed to seriously detest us. He split us up right away, of course, and then he sort of talked down to us. It was like he knew we didn't want to be there and hear him ramble on about frogs, and he was pretty much right. We were just doing our time and getting through it. I don't think he liked our cockiness or the way we dressed and smelled like cigarettes and all. He simply hated anything to do with the automobile and combustible engines, thinking we should all ride buses and so forth like they do in Europe.

He ran us down for hot rodding and would say, "You boys are ruining perfectly good family cars by tinkering with them in immature ways to make them faster and less safe!"

I think it might have bothered Mr. Pugsley that he didn't have the slightest idea of how one worked. To make matters worse, he drove a Nash Rambler station wagon, which was a mode of transportation showing absolutely no ego whatsoever. One day while he was handing out test papers, he caught me drawing a picture of a '50 Merc all lowered down with fiestas and pipes. Old Seymour went ballistic and he ripped it out of my notebook. He started squealing with that high-pitched voice of his and flashed it around so everyone could see it. He went wailing on about how disrespectful it was for to me to waste his and everyone else's time when I should be concentrating on the class and so on.

I guess this caught Billy as funny. He, who was sitting clear in the back, let out a burst of laughter that I could hear from way up front, where Seymour had me sit. I don't think Billy thought drawing a perfectly good impression of a cool car was any less important than listening to someone talk about frog balls.

"Get out of here!" Seymour shrieked while waving my paper toward Billy. "Take him with you!" he said, pointing to me. He was over the top now. "Take the other three while you're at it!" He pointed at every leather jacket in the room.

"Get out of here and go to the office!" Seymour squealed.

We knew the routine, and all five of us were on our way to the door by then. Billy, Joe, Miles, Gary, and I ambled along the hall in a swagger toward the entrance of the school, where the offices were. In our leather jackets and engineer boots, we looked like a flight crew crossing the tarmac on our way to a bomber. We knew we had a serious meeting with destiny coming, but we weren't going to let anyone know we were worried.

Upon reaching the school offices, we just waved at the secretary and went on into the room, with the big table where the school board met, and took our usual seats. Pretty soon, old Ashley came in from the rain and hung up his coat and hat, which were dripping wet. It was always raining.

He turned around, saying, "What's up, boys?"

Billy, since he was the oldest and usually did the talking for us, said, "It's Pugsley, sir."

"Oh," said Mr. Klink. "Why don't you guys sit around in here for a few minutes and then go back to class and try not to upset him like you do."

With that, he turned and marched out the door to keep the peace and right some wrongs or something. I don't think he cared much for Seymour either, because one of the secretaries told Gary she overheard Mr. Klink tell the principal that he thought Pugsley was a weenie and should just get over it.

About the time I actually started listening in biology class about something a little bit interesting, Seymour would drop it and start going on about his personal life, which I always doubted he actually had. He kept bringing up this wedding he was going to have up at the lake near John's Landing to this lady who was just mad about him. I think the whole class agreed about the mad part, but he would get on that and go on and on, holding his hands together and wiggling around, giggling with the girls he had sitting in the front row. God, it just about made you want to puke. It got worse. He would go on about what she was going to wear and what he was going to wear. The girls, of course, really dug it and hung on his every syllable. I was always hoping that Gary or one of us would come up with something so we could go see Ashley and get some peace and quiet. We would go totally deaf when he brought up the wedding thing, so we couldn't have known when it was going to happen.

Gary was always talking about this bitchin' car his aunt had, but we had never seen it, so we thought he might have been just shitting us about it and how cool it was. Well, the lucky bastard's Aunt Ruth died and left him the car. Gary got his license before me, and shortly after, he and his dad went up to the city where the car was stored and drove it back to Willamette. It was a light-yellow-and-white '56 Mercury two-door hardtop with factory yellow-and-white pleated upholstery. If that wasn't enough, it had one of those green glass moon roofs on the top over the front seat. If you had been sent out by General MacArthur to find a car to haul a princess around in, and to probably end up in her pants in, this was the car. It had a fancy radio and even had this clever little vacuum tube that sucked your cigarette butts out.

I could see one problem that stuck out and was obvious as hell. It was about a mile off the ground and poor little Gary could hardly see over the hood. I told him that he needed to take it down to Johnny Smith's dad's Ford dealership and we would remedy it for him. I explained that it was a simple process, and because of the type of springs it had, all we would have to do is relieve it of a coil or two and line it back up. I assured him that with that little improvement the rest of us might be caught riding in it once in a while. I guess he caught on about how important it was to us, because he let out the word that he would be down at Smith's Friday night to drop it off. When we all met there that night, you could tell he was still a little apprehensive about us taking a torch to his new car. It was like a sailor getting his first tattoo or a freshman getting ready for the initiation into a fraternity or something. We got a couple of beers down him while the other guys were removing the front wheels and up it went on the hoist, never to be the same old womanly car again. I took Gary, who was jittery as hell, over to the showroom to take a look at one of the new T-Birds when Billy popped the torch and the surgery began. Pacing back and forth, chain smoking, Gary looked like a man waiting for his firstborn.

After the task was completed, we were all slapping Gary on the back and congratulating him, and he was grinning, until he tried to back it off the hoist. It was so low it got hung up and wouldn't move.

"Jesus, Billy," I said," how much did you cut out of that thing?"

Billy looked like he had just farted in church and Gary had this horrified look on his face. Luckily, Joe and Johnny still had their wits about them and leaned down slightly and lifted on the front bumper and the car was released back into the wild.

Man, when that thing rolled off the hoist, it was like seeing a liberty ship slide off its mooring into the New York Harbor. We should have broken a champagne bottle over the hood. I suppose if we would have had champagne, it would have already been consumed. God, what a transformation! Having another big cruiser took a little pressure off Joe's '50 and we got to kind of liking having Gary drive us around.

One Saturday, Gary picked me up and we drove down to the Fletcher's station, where Billy and Joe were busy washing the '50. It's a real art to wash a car and people who don't appreciate cars just never get it. Some really, really like washing their cars. Joe, for instance, had his Ford painted with gray primer, and about every nine months or so, he would have to shoot on another coat because he just kept washing it off.

You should always wet the whole thing down first to soften up the dirt, then start at the top with some soapy, warm water and give it a bath. Wash a little and rinse it off and keep working down and so on. On a hot sunny day when the soap and water tend to dry quickly, it's a good idea to do the wheels and tires first, getting them out of the way. It's real important that you get the tires real clean, even on the black part. Wiping off the water spots is a good idea as you go, especially the windows and all the chrome and so forth.

Anyway, there was old Joe washing off his primer job and Billy was sitting there on a bucket drinking a Coke and shooting the breeze when we pulled up.

"Where we going this time?" asked Joe, who was wiping the soap out from between the louvers on his hood. By that time, we were outside and leaning up against the car, enjoying the sun. After I rifled a cigarette out of Gary's jacket pocket, I noticed the question was meant for me. I lit up with my Zippo and slowly let out the smoke like Humphrey Bogart, for effect and all.

"East," I said, thinking it would be kind of nice going towards the mountains for a change, since most of our daytrips were usually to the coast. I don't think anyone really gave a shit that day where we went; we just wanted to go. After putting away Fletcher's bucket and coiling up the hose, we were ready to shove off. As we pulled out, Billy opened the door and told Miles to get in. Miles gave his dad a kind of guilty look, and then jumped in with a little holler, and we were gone.

It was a typical spring day, with some sun and a shower once in a while, but pretty warm and nice. Gary motored us along past the fields while always veering east, staying off the main highways, but avoiding the gravel roads. The five of us were just reminiscing about the night before and who was doing what with whom and so on. It had been a normal Friday night in the spring around Willamette, maybe even a little more boring than usual.

Joe and Miles had been pulled over by Officer Morton for a bad taillight. After recognizing Joe, the cop just told him to get it fixed and let them go.

We stopped at the fish hatchery after turning right on Hillside Road. At the hatchery, the State had these rows of concrete swimming pools that were at least eight feet wide and about a mile long. In each pool there were different sizes of fish, from little fingerlings to great big trout. There were signs all over the place saying what you couldn't do to the fish, like feeding them, or whatever. While we were there, a whole slew of grade school kids were on the loose, running back and forth between the pools feeding the fish pieces of bread and popcorn. A couple of their mothers were sitting on a picnic table by a station wagon, smoking mentholated cigarettes and flicking the butts into the catfish pool.

As we swung out of there, Gary blew one of the moms a kiss, to her delight. Then we motored along Hillside Road, pipes cackling, until we came to the junction with the highway that went on up to the little town of John's Landing, by the reservoir. Turning left, we followed the rolling and hilly highway since we were getting into the foothills of the Cascade Mountains. Coming over the crest of one of these hills, we could see a stalled car practically in the middle of the road. Well, this sort of perked us up a little, thinking maybe it could turn into something interesting.

We could tell from the back it was a green Rambler, and of course, we all groaned, giving our opinion of what we thought of Ramblers and of who would ever drive one.

There was a skinny guy standing next to the car in the oncoming lane. He looked like he was undergoing some kind of excruciating pain with both hands on top of his head, stumbling around in circles going mad or something. Getting closer, Billy, who was riding shotgun, recognized him first. It was Seymour Pugsley, our beloved biology teacher.

He seemed to come out of his fit when he saw us and started waving us down. He practically threw himself in front of the Merc in fear we might not stop. A mixed look of ecstasy and loathing came over his face when he recognized his potential saviors. He started babbling and waving at the car and pointing at his watch at the same time. Come to find out, after we got old Seymour to calm down a bit, he was late to his wedding. He was wiping the sweat off his forehead and blowing his nose with the same handkerchief, while trying to explain what had happened. About all he could get out was that the car wouldn't go anymore and that he was going to be late for the service. He was begging, while holding his hands together like he did in class, for Billy to get out and try to fix his car for him.

Gary pulled his car off the road in front of Mr. Pugsley's Nash and we took our time in getting out. Seymour started spinning in circles again, holding on to his watch with his opposite hand. The first thing Billy did was put his shoe up on Seymour's bumper and re-lace it; being a Red Wing, it took some time. Upon finishing that little chore, he asked Mr. Pugsley if he thought the problem might have something to do with the motor and if he might happen to know where it was. All Pugsley could do was shake his head no and then yes and so on while wiping his brow. I want to tell you we were all starting to enjoy this little road trip.

Old Billy was on a roll and he wasn't going to let Mr. Pugsley forget this for a long time. With one hand, he reached down, released the latch, and raised the hood, to Seymour's glee. It was like we had made a great discovery and he was right in the middle of it. He had never seen a real motor before since he always had someone else take care of those kinds of things.

Billy surmised what the problem was right away and spun off the wing nut that held on the air breather. "What you got here is a float that is either set too high or is waterlogged," he said.

Old Seymour was nodding like a nutcase, making out like he understood.

"Do you know how a toilet works, Mr. Pugsley?" Billy asked.

Seymour was nodding yes and then no and then answered, "Yes, I mean no, I guess. Don't you just flush it and the water goes away?"

"Very good, Mr. Pugsley," Billy said.

Man, this was getting good. I was on the opposite side of the motor from Seymour, leaning on the fender with both elbows, watching Billy proceed with the operation. It was more of an operation on Seymour than it was on his little motor. Joe and Miles were leaning on Gary's trunk with their arms crossed, enjoying a smoke and watching the show, while Gary was sitting in the front seat of Mr. Pugsley's Rambler playing with his radio.

Then Billy said, "Mr. Pugsley, I want you to listen up because it wouldn't be fair for me and the rest of us here if I had to repeat myself ... now would it Mr. Pugsley?"

Oh, Seymour was nodding yes like a little kid when asked if wants to squeeze a puppy. I guess he didn't care what he had to go through, as long as he got to his wedding on time.

"There is a float with a valve attached to it in the tank on a toilet," Billy continued. "So when the toilet is flushed and the water rushes out the bottom, the float goes down, which opens the valve, which turns on the water, and that fills the tank up, got it?" Billy looked over at Seymour.

"Oh, yes, I got it," replied Mr. Pugsley.

"So in your carburetor here, you got one of these floats too," Billy said while reaching for his Swiss Army knife. Old Seymour shuddered when he saw the flash of the blade, like he was afraid Billy was going to cut something off him. Removing the screws from the top of the carb, Billy revealed a little tank that had overfilled with gas and choked the motor so it wouldn't run. Pugsley got a good whiff of the fuel and curled up his nose. You could tell he hated the smell of gasoline.

"See this little float?" Billy asked. Seymour nodded. "It's still floating, so all that's probably wrong is it got adjusted a little high and it's making the valve think that it needs more fuel all of the time, and it gets overcharged and here you are."

While he was lecturing, Billy removed the little brass float, adjusted the arm on the end of it and reinstalled it at the correct level. He slapped old Seymour on the back and said, "I think that might just solve the whole deal."

Scymour got out a choked grunt of appreciation. With the screws back in, Billy signaled Gary to try starting the stupid little car. Sure enough, after a few sputters and some smoke belching from the tailpipe, it smoothed out and started running like new. I guess I don't have to say how happy Pugsley was. He was hopping around shaking our hands and looking at his watch as he jumped into the car and started to take off with the hood still open. Looking a little embarrassed, like he had just flunked Mechanics 101, he sort of tilted his head for one last little bit of help. Joe leaned over and shut the hood. Seymour backed out onto the road and slammed on his brakes which brought the front bumper about a mile off the ground and killed the engine right on the spot.

We were all standing there just bewildered on how anyone like Seymour could get through life. He was so excited, he sort of rocked back in his seat with this big shit-eating grin on his face, and then he rocked forward, started her up again, and away he went. As he approached the next hill, he got way over into the oncoming lane but got it straightened out right before he went out of sight.

Back in biology the next Monday, things were different. After Mr. Pugsley's short honeymoon, he seemed like a different sort. He had a little spring to his step and didn't sit on the edge of the chair anymore. In fact, he actually had a little slouch about him. He was getting it figured out. I don't know if it came from his married life or if it was because he found out how a toilet worked.

Chapter 11

I can't remember when I met Ray, but he's about the only person in my life who I can honestly say I'd rather not have. He was one of those mysterious fellas you're drawn to but really never figure out. He always seemed to hold something back. He sort of picked out what part of himself he would share with you, but the rest was pretty blurry. Ray was a few years older than me, but I never knew how much, because he never went to a day of school all the time I knew him. He was tall, about six-foot two, and lean. He made his jeans look good; they were Wranglers that belled out over his alligator-skin boots. His jeans, with the big buckle in front, were pressed with a crease down the front and were long and tattered around the bottom, where they met the ground. He wore western shirts with embroidered ropes and rhinestone buttons, like Roy Rogers. Year-round he had on a straw cowboy hat, which he wore like a crown. It was important to Ray. His speech gave way to a slight Southern lean, which he called rodeo. He said they had moved around a lot and mentioned New Mexico, which is where, I suppose, he picked it up.

I was fifteen when I started going after junk with him. I think he hauled me along because I was pretty good at lifting things, from picking up hundred pound bags down at the mill. He called it going after *bads* and *rads*; *bads* for batteries and *rads* for radiators, both worth something for scrap. He would do the spotting during the week and then pick me up early on Sunday mornings. We would search out his predetermined locations for the piece or article he had found. Sometimes the finds would vary and included car parts and general used merchandise Ray thought was valuable. As he spotted and found the items, he would negotiate and buy it, so all we had to do was pick it up and haul it off. I guess it never occurred to me why we had to do the picking up at daybreak when none of the owners ever seemed to be around.

There is one thing I have to thank old Ray for; he introduced me to coffee. On mornings when he would show up at my house, he had two matching thermoses like the ones that come with picnic kits and include the boxes and look like they're made out of reeds or something. He drove an old International panel truck that had belonged to a plumber in town. It had once said *Acme*, with a big pipe wrench on the side, but Ray had painted over it because, he said, he didn't like bringing attention to himself.

Anyway, he would pull up to the curb outside our house in the dark and I'd be ready to go. Ray insisted that I be punctual, since he didn't like waiting long in one place. The panel must have had a good muffler on it, because it was quiet as a mouse. We would just slip away in the dark, drinking the coffee and smoking his Cavalier cigarettes. The dash lights were weak and everything was shadowy. Through the steam coming off the cups, I watched his boots work the pedals, clutching, braking, shifting, and throttling as we putted down the streets. The International had a good heater that would buzz along, and the vacuum-powered windshield wipers would labor away at keeping the water off the glass.

We made a few trips like this through the summer before my sophomore year. Once in a while, I would ride along to his place to help with unloading if he had an unusually heavy item. He lived with his family over past West Side, in the Bottoms, on one of those streets that turns into gravel and where the sidewalks disappear into unmaintained grass and blackberry bushes. Their house was past where you go under the railroad trestle on the right side. It was a big old structure that had a porch wrapping around two sides, and it looked as if it had some bedrooms upstairs. There was so much stuff on the front lawn you could hardly see the grass. In the middle, there was a load of firewood with an axe and a cutting block, as if each day they cut just enough to get through the night. It was always the same. His grandpa would be sitting on the porch with a pipe in his mouth. He just rocked away, petting the dog, like he was just waiting to die. Ray's little brother, who looked to be about nine, would be playing something on the harmonica, and I don't think he had ever seen the inside of a school. Ray's sister, Bess, stood between them holding a baby on one hip, with her bloated, pregnant belly showing, while smoking a cigarette with kind of a dazed look about her. She was pale, with red hair, and freckles everywhere not covered.

Each time we visited his house, Ray would pull around to an old garage in the back that was hidden from the road by blackberry bushes and old car bodies. Here we would unload. A couple of times, Ray's dad and brother-in-law were there and were either loading or unloading merchandise. They had a worn out Chevrolet 1.5-ton truck with side racks on it made out of an old billboard advertising Chesterfield cigarettes. Dale, the brother-in-law, was about as big a man as I have ever seen, with pink eyes, and he didn't have a hair on his body, so I figured he was one of those albinos I had read about. Like Ray's dad, he wore army surplus clothes with cut-off sleeves revealing tattoos on each arm. I saw him pick up a washing machine and slam it down on the truck bed with no more effort than a grunt.

I noticed that the items we brought in were never around the next time we unloaded. I mentioned this to Ray and he said that he had a way of spotting good stuff and it usually sold right away. Ray's dad and Dale, who both chewed Red Man tobacco, would make one trip a week to Portland in the old truck with a load of scrap. Dale would do the driving and Ray's old man would ride along, spitting juice out between his caveman teeth. The right-hand side of the truck had the stains to prove it, running down the *Sand and Gravel* sign painted on the door. Coming back, they would pick up a load of merchandise from their cousin's in Oregon City. These pieces ended up in the front of the house with *For Sale* signs dogged on them. Nobody around there said much to me, except Ray, and he hardly ever shut up.

Ray was quite a charmer and he had my mom thinking he was the real deal. One July afternoon when he dropped me off at home, I invited him in to meet my folks, because they were a little curious about who I was going off with early about every Sunday morning. Old Ray was polite as hell, telling Mom how young and nice she looked in her Sunday dress. Dad was a little less taken, and I noticed that Ray sensed he was being observed. I showed him around my room and the rest of the house and he seemed to scan everything, it was sort of mechanical with him.

Later, after Ray had left, we were at the dinner table having fried chicken when my mom went on about what a nice boy Ray was. Dad gave me a serious look and said, "I'd keep an eye on him if I were you, Sonny."

A week or so later, Ray picked me up like usual, and we headed out over the river going north, sipping coffee and smoking. Sometimes I would nod off and then wake up somewhere I hadn't been before. That particular morning, Ray seemed to know where he was headed, so I just blacked out, and was dreaming along when he stopped at this old farmstead on top of a little rise. It was just getting light and you could make out fir trees backing a meadow with a couple of milk cows near the barn, probably waiting to be milked. Right next to the road was this old cream separator that hadn't been used for quite some time but was now kind of an antique and pretty valuable, according to Ray. After we rolled it around and got it loaded up, Ray told me to have a look in the barn because there was an old car in there that might be available.

As I was opening the barn door, I noticed he had headed for the house. The inside of the barn smelled like spoiled milk mixed with manure and hay. Barns always smell this way if they are actively being used. It was built with large, wooden beams that were put together with pegs, so it was old. There were ropes coiled up and hanging around, along with wadded up bailing wire. The early morning sun was shooting beams through the knot holes, making the place look a little eerie. Sure enough, an old Ford was sitting right inside the big door, and it looked like it was used for daily transportation. I didn't have a clue as to why Ray thought they might like to sell it. I was thinking about how it would make a pretty good rod since it was a two-door sedan and it was either a '39 or '40 standard, when all of a sudden, I could hear Ray yelling, and by his voice, he was headed for the barn.

"Let's get the hell out of here!" he yelled as he ran by the door that I had just come in. "He has a gun!"

I was shocked, but I recovered soon. I rushed for the door to escape, hitting it full speed, which almost knocked me down.

"Son of a bitch," I blurted out. "The bastard locked the door on me!"

While I was looking around for a way out, it dawned on me what had happened. Ray was stealing the cream separator with my help and had been going to raid the house while I was busy in the barn. Doing so, he ran right into the owner's gun barrel. Ray was a quick thinker; he figured if he ran by the barn and locked me in, the farmer would be tied up with me long enough for him to get away in the panel truck.

As the door of the barn swung open, I was taking the stairs to the hay mow two at a time. I tore across the wooden floor and bolted right out the second story door without looking down. My feet were still going when I hit the fresh manure pile, which probably saved me from breaking a leg. Old Ray was grinding away on the starter trying to get the truck running when I heard the first shot. BBs were hitting all around me when I reached the panel's rear door handle, and I just barely got it open and jumped in when the rear tires started throwing gravel. Ray didn't waste any time getting off the hill. He came into the corners hard, sliding around them and straightening just in time for the next one. I was hanging on in the back, trying not to get squashed by this three-hundred-pound, iron machine that was rolling back and forth trying to kill me. I could see the reflection of Ray's face in the rearview mirror and it looked like a combination of terror and thrill at the same time. When he thought we were far enough away from the farm, he stopped and backed into a dirt side road. After leaping out, he ripped the back door open. I'll have to admit that I was a little worried about what might happen to me since he knew I was on to their operation and all.

"Help me throw this goddamned thing out of here. I'm in a hurry!" he said.

We dumped the separator and headed back down the gravel road. When he got us close to town, he stopped, saying, "Get out and keep your mouth shut or you're going to regret it."

I bailed out and hotfooted it for home. I had some time to think about what had happened on the way, and everything I had noticed over the summer began to make sense. About a week after I had invited Ray in to see my folks, Dad's single shot .22 came up missing. We never locked anything around the house, so I figured Ray slipped in there after we went off to church that Sunday and made off with it. I felt like a real idiot getting duped by a guy like Ray, but even worse was getting Dad's gun stolen.

By the time I had gotten home, I had a plan worked out as to a way I might get the gun back without getting myself killed. I hadn't gotten my license yet, so I convinced Billy and Joe to go on a little trip with me the next Saturday to Oregon City. I didn't dare tell them what had happened or what I was up to, or I'm sure they wouldn't have had anything to do with it. I stretched the truth a little and told them there was a car up there for sale I wanted to see.

Just like planned, we headed up towards Oregon City in Joe's 1950 Ford. Joe was my age, but had been driving for a while. The police who knew him kind of looked the other way, because they were aware of his home life and all. Some were also familiar with Sylvia, Joe's mom, from frequenting the bar downtown and might have been a little friendlier with her than they wanted people to know.

Billy had broken his transmission again, so I talked Joe into driving, which he was reluctant to do, because he felt Oregon City was out of his safe zone. I hadn't any idea where Ray's cousins lived, but I thought I could find it since I was betting it was just like Ray's house, with junk all around and a lot of used merchandise for sale. I was thinking they were fencing the goods they stole around our town with the cousins in Oregon City and vice versa. When Joe pulled the Ford into town, I saw a little store with a lot of pickups parked around. I figured it was a coffee hangout and told the boys I'd run in to find out where exactly the coupe we had come to see was. A little bell rang when I opened the door and all these farmers looked up to see who the stranger was. I gave one of my smiles and explained what I was after. They all agreed the place was up Deer Creek Road about a mile and a half and on the left.

I thanked them. As I was walking out the door, one of the guys said, "You be careful up there. They got dogs."

One of the others said something about them not being too friendly either.

I jumped into the car and told the boys, "Up the road about a mile, turn left, and it's only a little ways." Joe pulled out of the lot and we headed for parts unknown.

I was worried. What if one of Ray's family members was there? What if we got attacked by the dogs? How was I going to explain to Billy and Joe why I switched from looking at a car to buying a gun? I started thinking I should have been square with them, but it was too late, since right in front of us was the damnedest site I'd ever seen. It made Ray's look like an enchanted cottage. This place was like a compound with an army truck guarding the gate and two big bloodhounds waiting right inside with a hungry look about them. I guess I'd never seen anything quite like it before.

Billy and Joe hadn't either, because when Joe stopped the car, they both turned around in the seat with a "we aren't going any further" look. As I opened the gate and walked through, I noticed there was a coyote head nailed to the post still wearing its pelt. The sign wired to the gate said *No Thievin'*. I thought to myself how ironic that was.

The driveway had been gravel at one time, but was mostly dirt and rutted up. Both of the dogs converged on me at the same time, and where I got the constitution not to wet my pants, I don't know. One of them grabbed my pant leg and gave a pull like I was a new toy and the other one would have nothing of that and started pulling me the other way. About the time the war was going to start, I heard a whistle from up ahead, and they dropped me like old news. The dirt road angled up the side of the hill through a barrage of old wash machines and junk of every description. Some stuff was covered up with green canvas tarps that reminded me of the camouflage the German soldiers would throw off their machine guns to fire from their vantage point. It was in the morning, but already hot. My engineer boots picked up dust as I was putting one in front of the other, trying not to think of the consequences of what would happen if I was found out.

Before getting as far as the house, I came across an old dilapidated outbuilding with the roof falling in on all kinds of used building materials that had seen better days. There was canvas nailed to the top of the wall, stretching over an open area onto an old threshing machine, covering an area with a couch and some overstuffed chairs where they must have taken their lunches, since the ground was covered with old Shakey's Pizza boxes. Because of the shadows, it was hard to see the back of the lunchroom, but I could faintly hear a radio and the slow creaking of a rocker. In the rocking chair was the oldest person I'd ever seen. It was a woman, who might have been blind, wrapped up in an Indian blanket, listening to one of those fellers trying to talk her out of sinning. I was thinking the poor old thing couldn't sin if she wanted to. She couldn't have weighed 75 pounds dripping wet and only had a few strands of hair left. I walked on and could see some movement up at the house as I wove in and out of the refrigerators and such. It was a huge, old building, painted white at one time, and had a porch running almost all the way around it. Being as it was built on a side hill, the porch floor was several feet off the ground and reminded me of a fortress with the advantage.

I was pretty much trying to look straight ahead and not be very noticeable, but it was damned hard for me not to notice what was on that porch. I'd say she could have been as young as 17 or as old as 25. It was really hard to tell because she was about the most different-looking female I'd ever laid eyes on, especially since I was trying not to look at her. She was slowly swinging back and forth on a rope swing tied to the roof of the porch. She had on a cotton dress that came down to about her knees.

When she swung back her knees would come together, and when she came forward her knees would come apart and her shoulders would come through the ropes, and her hands would be behind her which made her breasts protrude, challenging the one button that was holding them back. Like I was saying, it was hot, and she was pretty wet. I could see sweat beads running down on her lips, which were full and angry. Her underarms were wet and so was her chest, and you could see her nipples that arced a little up and out. She looked straight into me with those pink eyes; she was an albino like Dale. She had pure white, long hair and had no color I could see.

I trudged on, feeling her eyes penetrate my back as I moved away. Up ahead, I could see an old Quonset hut, like what was used during the war. They look like half of a huge pipe lying on the ground and are used for storage. It was old and the galvanizing was partly worn off and rusty. The big sliding doors were shiny with use and cracked open, so I took a peek in. It was dark, with no windows, and all I could see were torches moving about. I didn't want to surprise anyone, so I made a quick assessment as my eyes became accustomed to the dark. I saw two guys cutting up a car, and not too carefully either. They were wearing dark-lensed goggles, so they didn't notice me, but someone did, as I felt a tapping on my back. I about crapped my pants, but was able to turn around to see a funny-looking little guy with a serious frown staring up at me. I'd say he was about five feet tall at the most and was a little wide in the middle. The guy had on one of those hats with a feather, like the carny rats wear at the county fair. His dark complexion was matched with a thin, dark mustache and stringy hair that was overdue for a cut. His hands were in the pockets of his checkered jacket.

"Whaddya want?" he asked, and I was thinking up a good answer and recovering at the same time.

"I'm in the market for a good .22 rifle," I said, thinking it sounded ridiculous anyone would come here for anything good.

He introduced himself as Cyrus, head of the retail department, and said he had a few .22s I was welcome to look at. He was also curious about how I found out about their enterprise. I assured him they had a big following and I'd heard they had a stellar reputation. He seemed pleased with that and motioned me over to a couple of semi-truck trailers that had stairs up to their rear doors, which were locked with padlocks and chains. Cyrus had this big ring of keys attached to his belt and picked out a big, gold-looking one, and after trying it, and about three more, got the door to open. I let him go in first, since I didn't take to getting locked in the last time.

He reached up and pulled a string, turning on a light that revealed a row of rifles all along the left-hand side of the trailer. He invited me to follow him to the end, where the small stuff was located. As I moved along the alleyway in the middle, I recognized a table saw and a couple of saddles I had helped Ray steal. Seeing this stuff made my blood pressure jump again. I was thinking I'd better finish this up and get the hell out of here as quick as I could.

Sure enough, I could see Dad's .22 up ahead, along with some others. Of course, he reached right up and brought down the most expensive-looking one, which had been built in Belgium. I looked it over and commented about how great it was, but I explained to him it was going to be a gift for my little brother, and since he was young, he probably should start out with a little single shot or something.

I could tell he regretted it, but he put it back and was reaching for a Remington pump, when I said, "How about that little Winchester on the end?"

He set the pump down on the counter with his right hand and picked up Dad's rifle with his left, while turning to face me. I didn't look at him, in fear of giving the whole thing away, and just took the gun in my hands like I'd done many times before. It was still clean, and you could smell the oil from the barrel and what Dad had rubbed into the stock. Trying not to act excited, I told old Cyrus the little single shot would probably do the trick if they didn't want too much for it. He rubbed his chin a little and made a remark about how well maintained it was and said he'd have to have twenty for it.

I was thinking how close I was, I had gotten it back, and all I had to do was fork over the twenty I had gotten out of my account down at First National. I had actually gotten thirty, because I was willing to go that high, even though I knew it wasn't worth nearly that much.

I heard this voice say, "Twenty sounds a little high; how about fifteen?"

My God, it was my voice negotiating with this guy when I should pay him, grab it, and run like hell for the car. He looked me over carefully with that finger on the chin thing. He said seventeen and that's it. I pulled out a ten and ten ones and gave him the ten and seven singles, pocketing the other three, while never letting go of Dad's rifle. I had the money stored away handy so I wouldn't have to wait around for change and all. I put the rifle in my left hand, shook Cyrus's hand with my right, and left the trailer without looking back. As I walked by the Quonset hut, I could see the flashing of the torches in the corner of my eye, which reminded me of the danger of being recognized, so I moved out in a hurry as casually as I could.

I passed the house within three feet of the porch, all that was there was the empty swing, still moving in the absolute stillness of the air. She had to have been there and seen me coming, and I will admit, I wouldn't have minded seeing her again. I hustled by the lunchroom and the old lady was gone, with her chair motionless, as if it never had moved. Fifty feet to go, and it was all I could do to keep from running for the gate. What about the dogs? What about the machine guns? It was all coming down on me and I could hardly breathe and walk at the same time.

Joe had the Ford turned around and the motor running. Billy had the door open, and he was leaning forward so I could bail into the backseat. The guys were ready, and as I hit the seat, the rear tires were scattering gravel. As we were heading down the hill, both Billy and Joe were looking at me over the seat, and I guess no one was driving. I sat in the middle, with both hands on the .22, trying to answer their questions, but all I could do was shake my head, because I couldn't get my breath.

I was starting to come out of it when we went over a little rise and caught sight of a vehicle parked in the middle of the road, facing us. I couldn't believe my eyes. It was Ray's panel truck and Dale was standing in front of it with a tire iron in his hand. Damn, I thought it was over, and here they were waiting for us.

I leaned ahead and somewhere down deep came my voice clear and steady. "Joe, whatever you do, don't stop this car, no matter what. Keep it in low gear so you don't stall it and be ready to hit the throttle if he tries to stop us."

Joe choked out a worried sounding, "Okay."

Billy was still turned toward me and had his arm over the seat with the other hand on the dash like he was ready for a ride. As we went by, I slid down in the seat with the gun between my legs like I was a witch doing a rollover. I could see the spider tattoo on Dale's neck as we passed by, and after fifty feet or so, I couldn't help turning in the seat, looking back. Ray was standing at the back of the International with a jack in his hand looking at us pull away. They were fixing a flat tire.

After a mile or two, I was able to regain my composure, and I filled the boys in on what had happened and what had led up to it. Nothing was said most of the way home. Neither Joe nor Billy mentioned anything about me misleading them, and I think they were both a little proud of helping me right a wrong.

I never witnessed my dad being surprised often, but when I handed him his .22 rifle, he seemed a bit jolted. Like most times, he didn't say a lot. He looked me square in the eyes and asked me if getting the gun back cost me much. I asked him if he meant in dollars and cents. He said, "Yes," and I said, "No."

Chapter 12

One Saturday, while sitting around the kitchen table, Mom brought up the fact that my sixteenth birthday was coming soon. It was one of her Saturday lunches, which filled the house with a warm, pleasant smell.

"I think you're going to hit the six-foot mark this year," she said.

Mom had always measured us on our birthdays and left the mark by the door to the kitchen. I would stand up straight to get that extra quarter-inch, and having a lot of hair didn't hurt either. It was dark and I liked combing it like Elvis, because he was it, as far as I was concerned. We had one of those new chrome and yellow tables with the vinyl top; the chairs were matching, and the whole set was bright and cheery. I guess we had reached the chrome age. New cars were loaded up with it; dealers were even saying that those quad headlights could look into the future they were so modern.

We used the table for everything; it was in the center of whatever was happening. The table had these leaves we would put in it for Christmas and Thanksgiving dinners, when my sister, Rita, would be home with her husband, Mark. They lived at the Air Force base in the coastal mountain range, where he spent all day in front of a radar screen hoping he'd be the first to spot a Russian plane coming over Alaska with a load of A-bombs.

From the table, you could see into the kitchen, and by rotating to the left, you could see the rest of the front room where the 21" Motorola TV sat on a small bench along with some *Life* magazines. The living room was a fairly small concern with a couple of overstuffed chairs and a couch with a blanket over it that sort of hid the worn and torn areas. Spooky spent most of her life lying between the chairs on an old blanket folded over a few times. It was in front of the oil stove that kept the house nice and warm in the winter. The other three rooms in the house included my bedroom, the bathroom, and Dad and Mom's room. All were connected together by a hallway, with the telephone on a little stool next to a dresser guarded by a stuffed deer head with a mournful look on its face. Since I had gotten Dad's .22 back, it had risen in respect and was perched between the third and fourth horns on the four-point rack, along with a box of shells on top of the dresser.

Anyway, Mom and I were discussing my birthday while she was finishing her coffee and Dad was having a cigarette. When counting off the days until your sixteenth birthday, the days turn into weeks and the weeks turn into months and so on. Man, I had been waiting for this for years. The independence and freedom of having a driver's license and your own car is like walking through a door that has held you back all your life. I suppose if they dropped the driving age to fifteen, you would just start craving it that much earlier. Fortunately for me, I had friends who were older and had already been into the world of cars, cruising, and drag racing, which in turn, opens up the universe of motors, oil, car wax, and girls.

Along with all the benefits, I was aware of the consequences of having your own wheels from watching my friends buying gas and paying for the dreaded liability insurance. Then came the speed equipment and the subtle changes that transform a normal family car into an envy-sucking personal rocket ship. As the Little Bastards transformed from bicycle riding maniacs to young adults with automobiles and other responsibilities, their own personal attributes and tendencies followed along. A teenager can tell a lot about other teenagers by what they drive. If you happen to see a guy standing beside an Oldsmobile hardtop dropped to the ground with lakes pipes, flipper hubcaps, and primer spots, talking to a guy who has a sweater wrapped around his neck and is holding a tennis racket and leaning against a Volvo wagon, you have seen an unusual occurrence. Kids tend to go their own way during puberty and early high school, following others with like interests. However, if you grew up next to the guy with the Volvo, you might be lifelong friends but just wouldn't hang around together much, if you know what I mean.

That year, Billy Wheeler had graduated with honors from Willamette High. He had grown up down the street from me and we became lifelong friends and fellow charter members in the Little Bastards club. Being older and interested in mechanics and other cool things, he sort of became my mentor. I don't know if it was his interests and accomplishments that made me want to do pretty much the same stuff or if we were just prone to do similar things in life. He was into model airplanes and trains and I was too. He and his dad built a soapbox derby car and I got to help paint it. His bike was cool so mine had to be cool. Billy had good morals and was raised by great parents, who included me in their lives when I was hanging around with him and his other friends.

When he had turned sixteen, cool things began to happen. We had buried ourselves in every hot rod magazine we could find until the pages were worn out. Billy pored over all the technical articles about welding, painting, and motors, while I scanned the way they looked and what was right. Half the cars from *Hot Rod* and the little books, such as *Hop Up* and *Rod & Custom*, were from California, and the rest were scattered all over the country. The East Coast boys had a little bit different approach, but came up with stunning rods and customs of their own. The drag racing rage took over America in the early fifties and it completely engulfed the country, and the little town of Willamette wasn't left out.

There were several hot rods on the high school lot, as well as mild customs that were lowered down with pipes and so on. Drag strips were being built and airstrips were modified to hold races on weekends. It became popular, because everyone could participate as a driver or a spectator. Classes were established to include the fastest built machines, as well as a mom's sedan.

This was us. The Little Bastards became "hot rodders" with passion. All we lacked were hot rods.

Billy was an ambitious sort of fellow and had worked and saved his money, so when the time came, he jumped. His dad pitched in a little, and with what he had stashed away, Billy bought a 1940 Ford standard coupe when he turned sixteen. They say people look like their dogs, or the other way around. Billy looked like his car. The 1940 Ford was one of Henry Ford's winners. It was distinctive in its simplicity. There was nothing about the machine that was not necessary; it was truly a work of art and function. That was Billy. He had dark hair, and by the time he was fifteen, you could tell he would be bald by the age of forty. There was nothing unusual about his physical looks. He was average height and weight, and that's where it ended. His father was a builder, and maybe that's where Billy got it. He was an innovator, a thinker, and was always out there in the world of wheels, motors, and grease.

We'd all be there on his porch listening to him explain how things worked as he leafed through a hot rod magazine one of us had scored. He seemed to like being with us and would talk with us, but he was way ahead on anything technical. He could talk to his teachers at school like he was one of them, adult to adult, but couldn't seem to communicate well with the regular-Joe student, and especially not a Jane student. He came off as being aloof, which made him fit with us, because we liked to think of ourselves that way, and we had a pact from early on that we would never smile for a photograph, like a James Dean or Marlon Brando thing.

Billy's '40 was stock as a rock and kind of a grey colored with 600x16-inch tires, which made it look like it was a mile off the ground. It ran good and used a little oil, which was pretty common for a car that old. We rubbed and polished and cleaned that car, but no matter what we did, it just didn't look like cars in the magazines.

Four of us got in that car one Saturday and made a trip to Portland to the Champion Speed Shop and came home with a $9 dropped axle. That little coupe was never the same again. With jacks, blocks, and wrenches we had borrowed, we had the front axle out and the new one in by dark on Sunday. We got in a tight spot because none of the steering parts lined up right after we installed the axle. According to an article Billy had read, we needed to heat some of the parts and bend them around and so forth. Johnny Smith was in on this too, so we pushed his dad's shop acetylene cart about a mile and a half from the Ford garage to Billy's house and back. The biggest lesson we learned that weekend was that with hot rodding, nothing ever fits. You have to take it upon yourself to alter by cutting, welding, bending, or hammering something until it finally gives in and fits.

After that episode, it was one thing after another. I helped Billy pull out the exhaust pipes and we threw away the mufflers and replaced them with straight pipes all the way out the back. Billy had me drive while he rode in the trunk with the lid open so he could listen and see if the sound they made was right.

If we weren't working or at school, you could find us over at Billy's house in the back, where they had a small garage that had become our new clubhouse. When we became the beneficiaries of Billy's wheels, we loaded up our 45 record player and the furniture from the old clubhouse in the blackberries and moved to the little shack in his backyard. We spent our time working on someone's car or just sitting around looking at magazines, smoking cigarettes, and listening to the radio. We were into rock and roll, and we had the record player above the bench with a stack of community owned 45s to choose from. Someone was always coming around with the latest hits, and we would stand around inside, out of the rain, and rave on with Buddy Holly or Elvis or whoever. Life was good. We thought we had it all. Brown leather bomber jackets all around, Levi's, and Penney's t-shirts, until it got real cold in the winter, and then we'd be wearing Pendleton wool shirts between the tees and the leather. We always said we were going to paint something on the jackets signifying to the world that we were the Little Bastards, but we never could come up with what we thought was appropriate, so we just went by reputation alone. A couple of the guys had attitudes and liked to push people around a little, even though most of us were pretty mellow, but we didn't take any shit from anyone either. If someone messed with one of us, they usually lived to regret it.

The Olsen girls would happen by if there was something special going down at Billy's garage, and that would add femininity, which we surely lacked. They had both gone to Lincoln Grade School with us and shared the values and lessons we learned growing up on the rough side of town. They were both turning into beauties and could have had any guy in school, but still liked being with us, which didn't hurt our feelings a bit. We were a pretty proud bunch in the way we walked and handled ourselves and it didn't hurt our game to have the Olsen girls with us. I think people thought we were a little cocky, but it didn't stop some of them from trying to join up or copy us. There were very few we brought in, like Archie, who weren't there from the start, and they were a special lot.

Most of the kids who were into the car scene and cruising around town liked hanging out at Pop's Drive-In out on Willamette Boulevard, the only four-lane highway in town. We called it the Boulevard. There was a gravel lot next to the restaurant, which became our headquarters. It was owned by a glass company, but since they didn't use it at night, we did. In the summer, we would pile up there around our cars, with the windows down, listening to music over some smokes and occasionally an Oly or two. Oly was short for Olympia, our beer of choice, which was brewed in Olympia, Washington.

I would pile in with any of the guys who had room, and we would take to the streets on a route that would take us out by Billie's Big Boy Burger, which had roller-skating carhops and such. Billie's clientele were mostly out-of-towners and kids who were a little afraid of Pop's. It was a good place to go because you could usually see something new, like a hot car or a girl nobody had seen before. We'd circle a couple of times and then hit River

Street and head downtown past the Paramount Theater to see if there was a live one there we might pick up. Of course, the idea was always to pick up girls, but most of us weren't very good at it, except Gary, who was good-looking and seemed to say what girls wanted to hear. To the rest of us, saying what girls wanted to hear didn't come real natural, because we thought it sounded girly and all, but it worked for Gary.

The Fletcher station was downtown and en route, so we would drop by there to see what was happening. Frank Fletcher was a great guy, and he didn't seem to have much interest in selling gas, because he let us hoodlums loiter around, using his hoist and washing our cars. Of course, having his son as one of us didn't hurt much either. Frank was a Mobil Oil Company jobber and delivered fuel and heating oil with his truck around town, and that was what kept him going, I guess.

From the station, we would drive to the Ford garage. Johnny Smith's dad was also a nice guy, and owning the business, he was a pretty important guy around the city and always wore a suit and tie to work. The way he treated people didn't go unnoticed by me; he was kindly and respectful no matter if they had money or how old they were. He would let us take over the shop at closing time. We would have it all night with all the tools and everything until morning, when he expected to have it back, all nice and clean and ready for his mechanics. A lot of times, some of the mechanics would stick around after work and help out with our projects. We seemed to attract goodwill. Everyone wanted to help and be a part of what we were doing. Most of us treated these people fairly and we were respectful and full of energy.

Anyway, the Saturday Mom mentioned my birthday we were finishing up lunch as Dad slid his chair back like he did when announcing something. I figured that we were going to the dump. Instead, he came out with something about Clarabelle Smith, this lady who went to the same church as Jim Wilson, and that she was going to trade her car in and he was wondering if it might be something I would be interested in. Well, he was right about one thing, I sure was interested in a car, but not any old car, and especially not some old lady car, since I was pretty particular and I wasn't one to like being laughed off the school parking lot. If it hadn't been for Mom asking Dad what kind of car Clarabelle was letting go of, that might have been all that was said.

Old Dad was just sitting there, and the corner of his mouth was just giving a hint of a smile when he said, "Oh, it's just that old '40 Ford that lady drives around town all the time."

I came out of my chair without sliding it back and almost upset the table. My mom gave me a look like I'd lost my mind and my dad broke out in a smile like I'd never seen. This little lady, her name unknown to me, had been driving this blue '40 Ford coupe around town as long as I could remember. My friends and I would slobber all over the car when we saw it parked downtown in front of the Monkey Ward building she frequented on occasion. The rumor was that she had lost her husband in the war and was still driving the car they had bought together before he shipped overseas. We could tell she kept it up, because we would see her enter the Ford garage for servicing and leave with it all clean and waxed. The word was that she would never part with it because of sentimental reasons and all.

I sat back down in my chair with a flabbergasted look on my face. Luckily, Dad took over and said if I was interested that I could have it for the same price the dealership had offered her, but she would like to take care of the whole thing in a week or two. After some spurting and sputtering, I got it across that I wanted it and would probably kill for it. I knew how to make money and how to save it, but I didn't know how large transactions were done, so I asked Dad to help me with the paperwork.

I hardly got a minute of sleep that weekend, and I sure as hell kept my mouth shut about that car being up for sale. I was down at the mill on Monday working since it was still summer vacation. I saw my dad come and go a couple of times that day, but he was busy with a broken seed cleaner out at Fernville. I didn't get a chance to find out anything until that night, and you can bet I was pacing back and forth by the door waiting.

When Dad showed up, he stopped at the doorway and leaned against it with a serious look on his face and told me about the deal. If I wanted the car, I had to come up with $400 this week, and he said he would buy my insurance until I was out of high school. *Oh boy*, I was thinking, because I had the money and quite a bit more just collecting dust down at the First National. Then Dad said he would go along with this and the insurance on one condition. I knew what this was going to be, and he said I must drive safely so I wouldn't lose the insurance and not to take the car all apart and ruin it right away. I stuck out my hand and shook his while saying it's a deal, and I even planned on making some improvements to the car. He nodded in a knowing way and that was that.

The next day, I got off some extra time for lunch, rode my bike down to the bank, and withdrew the $400. Dad met me at Rogers Insurance Agency next to Sears, where he bought me six months of liability insurance. After I got a little sermon from Mr. Rogers about how many people have wrecks the first week or two, we were out the door.

That evening, Dad, Mom, and I got in the Chevy pickup and went over to meet Clarabelle to see if we couldn't finish up the transaction. I was so excited I could hardly make a peep. She lived over in West Side in a nice, neat, smaller home with a garage where she kept the coupe out of the weather.

Clarabelle met us at the door and invited us in for coffee and cookies. Of course, old Dad and Mom couldn't turn that down, so I was downing cookies like a sugar fiend, hoping we would move on to the car. After about a hundred hours, she clomped back from the kitchen, as if in slow motion, with the title, and I jerked the money out, and we were about to do the deal, when she began to give me the biography of the car's life and what it had meant to her. She was leaving Willamette for a large city because of her work and she thought maybe she should buy a newer car. She also stated that the coupe had never broken down and had been a good car, and she couldn't see why it wouldn't continue that way if I took care of it. I thanked her very much. I said I would keep it nice and that I had admired her for how she had maintained it. She bent over the coffee table and signed the title, and I shoved the money forward like I was going all in, which I was, I guess.

My mother told her I had made every dime of that $400 myself and I had been saving it up for an occasion like this. Clarabelle smiled and shook my hand. Outside, Dad opened the garage door and there it was, the most beautiful blue object I'd ever set eyes on, and it belonged to me. Clarabelle backed it out into the street and my mom got in with me. I drove us home in my new car since I had my learner's permit folded up in my wallet where the four hundred had been.

Six days to go. Of course they went slow as hell, working down at the mill and still pumping back and forth on the old Columbia. I want to tell you I spent a lot of time with the car, after work mostly, just gazing at it and making plans. It was a deluxe coupe, which meant it was a little fancier coming from the factory than Billy's was. Mine had a wider grill with horizontal bars, a softer seat, a dash with ashtrays on each end, and a radio right square in the middle of it. It was more than I ever dreamed of.

My birthday fell on a Sunday that year, so I made an appointment with the DMV to take the driver's test on Monday. I then scheduled some time off from work at the mill late in the afternoon, thinking if I passed, I could drive around town a little, and if I flunked, I wouldn't have to go back out there and face all the guys at the mill, because they knew what I was up to and they would razz my ass if I failed. If I would have studied before my school tests the way I did before the driver's test, I might have graduated top of my class instead of where I did. I knew from interrogating my friends where the DMV routes were, how many, and exactly where they went. There were two driving instructors, Miss Yates and Mr. Mathew, and I knew each one's favorite route when testing a first-time applicant. If you failed the initial test, they would switch to a second route the next time and so on.

Finally, Monday came, and at 2:30 on the dot, I jumped on my bike and pedaled for home. Mom was ready and she rode with me out to the office, wringing her hands together, out of nervousness, I guess. The office was drab, with army surplus filing cabinets and painted green walls with small windows. A few minutes after I checked in, Mr. Mathew, who didn't particularly look as if he liked being there, came from out of the back with a clipboard in his hand, and after introducing himself to Mom, he motioned me to the door. After opening it, I held it for him, which seemed to make him uncomfortable, like he was excepting a bribe or something. Outside in the back parking lot, they had some parking spaces painted on the blacktop simulating downtown situations to see if you could parallel. I think they did this test first because some couldn't pull it off, so it saved going all over town for nothing. Mr. Mathew had gotten in and looked the coupe's inside over with what I thought was an envious sort of appraisal. This parking thing wasn't much of a challenge for me, since I'd been backing Dad's pickup around tight places when we were pheasant hunting. I backed her up and in, stopped and pulled up right in the middle, shut it off, and put on the emergency break just for good measure. Old Mathew sort of raised his eyebrows, which were those big, black kind that actually hung over his glasses, and wrote something on the form held by the clipboard.

He then had me start it and back up, and he told me we were going out on the Boulevard and north until we got to Oak, and then we were going to turn left. I could have told him right then and there where the rest of the route was going to take us, but of course, I stayed mum and let him give the orders. I shoved my arm out the window when we got to Oak, signaling that we were turning, while I looked in the review mirror and so forth. Again, his eyebrows went up and he wrote another note on his paper. When we got to the dead end of Oak, I stopped at the stop sign and pretended I didn't know we were going to turn left on River Street and head downtown. This time, sure enough, he just motioned with his left hand, with the yellow number two pencil in it. I signaled left again and away we went. Mr. Mathew was as predictable as old Ernest when he would come down the river at the same time on the same route like clockwork. I knew we were going to hit the one way on First and go into downtown and then turn on Franklin and back onto the one way on Second and go back out to the Boulevard and then to the DMV. I made the lane change he was after, signaling, looking back, and being alert and so forth, and he was writing like he was covering a horserace.

I got a chance coming back on Second to seal the deal when an old woman and her little dog were waiting to cross Washington Street. I slowed down with my arm hanging out the window signaling and stopped for to them to cross. She walked by the front of the '40 without even knowing what a momentous occasion she had been part of. When she reached the other side and stepped up on the sidewalk, I let out on the clutch and made a nice smooth launch. A little smile came across my face as I remembered that Sunday morning when I took the Olsen girls for a ride in Dad's pickup. As I figured, we took Second clear out to River Street and on to the Boulevard. Mr. Mathew was writing on his paper when he motioned me to park back where we had come from in front of the office. I pulled in, shut it off, and set the brake.

I saw him sign the bottom of the paper and I knew I was in. He ripped off the top sheet, which had carbon paper under it, and handed it to me, saying I could take it inside and they would take my picture. The paper I had would be my temporary license until one came in the mail with my photo on it. I got out and I was headed for the door when old Mathew made the comment that he was surprised how well I knew the one-way streets downtown and that he enjoyed the ride. I wasn't in the mood to stand around and talk about it, so I just nodded thanks and went into the waiting room, where Mom was waiting. She could tell right away what the outcome had been by the shit-eating grin on my face. I could tell Mom was pretty happy for me by the way she looked. She was unselfish and seemed content in making her family secure and happy.

I was called over for my mug shot by this undernourished, pale-skinned state employee, who looked as if she had just come from a funeral. She told me to stand by the wall between the two windows and smile. That must have been in her work manual, because I don't think she knew a lot about smiling herself. I gave her my rendition of Marlon Brando with a serious pout as she sprung the shutter. I dropped Mom off at home and she headed straight for the garden with a, "Drive careful, Sonny," over her shoulder.

I was over at Billy's house in a flash to give him a ride and talk over a couple of changes I needed to do right off, like drop it the way we insisted Gary do with his Merc. There was nothing worse than a kid having a car sitting about a mile and a half off the ground, driving around with bongo drums in the back window thinking he's got a cool set of wheels. You could have everything that old Honest Charley sells in his catalog stuck all over your car, but if it wasn't low, it just didn't get it. Billy hadn't gone to work at the Texaco yet since he had the evening shift, so we sort of cruised around, enjoying my new radio, making some plans on how I was going to personalize my coupe.

The following Saturday it was like déjà vu all over again, only it was my '40 and we were crowded in, heading for Portland to the Champion Speed Shop for a dropped axle. The bad news was they had gone up to $11 in the last two years, but the one I got was a little more smoothly made, coming from Mor-Drop in San Francisco versus the Dago axle that Billy had in his car. It didn't matter, since they both dropped the front three inches and had the same effect. That weekend was similar to before, except we took the car down to the Smith shop and used the torch set right on the spot. I left the car there on Monday so that John Burcher, one of the mechanics, could realign the front end so I wouldn't be wearing out the tires right away. After a week of enjoying my Dago'd coupe, I realized that the rear was going to have to come down a bit, since I was going to go with some new, taller tires in the back, which would about tip the car over on its front. The next Friday night, we pulled out the rear spring and I took it down to Anderson Bros. blacksmith shop on Fourth Street. We had old Newt flip the spring eyes, which brings down the rear about an inch, and then reinstalled it on Saturday night. We left out a couple of leaves, which brought it down another inch. Over at the Firestone store, I picked up a couple of 8x15-inch whitewalls and Joe came up with a couple of 15-inch Merc wheels that I painted black with a rattle can to match the 16s up front.

I was just about there, but I needed to do something about the interior. Of course, old Clarabelle had kept the seat and the rest of the upholstery absolutely perfect, but it had that old woman look to it. It looked like it should have been in a hearse or something, not at all like the rolled and pleated Naugahyde like the cars in *Hot Rod Magazine* had. I had read about taking cars to Tijuana, Mexico, for upholstery, which was in my plans but a long way off. I noticed one of Dad's green army blankets hanging on the clothesline over by the garden, so I just whipped it off and threw it over the seat. I was set for my junior year of high school.

Chapter 13

A year later, since Billy was home from college for the summer and Joe and I were going to be seniors, we had been planning on doing something special. Life as we had known it was coming to a close. Ever since I had gotten the '40, I had been planning on taking it to Mexico for an upholstery job. Billy had gotten his done right there in Willamette and it was good, but I was thinking of the adventure of a road trip and getting out of the country. I got to thinking that since the flathead was a good, reliable little motor, I'd better get the trip and the interior out of the way before I pumped the thing way up with a wild-ass motor.

We had been talking about making the trip, and it looked like it was coming down to Billy, Joe, and me. My dad thought it would be okay, because I usually had a couple of weeks after school ended before they got busy at the mill and I would have to go to work. Well, with Mom it was a different story, and she was truly worried. The fret was on. She had never been out of Oregon, while Dad had been all over the world in the war.

One afternoon she finally gave in and said, "Sonny, if you can get the other parents convinced, I guess it's okay with me."

"Thanks, Mom," I said as I gave her a little squeeze.

About a second later, I was at Billy's house with the news. He said that was exactly what his mom had said, so we just swapped permissions, so to speak, and of course Joe's mom didn't care, so we were ready to go.

Researching back through our archives of hot rod magazines, we studied stories of Tijuana, Mexico, upholstery jobs and what they cost. Tijuana, a border town situated about fifteen miles south of San Diego, California, had always been a favorite of American tourists because of its close location. Frank gave us a Mobil Oil Company map of California and we pored over it, planning routes and backup routes, weaving a trail south that would include some interesting spots, such as anything famous that had something to do with hot rods or surfer girls. When the time got close, I had the '40 on the hoist down at Fletcher's and gave it a good going over. We changed the oil and greased it up good and even replaced a couple of the tires that looked as if they might not make the trip. Frank loaned us the spare parts he thought we might need, and we replaced the fan belts and flushed out the radiator.

Finally, the morning came. After getting a tearful hug from Mom and a good luck from Dad, I fired up the coupe and backed out. I saw Spooky looking at me as I spun the wheel around. I waved a goodbye to her and subconsciously hoped she would be there when I got back, since she was getting pretty old. I suppose in dog years, she was about 150, because she'd been around as long as I could remember.

I went straight to Billy's house, where he was getting about the same sendoff. His mom had made us some cookies for the trip and was kind of wringing her hands in her apron when we left. Joe got a rare hug from Sylvia on the porch and she actually looked as if she meant it.

We could hardly control our excitement with the anticipation. I made a slight detour so we could swing by the Ford garage and honk at everyone as we went by. Fred and Ronald, two of the mechanics, were pushing a used car into the shop as we putted by with the window down for a wave. When they saw us, Ronald began pumping air with his fist and Fred yelled, "Don't get any on ya down there!"

I gave them a grin and we were gone.

Eisenhower was building a freeway system of highways about this time, and some of it was finished and some of it was still in construction. They started and finished the areas closest to large populations with heavy traffic first and then tapered off to less traveled areas. Willamette happened to be included in the route chosen to hook California up with Portland on the way to Canada. This was the northern end of what they were calling I-5, and eventually, it would go south all the way to Mexico. Since the whole thing was somewhere in the middle of happening, we would be on and off the finished areas. We sure didn't care. It was a new adventure and we were headed south.

Once we started into the hills, it was unchartered territory for us, and we were digging it. Passing construction sites meant getting on and off gravel and dirt ramps and stopping for flaggers. It was an education seeing a major highway literally being cut through mountains and bridged over waterways. Having a lot of time to talk, we discussed the usual topics of cars, music, and girls. Passing through different areas, we were picking up radio stations and hearing music we hadn't heard before. We had entered western music country and it was twang this and twang that by artists unfamiliar to us. As I'd mentioned before, Billy was pretty bright and was always good at solving problems. He had come up with this idea during the planning stages of the trip to pool some of our money in an envelope and put it in the glove box for gas and food and all. This saved us from having to dig for cash all the time, dividing by three, and so on.

Upon reaching Ashland, the old Ford was running on empty, so I pulled off at a Shell station. It had a sign over the door: *Jack and Frank's Friendly Service*. When Frank came out the door, we had already gotten out and were sort of stumbling around stretching and groaning. I was guessing this person was Frank, because she was wearing a tan Shell Oil Company shirt that said *Frank* on it. Cocked on one side of her head, she wore one of those work fedoras that was waterproof and had some extra wooden matches stuck in the band. She had a cigarette going that sort of bobbed up and down when she spoke.

"What'll it be, boys, ethyl or regular?" she asked, kind of leaning back so the smoke wouldn't get in her eyes.

I looked over at Billy and said, "I think we're going to need everything we've got by looking at that mountain."

Frank was pointing up at the mountain while she was jamming the nozzle around trying to find the gas tube. "That son of a bitch is about straight up all the way to the California border," she said, the cigarette dangling over the gas tank.

We had been warned about this part of the trip by more than one who had traversed it. It was comforting to see all the vehicles coming down off it, which made it seem conquerable. I'd never seen so many log trucks and dump trucks. It was springtime and they were covered with mud from top to bottom. They always seemed to have their foot in it, with the black smoke bellowing out pipes and the motors bawling. She filled us up and checked our oil while Joe, Billy, and I took turns at the bathroom out back of the station. With the change from the five dollar bill, Joe got us a Milky Way and two Hershey's, and we were on our way with a wave goodbye to Frank.

Luckily, the first part of the highway, to the top of the Siskiyou Mountains, had been replaced with the new, wider strip of concrete, and there were three lanes going up and two down. We got in the middle lane where we could keep up with the empty log trucks. We must have met a hundred with loaded trailers coming at us. Things were happening: logging, highway construction, and new building everywhere you looked. Times were booming. After reaching the top of the first hill, the highway turned back into the two lane affair with turnouts located in strategic spots. An occasional truck would be stopped along the side with the driver filling the radiator or just kicking the tires. It was a gruesome grind up the hill for sure. We came across an old Hudson that looked as if it was abandoned, but had a dog leashed to the trunk handle and a temporary camp set up with a tarp tied between the car roof and a couple of pine trees. An older guy had the hood open and was working on the motor. There were feet sticking out from under the bumper that must have belonged to another amateur mechanic. They had a little fire going with a pot hanging over it and with a gaggle of kids pressed around it waiting. You could get a good look at the landscape while traveling by because of the slow pace. Once, I had to go clear down to low gear, which was a trick because the '40 didn't have synchronizers between first and second and you had to sort of double clutch it and hope for the best.

Seeing the Summit Cafe we had heard about was a treat, I'm here to tell you. As I rolled into the lot, I congratulated myself and the old Ford for making it to the top. I parked up close to the screen door that was banging open and shut with working men coming and going. The smell of cooking food that followed them out was having its effect on us. The place was full, but we got stools at the coffee bar, where we gobbled down some biscuits and gravy, a hardy meal that fit our tight budget. We paid up and left a nice tip to the sweet little lady who suggested her famous biscuits.

"You darlings have a nice trip, you hear," she said with a wink as we slammed the door.

I was about all driven out and it was getting along about late afternoon, so I asked Billy if he wanted to take the wheel for a while. That old Frank was right about how steep the hill was going up, but the other side was just as steep and a little scary. Billy took it easy on the brakes, and we rolled on most of the steep areas in second gear, just letting the little flathead cackle.

A few miles down the road, we came to the California border station where they check to see if you have any agriculture, produce, or illegal commodities in your rig. It was pretty quiet by then because of the time of evening, so there weren't any other automobiles in line but us and a couple of freight trucks over in the weigh line. It was a big old place that kind of reminded me of a huge service station with tall ceilings to make room for the trucks and trailers with their high loads and such.

As we were sitting there with the motor running waiting to be inspected, we were commenting on how well lit up the place was, and then this attendant, for lack of a better name, came over to look in. She had to be one of those Amazons I'd heard about.

I'd guessed about six-foot five.

Joe, kind of under his breath, said, "Six-foot seven, at least."

She sort of sauntered over like she wasn't in any hurry, I guess because we were the only ones in line at the time. She was wearing this California highway patrolman uniform that was all pressed and starched, and there wasn't a wrinkle to be seen anywhere, from the shiny black boots up about four feet of tan slacks, with a black belt holding a revolver and a pair of cuffs. Further up, she had on a white cotton shirt that looked as if it was made out of metal it was so straight and tight, and she had a pair of enormous knockers that made her silver star look little like one of Gene Autry's buttons.

Stopping at Billy's window, the first thing she did was lean over the cowl and pick a butterfly out from under the wiper. It was a pretty yellow bug with black spots that we had been looking at ever since we left Ashland. Being as tall as she was, she had to step back to bend down enough to look at us through the window.

"Now look at what you've gone and done here," she said with a pair of the biggest, reddest lips I'd ever seen. You couldn't really tell what she looked like because of the mirrored sunglasses she wore, but she had a lean nose and I'm thinking her eyes were probably stunning, but I wasn't asking.

Billy answered, "That happened in Oregon, ma'am." Then realizing how dumb that sounded, he froze up and couldn't get out another peep.

She dropped the bug into the wastepaper can behind her without ever taking an eye off Billy. Another car pulled up to be inspected on the opposite side of ours, which got the officer's attention. She raised her arms up and folded them across the top of the car, giving the other driver the sign to stop. This movement of her anatomy caused her breasts to fill up the entire driver's side window, and instead of finishing with us first, she decided to interrogate the other motorist from her existing vantage point. Poor old Billy was froze up, looking straight ahead with both arms stiff and hanging on to the wheel while the left side of his face was getting a rub down by those enormous knockers.

This went on for a while, because the other driver kept asking about what kind of fruit she was looking for and that little Peter had part of an apple in the backseat. Finally, the guy got it through his head to leave and that brought her full attention back to us.

She leaned down again, releasing Billy's still frozen face, and asked, "Where you boys think you're going in this cute little car?"

Billy still couldn't get out anything but a little whisper about something to do with the seats. The officer then leaned her face into the car a little like she couldn't hear Billy, and I could smell her perfume. I'm sure Billy could hear her breathing, because I'm sure he had stopped. Joe piped up about how we were needing to get down to Sacramento because his grandma was in the hospital and the doctors didn't know if she would make it through the night. I guess Joe was a pretty good liar if he wanted to be, because that sort of brought Billy out of it, and I was looking at Joe with a "what's this shit all about?" look.

I could tell that the officer wasn't liking to let the conversation go anywhere where we wanted. She thumped Billy on the shoulder a couple of times and asked if we had any produce, pointing to the sign behind her that stated no fruits or vegetables beyond the line. Billy just shook his head, still looking straight ahead. I guess she was done with us, because she did an about-face and walked back to her little cubicle.

Chapter 14

Driving through the night, I must have gone to sleep, because the next thing I knew, we were in a service station in Redding. We all stretched and went to the bathroom, which was getting kind of routine. After waking up the attendant, we got some gas, and I dumped in the first quart of the Mobil Special 30 I'd gotten from Fletcher's.

Billy was done in, so he took shotgun, I moved to the middle, and Joe got behind the wheel. That was the way it went all the way down and back. When your turn to drive was finished, you got by the window where you could get some sleep, and the window guy moved to the middle, and so on. After checking the map, which we had totally memorized before we left, we noted that we needed to veer off at Red Bluff and head diagonally for Sacramento. We had entered a hot climate, so we were traveling with our windows down and our jackets were in the trunk.

On the occasions I was awake, I noticed we were in orchards. Miles and miles of orchards. It was dark, but I figured they were some kind of nut, and then I was pretty sure we got into some olive trees. I woke up for good about Marysville, and it was getting light out, so we decided to stop at a little cafe along the highway, since we were all hungry as hell. We needed to burn a little time because we didn't want to hit Sacramento during rush hour. Joe suggested we load up pretty good since we might not want to eat anything big until that night. We each had a big breakfast with ham and eggs. The place really piled it on with potatoes, gravy, and all the toast you could get down. It's funny how hungry you can get just riding along sitting in a car like that. The joint was filled with farmers coming in and out of a screen door matching the one on the mountain, except this one had a *William's* bread sign on it that was worn from big hands banging it.

We hit Sacramento about midmorning, and the multiple lanes of traffic going both ways were already full with commuters in a hurry. They were honking and darting here and there like this was their last day on the planet and they had some stuff to get done or something. I was back at the wheel, and we were all rubbernecking around looking at the tall buildings while trying not to get run over. After twenty miles of white knuckles, we were shot out of the tube and it got pretty quiet again.

Motoring along, we enjoyed the fields of everything from rice to tomatoes, all new and different to us. While cruising through Lodi, we were passed by one of those Ford retractable hardtops. We might not have noticed it, but it was a brand new '57. It still had the temporary license sticker in the rear window and a dealer logo where the license plate went that said *Worthington Ford, Long Beach*. It was a beautiful car, all turquoise and white with full hubcaps and white walls. It was traveling fast and we couldn't stay up with it. I figured it probably had one of those new interceptors in it with two four-barrels or even a blower.

What really stood out was who was riding in it. We decided she had to be some kind of movie star or something because of what she had on with the sunglasses and all. When the car went by us in the morning, she was wearing a tiger-skin coat, her blonde hair was long, and she was smoking. You could even see the lipstick on the cigarette for a spilt second. About Manteca, they passed us again. The top was down and she had a scarf on her head and was wearing a movie-goddess-gold dress, still smoking. The driver was a sophisticated guy wearing a straw fedora and smoking a cigar. We thought she was flirting with us, because she would slip us a little smile whenever they passed, and it was getting routine for them to overtake us every so often. I think we were all daydreaming, I know I was, fantasizing about how she was going to notice me somewhere in L.A. and we would have a nice little one-night stand and I would be the one driving the retractable.

I whipped into a rest area out of Madera, since I needed to stretch and Joe said he had to piss like a racehorse. We had been drinking Cokes all morning to keep awake, so we could enjoy the daylight and see the sights. The rest area was a ways off the main highway, but it could be seen from there. Coming in, we noticed a young, dark-haired boy of about thirteen sitting on a large rock with a crutch under his arm. He was petting a sheepdog that was standing next to a sheep. Not a full grown sheep, like a ram or something, but an almost grown lamb. While Billy and I were washing up, Joe went back to have a talk with the boy. While waiting for Joe, I washed the bugs off the windshield and Billy checked the oil, and then we looked the tires over.

Old Joe must have been learning the kid's whole life story, because it seemed to take a while. Finally, he showed up with this concerned look on his face he gets sometimes. Billy and I were leaning up against the car there enjoying the sunshine while Joe brought us up to speed about the kid. It turned out the boy, whose name was Luix, was a Basque. He had been up in the foothills with his Uncle Belasco, herding sheep all spring, and their cart got away from them coming down a hill. It had rolled over a couple of times, which broke the uncle's leg and sprained Luix's foot, or so they thought.

Anyway, Joe went on to tell us that Luix needed a ride into Fresno where his family owned a hotel so his dad could get back to the sheep camp to rescue Uncle Belasco.

I said that I didn't think it was a problem; Fresno was right on the way. I suggested we load him up and he could set on one of the jump seats in the back and we would keep moving on.

Joe was kind of looking down at his feet when he said, "Well, there is a little hitch."

That sounded a little suspicious, so I asked what that was all about.

"He won't leave his dog," Joe said.

"Jesus," I said. "I never even let Spooky in the car and she's my dog."

"Well, all the same, he won't leave it, and he's in a lot of pain."

I noticed Billy was looking at me like I was the biggest shithead in the whole world. So, of course, I gave in and drove the '40 back off the hill while Billy and Joe walked down to where the kid was.

I got out and put one of the little jump seats down that came from Ford, because it was a Deluxe Opera coupe and I guess they were a little bonus. The way Joe and Billy were standing there together, I began to think there was even more to this than they were letting on.

Not unfolding his arms, Billy said, "And he won't leave the sheep either."

It was one of those times when you know you're absolutely right about something and everyone else is absolutely wrong and you can't do a damn thing about it. Luix, or Louie or whoever he was, looked at me with those big, brown eyes with pain in them, and I could see what Joe had been going through.

I threw up my arms and said, "Get in. All of you."

As I was holding the door open, I asked anyone who might be listening if the sheep had gone to the bathroom lately.

So I headed out on the highway with my arm on my forehead like I had a splitting headache, which I was sure I was about to get.

Joe said, "Shit, Sonny, what do you care? You're

going to throw all this upholstery away in a couple of days anyway."

We were buzzing along the countryside when I saw the green and white Ford in my rearview mirror. I bumped Joe with my elbow to wake him and Billy, because I knew they would want to see if she gave us another little sign. When the movie babe got right alongside, she was smiling, and then she started laughing her ass off as she put her hand on the fella's shoulder to get his attention. After he took a peek at us, he broke out laughing too. So, of course, we got to wondering what the hell was so funny and what all the cracking up was about.

"Oh my God," Joe roared as he looked over the seat.

Billy did a 180 and was looking in the back with his knees on the seat and he let out a yowl too. By leaning my head to the left I could see through the rearview mirror what everyone was admiring so much. Luix had fallen asleep on his chair, while the dog was asleep on the floor, and the sheep was sitting on the other jump seat looking out the window at the movie star. After I recovered, and it took a while, I asked little Luix back there what exit we should make when arriving in Fresno to take us to the hotel. He came to be known to us as Little Louie since none of could seem to pronounce his real name right. The poor little guy had the idea that we were going to just dump him at the exit and be on our way, but I assured him we were going to take him all the way to his doorstep.

Fresno is laid out all nice, square, and flat. After we left the highway, we did a lot of lefts and rights, hoping Little Louie knew how in the hell to get home. I noticed we kept sinking into the older, tougher part of the city by the scary way people looked and the rundown shape of everything in general. I made a mental note to myself that it might be prudent to get packing as soon as we attended to Louie. Sure enough, right on the corner of Main and First Street stood this old, square, brick building with a dilapidated sign painted on the bricks that said *Hotel Fresno*. Little Louie motioned for us to park at the curb right in front of the double wooden doors.

Joe got Louie out and up to the hotel, while Billy attended to the dog, which left me with the sheep. We were met at the door by an olive-skinned, middle-aged woman who looked to me like she might have been a gypsy by the way she was dressed. Obviously, she was Little Louie's mother. We learned her name was Angela. She was hugging him and asking all these questions in what sounded like Spanish. Angela sent this little boy, who was peering at us from behind her skirt, off to find the dad, who we found out later was named Gorka. Several people, the dad included, showed up at the same time, and Louie was carefully rushed through a door in the lobby into what appeared to be the family quarters.

This left the three of us standing in the old lobby, which had a high ceiling and tattered wallpaper and pictures of sheep and herders hung all over it. There was a fan gently turning over the bar, which was situated on one side of the room toward the middle and opposite the door Louie had been ushered through. I was looking around for a place to tie up the sheep so we could leave, when the door to the restaurant opened and this little old guy appeared. He was grinning, showing a remarkable set of white teeth for a man of his age. He was badly wrinkled, with thinning hair and a mustache, and wore a leather vest over a white cotton shirt. Around his neck was a western tie, one of those little rope affairs with a silver button in the middle with some kind of blue rock stuck to it. He actually looked like he could have been a Gaucho from Argentina or somewhere else near the equator.

"I'm Barea," he said as he distributed three small glasses on the bar. "Luix's grandfather."

He muttered something with this foreign accent about how thirsty we must be as he was reaching for a bottle, and before we could get out a no thank you, we were looking at three shots of some kind of liquor. Old Barea became Barney to us, and suddenly, we were fast friends. He asked us all about how we met up with Luix and told us the whole family appreciated us delivering him safe and sound and so on. To show their thanks, he said there wouldn't be any charge for the drinks. Looking back, I'd say it was some kind of brandy, made from apricots or something.

He told us, while pouring a second round, that it was a Basque before-dinner drink and you really shouldn't eat without a couple beforehand. After we downed the second one, Angela, Little Louie's mom, came back out from the family part of the building wearing a long, cotton dress with red and black print. She looked traditional, reflecting what her ancestors wore in the old country. She had the news that Louie was doing fine and her husband was already on his way up north to rescue his brother. With that, she showered us with thanks about getting Little Louie home and insisted we stay for supper, which would be coming up soon. While leaning on the bar getting a little sloshed and visiting with Barney, we noticed customers, some Basque-looking and some like us, milling around the lobby, drinking and visiting, waiting for something, which turned out to be dinner.

I was getting a little worried about the car and made a comment about it to our new friend Barney, and he said not to worry, it was safe. I gave him sort of a questioning look and he gave me a look back that meant, "I said it was safe."

I figured that they must have had someone patrolling the area around the property and imagined this big, tattooed, bald guy with a sword in his belt and a dagger in his boot.

The doors to the kitchen opened at exactly 6:30. We were called by a young girl, who we found out later was Little Louie's sister, Katelin. She had long, black hair with dark, soft skin and these big, brown eyes that looked us over so quickly that if we hadn't been doing the same, we wouldn't have noticed. She was striking, in a genuinely pure way. She looked like a cross between an exotic princess and a peasant girl. Grandpa Barney shot us a look that told us she was not available and to even think about it was way out of line.

The dinner was family style, with everyone sitting down together at wooden tables showing years of wear. They, like the benches we were sitting on, had cigarette burns and were scarred up like they'd seen more than one dinner. Between every other person sat a wine bottle with a loose cork. We were told by one of the guests that the Basques made their own wine in the Central Valley somewhere, and it was always the same, a red table wine that was good with about anything.

We sat across from a middle-aged couple from Boise, Idaho, who said they ate at Basque restaurants anytime they got a chance. Joe told them we hadn't known there was such a thing until about five minutes before and filled them in on our episode with Little Louie and his sheep. As we were eating our salads, which consisted of only lettuce and some vinegar, the lady wanted to know every little detail of our trip, and she seemed genuinely interested. We noticed that the other guests, a mix of average tourists and Basque people, were helping themselves to the wine, so not ones to be left out, we were lugging down our share.

As I was eating the pinto beans and bread that came next, I began to feel a nice little glow come over me and the wood seat I was sitting on seemed a little softer. Everyone was into the wine pretty well, and as the time slipped along, the room got noisier with just normal conversation. Every once in a while, one of the Basques would slam his fist down on the table and come out with a few verses of a song from the old country. One of the younger men would hit the one next to him on the shoulder with a laugh and then calmly wait to be hit back by the victim and then they had their arms around each other laughing.

Of course, keeping with the theme of the day, the main course was lamb. I'd never heard a lot of good about eating sheep. It had gotten a bad reputation in the war because it was overused and called mutton. However, this was delicious, and the three of us had our share and finished up with chocolate cake that also went well with the wine. As the guests were finishing up and leaving the restaurant area, we all attempted standing at the same time, without much luck. I was pretty well on my way and I knew I couldn't drive, so I began to contemplate spending the night in the '40 under the protection of the man with the sword.

Angela met us at the cash register that had become just a little, fuzzy, funny-looking tool with buttons on it and informed us that there was no charge and we would be spending the night at the hotel. Our old friend the bartender and Louie's little brother, who had gotten over his shyness, helped us with our luggage. We were shown our individual rooms and where the community bathroom was at the end of the hall.

When I woke up in the morning, I still had my shoes on. My head felt like it was full of cotton and my mouth full of dog shit. When I got to the lobby, Billy and Joe were nursing coffee in silence, and it was easy to see they weren't much better off than me. Angela insisted on feeding us breakfast. This was a total failure, because we couldn't swallow yet, so she turned the whole thing into sandwiches that she bagged up for us to take along.

After a few hours on the highway going south, with the windows down, things started to turn right side up with drinking Cokes and eating sandwiches. Stopping in Bakersfield for gas and more Cokes was the same old drill. I dumped another quart of oil into the motor, and off we went with clean windows, still heading south. Staying the night at Louie's hotel cost us some time, but we all agreed it was well worth it getting to meet everyone and having a nice bath that morning, even if it was a little tarnished with the headache and all.

Getting to the Grapevine was something we were looking forward to since we had heard about it, and it was a real treat to just sort of coast down and around until we got to the bottom. From then on it was traveling through a mass of humanity we had no way of being prepared for. We stayed on the I-5 Freeway, or tried to, all the way, but the names would change from numbers to names and back to numbers. We missed a couple of times, but recovered and actually made it through in pretty good time and missed the rush-hour traffic. Upon reaching San Diego, we decided to find a place in Chula Vista, a little town right above the border, to crash for the night and then cross the border and get the job done and get back over before night the following day. The thought of spending the night in Mexico wasn't our idea of smart.

We asked the lady at the hotel if she would wake us at six and then flipped a coin to see who got the bed. Billy and I slept on the floor in our sleeping bags until we got the knock on the door in the morning. After everyone showered up, we headed for the border.

The crossing itself wasn't unlike the one going into California from Oregon, except it was on a long bridge with a small block house where the guards would hold up. We rolled in about 8:00 in the morning, and three of the Mexican officials came out, mostly to look at my car. They were nice enough, asking for our IDs and what we planned to do in their country, whether it was for business or pleasure and things like that. A moment later, we were across the bridge and witnessed the transformation from America to a third-world country.

At their end of the bridge, we were met by a little army of young boys with dirty clothes and no shoes selling gum and almost anything else, including advice. One of the older boys swung up onto the running board of the '40 and introduced himself as José, saying he would help us during our stay. I asked him where the upholstery shops were and told him we were looking for a good, honest place to stitch the car he was borrowing the riding on.

"Oh, *sí, señor*," José said. "My uncle is the best upholsterer in all of Tijuana."

About that time, a cohort of José's jumped on the opposite running board while waving the other troops off. José motioned me forward and, using some pretty good English, said he would show me the way. He pointed left onto Revolutionary Street and we drove by the most amazing things I'd ever witnessed. It was the street with all the bars advertising shows of everything under the sun, and most of it wasn't nice.

The street was full of sailors and marines swarmed over by hookers. There were pigs and chickens being carried by donkeys in tow of entrepreneurs in search of deals. Cars were trying to squeeze through, including ours, horns were honking, and people were yelling at the top of their lungs, and this was first thing in the morning.

José was yelling and hollering like he was escorting important dignitaries and directing us out of the calamity onto a street that turned into a neighborhood of automotive repair shops of all kinds. By then, we had quite an entourage of kids running alongside and were picking up more all the time, and they were yelling, "Hot rod, hot rod!"

I pulled the car up in front of an open building with a corrugated roof and stucco walls and a sign overhead that said *Cadillac Upholstery*. José hit the pavement running. Our little crowd sort of milled around close while our other escort motioned for us to stay put. There were people everywhere looking busy, and some not so busy, but all were curious about the three gringos from the *Norte*. José appeared again, this time with his uncle, who looked as if he owned the enterprise. Uncle Abel greeted us friendly enough, and through José, I explained to him what it was I wanted with the upholstery. I told him how I wanted the seats pleated, rolled blue and white, with the headliner and door panels white with blue piping.

We came to an agreement of $119, which would include the trunk and a pleated diamond on each of the door panels. I coughed up half of it up front, and he promised to have it done late in the afternoon, giving us plenty of time to get back across before it got too dark. It was quite an event to see the whole thing come together so quickly. There were three sewing machines going. Meanwhile, I assume they were all family, another half-dozen Mexicans were cutting and fitting while jabbering away and laughing like they'd never had such a good time. We just hung around drinking Mexican beer, eating tacos, and waiting to get sick. With help from little marauding salespersons, each of our moms ended up with a nice, hand-carved purse, and we ended up mildly drunk.

When they finished what I thought was an amazing accomplishment in such a short time, I paid off Abel and gave him the old upholstery, which he seemed to cherish. With José and his number one man riding security, we made for the border. As I was pulling away from where they had to get off, I looked in the rearview mirror, and José was grinning and waving goodbye with the five dollar bill I had just planted in his hand.

Up ahead at the blockhouse, we saw a cab coming from the American side that looked like it had been lowered. Come to find out, it was full of sailors who were unloading and having their IDs checked. You could tell they had been having a good time before they arrived by the way they were weaving around and trying to stay standing. As we were passing by, one of them, who was a high school kid just like us a short time ago, drew up to attention and saluted with, "Seaman First Class Jahns, United States Navy."

Old Joe swung around in the seat and saluted back with, "Joe Harden, Little Bastards, Willamette, Oregon!"

With that, I hit the throttle and raced back into the country.

Our trip back was uneventful. We stopped at one of the beaches we had heard so much about. Joe stripped down and made a banzai run for the water and came out looking like a blue Popsicle. It wasn't nearly as warm as the Beach Boys had led us to believe.

It must have been the Amazon's night off when we slowed down for the state border crossing, because all we could see was this little guy, about four and a half feet tall, wearing a Smokey the Bear hat and using a flashlight to check the cars coming in from Oregon.

Chapter 15

One sunny afternoon in the summer before my senior year, Gary and Joe met up with me at my house, and we drove down to the high school to register for our last year. After signing up for another sentence, we returned to the parking lot, hopped into the '40, and lit up while discussing the new crop of girls showing up for their freshman year. Of course, we weren't supposed to smoke on school property, but we were on the edge of it and we liked living on the edge.

As I pulled out, I saw some cheerleaders who had been having tryouts in the gym walking away from us along the sidewalk and in deep conversation. To get their attention, I goosed it a little, chirping the tires, and then I backed off and let my pipes cackle as we went by. Joe had his head hanging out the window making some goofball face he was known for. In the mirror, I could see them giggling, a common reaction to our confidence, which was usually over the top when we were at a safe distance from the female kind.

We were making for Elmer's wrecking yard to see about getting some Lincoln wheels I heard showed up the day before. The wheels had the early bolt pattern, but were wider and would take a bigger tire. They were unique in that they would fit the older Fords and made them rare as hen's teeth. Elmer was a kind, old guy and let us have the run of the place. We had spent many a Saturday pawing over the piles looking for treasures.

I noticed this black Chevy following me in my rear-view mirror. I'd seen the car around lately. Rumor had it the driver was going to be a new student at W.H.S. and was from the coast somewhere over by Newport. I could tell by the car he had it together, since it was low and painted with black primer. It had a nice, smooth cackle, which sixes are known for, when he downshifted as he came down the street. As I stopped on Muddy Creek Road, getting ready to turn right for Elmer's, he came up beside me and thumped the throttle a little to get my attention.

Gary gave me an elbow in the side like he knew something was coming down. This fella, who was sort of slouched down in the seat, looked older than his years. He was comfortable with himself and his ride. He piped up with, "It was nice of your mom to let you drive the car today."

I wasn't going to let it go, especially right in front of Gary and Joe, so I came back with, "My grandma's car could beat that little mousey thing you're in."

I was pointing my finger towards the straightaway on South Muddy Creek Road. He got the picture. I pulled out into the left lane so he could move to Joe's side for the countdown. On one, we both slammed the gas to the floor and on three we dumped the clutches in unison. I could hear his tires squealing as they were burning rubber. All I got was a little chirp and a puff of smoke. This gave me the jump on him, but he was pulling up at the top of first gear, and when I slammed second, we were neck and neck. I glanced over in time to see him pulling away and he was looking back at me like he was galloping away on a stolen horse. At the top end of second, I was reading his license plate and I wasn't liking it much. Luckily, we had to slow down for an S corner coming up, or it would have just gotten worse. He swung into the old abandoned Anderson Sawmill and stopped in the gravel turnaround.

I stopped alongside and he offered to run back the other way. I said I didn't think there was much use in it since he beat me fair and square.

We got out and I introduced myself. He shook my hand, saying his name was Bruce and that he had been admiring my car around town.

"Thanks," I said. "This is Gary and over there is Joe."

He told us he and his family were from Newport and had moved to Willamette for a job his dad had landed out at the mill.

"What about popping the hood?" I asked. "I'd kind of like to know what you got in there that kicked my ass so good."

"It's just a little ole six I got out of Uncle Bill's beer truck," he said.

After seeing the contents between his two front fenders, I was feeling a little better about my little 239 CID stock Ford flathead. Instead of the '50 Chevy six I was expecting, it was a 270 CID GMC he had gotten out of a delivery truck, and it was all chromed out with three carbs and a split manifold right below the Vertex magneto. Hell, it was a full-blown hot rod. After we were done slobbering all over his motor, I told him we were glad to have met him and that he was welcome to swing by and see us at Fletcher's any time.

There was a group of people, like an outer ring, that we let hang close to us but not real close, never to be part of the heart and soul of the Little Bastards. Bruce earned his way into this echelon that day by beating the pants off me fair and square and being good about it. However, as much as I was taken with Bruce, I didn't take to getting beat that bad, and especially by a six. It got me thinking about hopping up the flatty or maybe replacing the thing altogether. I had endured being about the slowest thing on wheels around Willamette for more than a year and it was getting pretty old. After rebuilding my war chest down at the First National by working at the mill and helping out down at Fletcher's, I was in the market for some horsepower.

One evening, on a school night, the very person who gave me such an ass-kicking out on South Muddy Creek Road called me up to tell me about a wrecked car he had towed over to Elmer's wrecking yard the night before. Bruce had been working for AA Towing in town, driving wrecker, and business was good, since highway 99E was getting way overcrowded and becoming a bloodbath. Especially south of Willamette, there were some long, straight stretches where people would really get to hauling ass and get into trouble. Anyway, the night before, he had towed in this hardtop that might be just what I was looking for.

Bruce was into cars, from working on them to driving them, had the need for speed, and seemed to have the natural ability to get it. The car he called me about was a practically new '57 Olds 88 with a J-2 high-performance motor. According to Bruce, it had been wrecked on a corner down south the night before by the owner, a banker from one of the little towns below Willamette.

"Look, Sonny," he said over the phone, "I think the insurance company will total the whole thing, since there isn't a straight piece of tin left on it except right in the middle of the top."

"What about the motor and tranny?" I asked.

"I think it'll run, but nobody's going to try it because the radiator's crushed," he said. "Hell, the whole thing's almost new. The paint's just barely burnt off the manifolds."

I agreed to meet him at the yard right after school the next day and we would give it a look-see.

I knew quite a bit about the Oldsmobile V8 engines from reading the *Motor Life* magazines the school subscribed to in the library. That was about the only reason you ever caught one of us Little Bastards in the room of doom. Well, that and one other reason: The new librarian wasn't hard to look at. Her name was Kathie, and she had come out from North Dakota for college and got on at our school after she graduated from the university. She was all young and bubbly with a knockout body and seemed genuinely interested in us guys who weren't jocks and didn't play tennis or anything.

Anyway, I had read an article recently about the new General Motors performance line, which included the new Olds J-2 engine they had gotten out just in time for the big race in Daytona. They used the basic block that came out in 1949 and increased the size from 303 CID to 371 CID, while also increasing the compression. This optional motor also included three two-barrel carbs, a hotter cam, and solid lifters.

I figured with that much horsepower in my light little Ford, I'd earn the title "Mr. Fastest Man in Town," which I thought had a nice little ring to it. All I had to do was buy it and get it in my car. On the way out the door in the morning, I lifted my dad's tape measure from his tool box and headed for school.

I met up with Bruce in the parking lot the minute after the bell rang. He jumped in with me and we roared out to Elmer's, where the Olds was sitting in the bullpen. The "bullpen" is what Elmer called the fenced off area where he put the cars to wait for the insurance companies to decide their fate. Elmer was there and unlocked the gate for us, swinging it open. After working all day, his overalls were still neat and clean. He was one of those guys who could be around dirt, grease, and oil all day and never get any of it on him. I was pretty much the opposite; if I looked at it, I was wearing it.

Bruce was right, there wasn't much left of the outside of the car, except the windows weren't broken, and that's probably why the old poop made it out of the thing without a scratch. While I was assessing the damage, Bruce filled me in on what had happened the Thursday night of the accident.

Bruce had just locked up at the lot where he had dumped off a repossession for the bank, when he got a call over the Motorola two-way from Howard, his boss. Howard had just gotten off the phone from the county sheriff's office notifying him of a wreck on 99E that they wanted AA to handle. Bruce said he was driving the new Ford 600 that night, so it didn't take him long to reach the scene. The car was hard to miss, being painted pink. It had come to a stop with the front wheels on the edge of the pavement and the rear hanging over a ditch that was scary deep. Upon his arrival, Bruce had noticed an older couple sitting in back of one of the police cars.

After getting the Olds hooked up and pulled out on the shoulder of the highway, headed north, he was approached by the county deputy who had some papers for him to sign on his clipboard. The deputy asked Bruce if he would mind dropping off the couple at their home since it was on the way back towards Willamette. There had been another call and the cop said he needed to push on and deal with that. This was a pretty common practice, and of course, it was fine with Bruce. The officer introduced Bruce to the old couple, whose names were Flo and Floyd, explaining to them how they would be getting home.

Floyd had to go back to the Olds to get the blanket since old people never drove anywhere without a blanket in the car, a habit from the days of horse and buggies or whatever. Floyd had on his suit and tie and was wearing a small-brimmed fedora with a little feather in it, while Flo had on a nice, pink dress, white shoes, and a hat with flowers. Bruce could tell by the way they were helping each other into the truck they were both smashed. Come to find out, they were on the way home from a party at the Elks Club.

According to Flo, they were going way too fast when a deer ran in front of them. Old Floyd swerved to miss it, and suddenly, they were going backwards down 99E, scraping the guardrail. She had to stop and blow her nose on Floyd's handkerchief, which gave Floyd a chance to explain he was only going about 60 and how it was hard to hold these cars down, because they were made to go faster. Flo started in again, while handing back the handkerchief, about how, all of a sudden, the car started turning, going sideways, scraping the front of the car, and then they were going frontwards, scraping the opposite side of the car, before it finally stopped damn near in the ditch, where she said they could have both been killed. She was holding on to the blanket, crying, as old Floyd was consoling her. She finally sort of dozed off or passed out in his arms.

Floyd relaxed then and began to talk.

"I'm really going to miss that car, you know," he said.

"We only had it for a few months."

Bruce asked, "So, why did you happen on that car with the two doors and a big motor with a stick shift?"

"Well," he said, "it was the color."

Floyd went on to say how much Flo liked pink. The car was pink and white, and it was right there in the showroom ready to go, so it seemed like the thing to do. Flo hiccupped and woke up just long enough to reach for the hanky again and then she was out like a light.

While I was getting the rundown about the wreck, I was rolling around under the Olds measuring the driveshaft, length of the transmission, and any other thing that was appropriate for a complete motor and running gear swap.

"That's about it," Bruce said. "I helped them into the house and Flo hit the couch with a box of Kleenex. Floyd covered her with the blanket and showed me to the door. Oh, I almost forgot, Floyd slipped me a ten when I was opening the door to leave. He's a good old fart."

To make this as short as possible, the insurance company decided to total it and put the remains up for sale. Elmer helped me negotiate the price down a little. I ended up buying the whole kit and caboodle for less than I could have spent up at the Champion Speed Shop in one afternoon. Elmer wanted what was left after all the hardware was gone, so I gave it to him for helping me dismantle everything.

Billy was taking summer classes at college, but we corresponded frequently, and I couldn't wait to call him up and relate the news. He was planning on being home for the break before fall term and said he would help me with the "switcheroo," which is what he called it. I made arrangements with Johnny's dad to let me use the Ford shop for the job, because I knew it was not going to be as simple as Billy made it sound.

A few days before the break, I followed Billy's suggestion and pulled the front fenders, grill, and radiator off the '40. This made me a little nervous, because I hadn't been without wheels since I had turned sixteen. I was back to riding with Joe, and he ribbed me about it a little, but I kind of enjoyed his company.

Bruce slipped by with the wrecker on the evening before Billy was slated to arrive home and we towed the coupe over to the Ford garage. During the week Billy was home, we burnt the midnight oil and daytime oil too. We hardly noticed the crowd watching the ordeal. Sometimes you could see a dozen pairs of shoes from under the bottom of my car. There was lots of advice floating around, with all the other bullshitting, through the nights and days. The Olds' rear end, wheels and all, were narrow enough to fit right under the Ford fenders, which was a pleasant surprise. We simply welded the spring mounts from the '40's rear end onto the Olds and then attached the new shocks off the Olds. Then we had the driveline shortened down at Johnson's machine shop.

Joe and I hauled the radiator over to old Gene on First Street, and he plugged up two of the holes that weren't needed by the new motor, while Billy was welding in the transmission mounts we robbed from the 88, along with the ones that held in the motor.

One of Mr. Smith's mechanics helped us with the wiring that had to be changed over to 12 volts. We had to remake the battery box, hook up the speedometer, as well as the clutch and throttle linkage. The Ford shifter worked alright after we grafted the rods together.

We were about done. There was an air of excitement ramping up as we were getting close to completion. Everyone knew the outcome was going to be a game changer. It was the big motor, little car syndrome. If I could keep it on the road, it was going to be a bullet.

The swap wasn't as simple as it sounds here, but we overcame each little problem as it arose and beat it into submission. Billy insisted we put the hood back on before we test drove it, which is probably something that I wouldn't have done. He was just that way. It was just the two of us there when we rolled the door up and left the shop. We took it out to South Oakville and ran it through the paces. I could burn rubber all the way through first and most of second gear, so I knew I was going to have a traction problem. We made a few adjustments to some of the linkage and set the timing, but that was about it. The motor was practically new and was still clean and nice, so I didn't even have to paint it.

The only noticeable differences in the appearance of the car were how it sat a little lower in front because of the weight of the J-2 and the badass noise coming out of the larger exhaust pipes.

Chapter 16

Late that summer, after we did the motor swap, a tragic thing happened. Miles Fletcher was killed in a car accident while riding in his '46 Mercury.

His cousin, Theodore Wilson, was the driver. He always insisted on being called Theodore, not Ted or Teddy, but Theodore. His mom had brought him down from Seattle for a couple of weeks each summer ever since we were kids riding bikes. T is what we called him, because we didn't care what the hell he wanted to be called, and Theodore was just too long.

T was wild, from the first day I saw him until the last. If we were making jumps with our bikes, he would have to jump higher. If someone skated off a cliff, he would skate off a higher cliff. He was always taller than us, skinny, with blue eyes that glowed with enthusiasm. He had brown, wavy hair that just always seemed to fall in the right place, while we weren't having much luck because of cowlicks and years of hair just plain going the wrong way. His mouth was never quite closed, and his tongue was always hanging out the left side a distance, depending on how involved he was with a wild-ass scheme. He reminded me of a wolf circling, his mouth partly open and tongue hanging out. He was always wiping the saliva from his chin with his arm. He was hard on stuff; model airplanes and trains seemed to just get crushed when he was around. I think he meant well; he was just wild.

When Miles was approaching sixteen, his dad bought him a '46 Mercury convertible without an engine, and a few other necessary parts were missing too. It was a project for them to fix up together with the help of us guys who were always around the station. They did it on the cheap with junkyard parts. We shot it with gray primer right out back of the station on one of those mornings when it was nice and calm and the bugs were still asleep. It ended up with a '49 Caddy engine and its automatic transmission. They kept the old suspension, which made the car handle badly at high speeds. It wasn't real fast in the quarter, but when it got going, it would really fly and would scare the hell out of you.

Miles was a careful guy. His folks were cautious with him and seemed to feel he needed protection. You could tell they worried about him when he would jump in with us and we would motor off like we hadn't a care in the world. It was like they had a premonition of something really bad happening to Miles, like they were cursed with it and had to live with the thought. When T came down for his summer stays, Miles wouldn't let him drive because of what he thought might happen. But T was always after the keys.

Of course, T always wanted to be in the Little Bastards club from day one, but we wouldn't let him be a bona fide member, because he wasn't around the whole year, at least that's what we told him, and he seemed to live with it. He showed up with a leather jacket the year he was 14, and of course it wasn't a brown bomber like ours, but a black motorcycle jacket with silver stars and buckles and the like. It was a little over the top. Speaking of over the top, if we ever got near water, he would end up wet. He always fell in and would usually take someone with him, whether it was on the dock in Newport, up at the lake, or even when we were kids, on the log rafts down on the river.

You could tell he liked drinking from the very first time he upended a beer. We had found a six-pack in the trunk of an old car abandoned near Billy's house and decided to try it out one evening after Frank had left the station for home. The beer was warm and had been around for a while. The rest of us couldn't get much of it down, but T managed to drink enough that he got all goofy and was stumbling around and was kind of pissed when we got to pouring ours out. He was getting kind of scary and we weren't liking it; we decided he didn't need any more gas for the fire he was flaming.

It was like that from then on. T would always drink a little more and a little faster and get stupid when the rest of us could usually handle it. Sometimes, there were exceptions and one of us would get tipped over, but it was not the norm.

The night of Miles' death was just another night in late summer and most of us were down at the gravel lot beside Pop's Drive-In. We were having some beer, listening to music, and smoking as usual when Miles came driving through.

It was during the two weeks that T was in town. He was with Miles and had gotten his hands on a bottle of 151 rum and was wondering if anyone of us had the balls to try a gulp. We each took a gulp to be social, but I noticed Miles was swigging it down pretty good before pulling out to head for Billie's Big Burger, where they had heard some Portland girls were just waiting for guys like them to show up. Miles putted the convertible out onto the Boulevard going north at his usual careful speed of slow.

During the night, I saw them two more times, meeting them on the route we took while running the gut. Miles was driving and T was riding shotgun with his mouth open and his tongue hanging out a little more than usual. Once, I saw him upend the bottle from a brown paper bag and take a snort before handing it over to Miles. I was thinking they must really be on their way by now.

The last time I saw Miles alive was when they came into Pop's and T was driving. It looked as if Miles was passed out, leaning back on the seat kind of in the corner by the door. T roared right out into the gravel lot and cranked the wheel to the left and hit the throttle, throwing rocks all over everyone and everything near. He went clear around, then whipped the wheel all the way to the right and did it all over again. With the rear wheels still spinning, he came out right between my car and a red Pontiac and reentered the Boulevard. Then he was gone, with a dazed look in his eyes and his tongue hanging out.

If I had known what I know now, I would have leaped over the side of the car and gotten the keys away from him. But at the time, I thought we were all invincible. I soon found out I was wrong.

It wasn't long after that we heard a couple of sirens in the distance and then a fire truck came by with its lights flashing and siren wailing. Of course, we had no idea who was involved, but like always, Joe, Johnny, and I jumped in a car and followed. I don't know what causes people to want to see somebody get hurt or even see something morbid, but they do, and we couldn't wait.

We followed the fire truck through downtown and over the bridge. We could see the lights flashing up ahead, and before we could get close, we were turned back by an officer who told us the road was closed and probably would be for some time. Joe parked off the road and we walked towards the accident with our normal manner of laughing and talking, genuinely looking forward to seeing a good wreck. The first thing I recognized was the AA tow truck with its gumball rotating. I followed the cable with my eyes to where it was hooked on the front of Miles' Mercury, which was totally wrapped around a power pole. My heart just sank.

There were two firemen at the scene cutting the car in half with an acetylene torch hooked to the tow truck by a long pair of hoses. Bruce was standing there holding up the hoses. When he saw me, he just sort of shook his head and motioned for me not to come any closer. I couldn't help myself and approached further. Bruce dropped the hoses and cut me off so I wouldn't see what he was enduring. He caught me and held me back, but over his shoulder, I could see one of Miles' engineer boots dangling on the end of his leg, hanging out of the right side of the car where the bottom of the door had been ripped off. I heard Bruce say Miles was dead and T was unconscious.

I turned back to the other boys and noticed a shiny object lying in the grass by the roadside. It was Miles' glasses. They must have been thrown during the impact. I picked them up and folded them into my pocket, which momentarily gave me something to think about rather than what I had just seen.

I'm sure that moment changed my life forever. My mind exploded with a thousand thoughts at the same time. To have a lifelong friend warm and happy in just another day of his life one moment and then suddenly gone and the whole thing is over for him and he won't be back tomorrow was more than I could wrap. I had hold of Joe and Johnny by their jackets, dragging them along through the crowd of people who were watching all google-eyed, and I hated them for it, but they were just me before it got personal.

By the time we got back to Joe's '50, we had lost control and were crying like children. Johnny started throwing up and nobody could talk. It took us a long time to regain enough composure to notice the ambulance come and go, and then the car from the mortuary showed up and then they left too. The crowd began to file away, leaving room for the squad cars to get past. Last was the tow truck with Bruce towing Miles' car. He was white as a sheet and you could tell he was worn out. When he saw us he stopped the truck and just let go; with his hands locked on the steering wheel, his chin dropped to his chest and he was heaving. I guess he just held it all in until his job was finished. He'd been around a lot of wrecks and some fatalities, but never someone he knew like Miles.

As soon as Joe let me off at my car, I headed right home and not too fast either. All of a sudden, cars looked more like weapons than rolling mechanical marvels. I finally got to sleep after laying there most of the night reliving my life with Miles.

In the morning, my pillow was a pool of tears I woke up floating in. Dad and Mom greeted me from the kitchen table and they, of course, knew what had happened. News traveled fast in our small town. They were silent the whole time I was explaining how it had happened, and you could tell by the looks they gave me they had been there too, at one time or another, but it didn't help. I don't know if they felt sorrier for Miles or for my friends and me, who had just gotten our world tossed. Mom was crying and Dad was smoking, but you could see the red forming in the whites of his eyes, which sort of gave him away. They both knew Miles well. In fact, Miles had spent some time right there at the table where we were sitting.

When I finished, Dad began picking up the dishes and taking them to the sink, which was the first time I'd ever seen that happen. Mom turned in her seat, looked straight at me, and started coaching me on what I needed to do. This was good; she was telling me I had a job to do, so life must go on. She told me to round up all my closest friends and get over to the Fletcher house, no matter how hard it was going to be. She said they would be awful glad to see us and we would understand when we got there.

It was hard to find a place for us to park our cars when we showed up. It was Joe with a carload, along with Johnny and Gary in his Merc, and I had Billy with me. I was glad it was still summer and Billy hadn't left for fall term yet, because having him there was a comfort.

There were people Miles' folks' age carrying plates of food up the concrete steps onto the porch. The same steps I'd been up a million times. Miles' black and white cat jumped off the railing and met us on the sidewalk like he knew Miles would be with us since he'd seen us together so much. The whole affair reminded me of a potluck dinner where everyone brought a plate and carried it down into the basement of the church, only this was more solemn, with people just kind of slowly shaking their heads and trying to make conversation.

In the Fletcher living room, the table was covered with plates of food, and I was wondering how anyone could eat all of it, because I was having trouble swallowing. My dad was in the hallway talking with Johnny Smith's dad and they gave us a nod when we went by. The Fletcher house was large compared to ours and they had another room off the kitchen they called the sitting room. It had a carpet that covered most of the floor, and it was wallpapered real nice. They used the room when company was over and it had always been sort of off limits for us kids. The only time Miles saw the inside of that room was when he had to practice the piano, which was in the center of one wall.

This is where we found Mrs. Fletcher sitting, surrounded by her peers, one of which was my mother. Geraldine was her name, and she was there on the edge of the bench with her back to the piano, a hanky in each hand. When she looked up at us with those tired, red eyes I almost lost it again. I had a knot in my throat that was as big as a baseball. She got up and got hold of the front of my jacket and pulled me to her and started to say something about how nice it was for us to come, but it just turned into sobbing, and she buried her face into my chest. I put my arms around her, and as I was looking over her shoulder, I was looking into a framed picture of Miles' face on the top of the piano. It had been taken a few years earlier, when he still wore those cockeyed glasses Billy had fixed for him. Geraldine's legs were sort of coming out from under her, so I gently sat her back down on the bench where she was given another dry hanky.

This gave me a chance to look for Frank. I found him with some other gentlemen about his age in the kitchen. When I got close, I stuck out my hand holding Miles' glasses. After taking them, he grabbed my arm and sort of pulled me into a kind of half-hug that was alright for a man to give another man, and I appreciated it. My cheek sort of brushed the side of his chin, and I could tell he hadn't shaved that morning, and I could smell some kind of hard liquor on his breath. One at a time, we all tried to express our condolences like men will do, but none of us were very good at that sort of thing yet and most of it just came out wrong. Old Frank got the point, I'm sure.

There might have been more to Miles than I thought. Dad advised me to get to the church early for the funeral because it was going to be big. When we got there we were truly amazed. They had chosen to hold it at the Presbyterian, the biggest church in town. Miles never talked about going to church or Sunday school, so I don't know if they were of the Presbyterian faith or not. We had to walk a couple of blocks from where we parked, and I was with the same bunch that had gone to visit the Fletchers, plus a few more.

Mrs. Fletcher told my mother she would like to have Miles' friends, meaning the Little Bastards, to be his pallbearers. She thought Miles would have liked us to wear our jackets and sit together behind the family. I guess we looked like a small platoon when we marched down the aisle to where our seats had been saved for us, because we got some unusual looks from some of the mourners. Frank was sitting next to the aisle in the front row with his arm around Geraldine, who was leaning into him. Her sister, Ruth, Theodore's mom, was on her right and was enduring pain of her own. T was in a coma at a hospital in Portland, and according to the doctors, there might be brain damage, if he was to wake up at all. To Ruth's right was the rest of the family in order of how close they were in age, as near as I could tell.

Right in front of the family was Miles in his casket, the lid closed and covered with flowers. I didn't have to ask why it was a closed casket affair after seeing the shape the car was in. I recognized a lot of students from the school, and they included about every social branch that schools tend to have: the jocks, the brains, and the rally squad types. Everyone had one thing in common: They were sad and blue. I'd never seen more outpouring of grief and love for any one in my life.

The minister was a young fellow wearing a normal black suit and tie. He gained my respect with his ability to carry on after such a tragic event, everyone coming apart and that poor boy who had been cheated out of most of his life on earth lying right in front of him. When the service was over and after the family had filed out, we carried Miles out to the hearse for his last ride. We all crammed into one of the limos the funeral parlor provided and the family rode in the other. The procession was escorted by two city police officers on Harley Davidson motorcycles with their headlights on, and they gave a little blip with their sirens as we crossed interchanges on the way out to the hill north of town.

As our driver was rounding the last corner at the top of the cemetery, I looked back and it was as if we were the head of a long snake winding up the hill with little glitters between each joint. It was a beautiful day up there among the freshly planted trees and shrubs and new asphalt. It seemed fitting to me that Miles was going to start out eternity in a nice, new place with only flat surface headstones since he was also so young. After it was over, we were standing there around the casket when a kid who looked as if he might be about a freshman used a Brownie and shot a picture of us all taking our last moment with Miles. The image of us with our wrists crossed over our belt buckles showed up in the next year's school annual on a page memorializing Miles' life.

I spent a lot of time after that down at the station helping Frank out. I guess we all did, hoping it would help in more ways than just getting rid of gasoline and occasionally some grease. It was some time before anyone even mentioned the words beer or drinking or even car performance, but gradually, we all sort of drifted back to our old ways, although not completely unchanged for life.

Chapter 17

Miles' death cast a shadow on our senior year, but we recovered, not completely, but enough to make our last year in school another memorable one. In time, we got back to our old cocky ways. We ruled the hallways when we cared to and showed the leadership expected of seniors, like teaching Drinking 101 and helping in the advancement of showing off. When we left the parking lot in our parade of hot rods, it was a wonder that did not go unnoticed by the envious. The teachers and the hierarchy of the school accepted us and started calling us by our first names, which made us a little uneasy. Mr. Klink was promoted to superintendent and replaced by a woman, showing us it was a new era.

Our one and only involvement of sporting activities happened that fall behind the grandstands during homecoming. The homecoming parade always started out downtown with all this pompous crap and ended at the football field, where they would light the bonfire and celebrate with the jocks and cheerleaders. We had been noticing the progress of the preparations all week, with the stacking of orange crates and boxes and any other discarded stuff they could round up and put on the pile. Some parents were into it, helping haul with their pick-up trucks.

One afternoon, in bonehead English class, Joe got this idea that we should help out with the bonfire. It seemed like a good idea to us since we were seniors, like it was sort of our obligation. We made a plan, and almost all of us were in on it, including the Olsen girls. It took some coordination and timing not unlike the plan to get old Ernest, since the bonfire was guarded twenty-four hours a day by these guys from the cheer squad who thought they were pretty hot shit.

On Thursday afternoon, about the time the parade was to start, Gary and Johnny came rolling up to the bonfire pile in Gary's Mercury with Meg and Denise in the back-seat. The girls always started a stir wherever they went, and this was no exception. The bonfire guards came lumbering over to the Merc like a couple of puppies after a bone as the girls were unfolding their legs and exiting the car. Meg and Denise immediately got them into a deep conversation about their biceps or something, while Gary and Johnny leaned against the front fender and had a smoke. At the predetermined moment, Joe and I came running out from behind the grandstand with two Oly bottles filled with gasoline. We were on the opposite side of the pile and weren't detected by the guards, who were as busy as two young bulls smelling flowers. We sloshed the gas up and down the upwind side and then lit it with our Zippos as we turned and made our escape back to the grandstands.

Suddenly, the Olsen girls lost interest in their conversation with the guards and loaded up in the Merc that was already creeping away. The bonfire exploded into an inferno almost immediately and was met by the gaze of the hundred or so would-be revelers tromping through town blowing on horns.

No matter what we did that winter, our hearts and interests always returned to our cars. We tuned and rebuilt and planned those rainy days away with the anticipation of the upcoming summer, which would bring racing back to the streets.

Willamette began to be known as the hub of drag racing in our region. There was a core of us who were hooked, building cars and rebuilding them to perform better and faster.

After taking my coupe to Portland the previous fall to an organized, legal race, I realized I had to rebuild my rear suspension to keep the tires on the pavement. Fortunately, I had kept the Olds' rear springs, which I put under the '40, and I built some traction bars like I'd seen in *Rod & Custom* magazine. Along with the lower gears I had put in the rear end, the whole combination came together with the horsepower, making my little Ford the fastest car in town. During my senior year, it seemed that on any given weekend, someone was in town looking for me. I was kind of the fastest gun. Like the western movies, I could hardly keep up with my reputation.

At school, I would be asked about racing some guy with a car that I'd never seen, from a town where I'd never been, and of course I always won. My reputation was self-inflicted to start with, but it got away from me and became somewhat of a curse. It was helped along by this guy named Eddy, who was always around and knew all there was to know about every hot car on the street. It was kind of his deal, like he was a stats keeper for a baseball team or something, except it was about illegal street racing. Anytime he would see me pulling into one of the hangouts alone, which was frequent, because I would take that route after closing up at the station just to see what was cooking, he would jump in with me to bring me up to date on what the competition was doing and all. It wasn't just me he did this for, but I was the most common, it was like he was my agent or something.

I saw him on many occasions go right up to some stranger with a hot car and start interrogating him about his ride and what he had in it, and then I would see him point over to my car and start taunting the poor guy. Pretty soon, the race was on. We'd head out of town to a straight stretch without power poles where we had painted lines designating a quarter-mile, and I would beat the guy once or twice, depending on how he liked it. Eddy really got off on flagging us with a flashlight or just a drop of the hand. He would be jumping up and down and whirling around when I came back for him. He could tell by the sound of my headers whether or not I was using everything I had. There wasn't any reason to beat anyone any more than was necessary, because it sort of discouraged the competition and was hard on equipment.

Of course, when we got back to Billie's Big Burger or Pop's Drive-In, Eddy would have to let everyone in on the outcome. He'd just bounce from car to car with the blow-by-blow account of the race. Eddy was a skinny kid a year younger than me, but a couple of inches taller. He drove a Simca wagon with this fake painted wood on the sides and a decal in the back window that said *Minnesota Land of Lakes*. It had about one horsepower and he would putt out to Pop's to watch and wait for a chance to jump into something fast. I developed a fondness for him, even though sometimes he was really hard to like. He would never shut up. He was always wound up like maybe his folks wouldn't let him talk at home or something. He would be talking the second he was reaching for your door handle. He never said hi; he just started in.

During the summer after my graduation, there was a place about 10 miles out that was getting to be a popular racing and beer guzzling venue. It was named Otto's, after the farmer who owned a place adjacent to the highway that happened to be straight and desolate. Otto enjoyed having the gigs, and he would actually drive his old flat-bed out to the road and sit in the back with his wife and watch the racing. He'd have the cows out behind the barn in a different pasture come race night, so we could all park in his front field for tuning and beer drinking. It was a made-to-order deal, and people started showing up from all over, because the word gets around when kids are having a little fun. Another great advantage the location offered was that you could see a car coming from three different approaches for miles before they could get there. On a big night, we would have some spotters give us the lights if they saw the law show up and we would just resume our harmless, innocent existences until they would give up and go back to town.

One such representative of the law was Sheriff Buster Cleveland. He was known as an "always got his man" sheriff and was having difficulty getting used to the idea that he just couldn't catch those little bastards out at Otto's. It seemed every time they would get the call that there was a big race going on, by the time they got there with a couple of squad cars, the place would either be empty or it would be just a bunch of hoodlums sitting around listening to that new rock and roll on their car radios. It about drove old Buster off the wall. He was nearing retirement but was still in good physical shape and was sound of mind. He actually looked a lot like the television star Phil Silvers, except Buster had about thirty pounds on him. He wore these black-rimmed glasses that sort of bounced up and down when he got excited while he was talking, and he seemed to get excited pretty easily and often. He wore a tan fedora while in uniform, which wasn't code, but he thought it gave him an air that set him above the common cop. Buster's one and only deputy was his nephew, Buddy Cleveland, whose father was Buster's brother. Buster must have owed his brother a pretty big favor, because Buddy wasn't really the best law enforcement material, even though he tried awful hard.

The old sheriff developed a plan one morning over donuts and coffee with a couple of state highway cops at Lucy's Cafe, a truck stop out on the highway. This was all according to Lucy, who told me the whole story sometime later, including details of the fateful night, which she picked up from the sheriff after the fact. It came to him while he was looking at the three donuts there on the table in kind of a triangle. He'd been complaining to these officers for months about not being able to nab the racers out at Otto's place, so they were tuned in to what he was going on about. Buster was chewing away on his cigar while in deep thought about the raid, when one of the staters made for a donut, just to get slapped by old Buster.

When he came out of the trance, the cops dropped their eyebrows back down and sort of hunkered and leaned forward like they were going to be part of something big. Sheriff Cleveland always thought that way. He was thinking a big bust like this had never happened around there before, and it would be the one thing he could hang his hat on after retiring from the force.

"Damn, I shoulda thought of this a long time ago." Buster slammed his fist down on the table, almost spilling the coffee. "What we need is a plant. A man on the ground at the scene during the action who could document each and every infraction. Then we could cross reference that with their car license plate numbers when we catch 'em in our net!"

He was looking over his glasses at the staters and added, "That'll be your job. You guys will seal off this donut, I mean road. And this other one coming from the west, and I'll cut 'em off from going out north, and we'll have 'em."

Old Buster was rubbing his hands together with glee at this point. The officers, finishing up their coffee, were nodding in agreement, and one of them asked, "Now, Sheriff, who do you think we should get to do the dangerous work of being on the inside and all?"

All three were sort of stumped with that one, when Lucy, who was standing there with the coffee pot, chewing gum like always, suggested, "Why don't you just ask Buddy to do it?" Cleveland hit the table again while looking up at Lucy and said, "Jesus Christ Almighty, have you been listening here to everything we've been saying?"

"Well, sure, Sheriff," she said, "I've been standing here with my hand on your shoulder the whole time. Damn, what does it take to get noticed around here anyway?" She gave Officer Jones a wink.

Just the mention of Buddy's name caused a general deflation of the euphoria that came about by the sheriff's plan for the mega bust. It was like hearing a tire go flat with air and enthusiasm escaping.

"Don't worry, fellas," Buster was saying as he slammed the screen door on the way out, "I'll devise such a bulletproof plan even Buddy couldn't screw up."

The Sheriff spent most of the next week out at Otto's place mapping out his strategy. It was easy for him to find the exact point where the infraction would occur from the painted lines that marked out the starting line, as well as the finish. Which end was the start was obvious in that it was marked up with black rubber stripes made by spinning rear tires trying to get traction. The evidence was all over the place with the mapped out track and beer bottles scattered all over the place. He gave Otto a wave as he was doing his detective work. He knew the old farmer was sort of an accomplice, but he decided not to go that route, since public sentiment would likely fall on Otto's side.

Buster decided to use the old gravel pit overlooking the farm for his base of operations, from where he could see the entire battlefield, so to speak. It was far enough away that he didn't think he would be noticed. From his perch, along with the Motorola two-way, he could conduct business right from the seat of his black and white. He knew he couldn't make out the individual suspects from that distance, even with his binoculars, and that was where Buddy came in. The sheriff noticed there was a sizable oak tree within a reasonable distance from the finish line that an inside man might be positioned in to see the license plate numbers as they crossed the finish line if he was equipped with a strong pair of lenses. From his headquarters in the rock pit, he figured he could receive messages from Buddy over the two-way radio the deputy would have in his forward position, along with some other supplies.

The sheriff arranged with the road department to supply the tree with a deer stand seating arrangement, which they installed with the use of their boom truck under the ruse of normal highway maintenance. Sheriff Cleveland had sort of a sixth sense about him when it came to setting traps for facilitators of illegal activity from years of catching poachers and cattle thieves. He felt this net was coming together nicely. The easy part was locating positions where Officers Smith and Jones could head off the escape to the south and to the west when the sheriff decided to spring the trap. Not only would he have radio contact with the staters, he would have a visual on them from his vantage point on high ground. Before calling another meeting with Jones and Smith, which would also include Buddy, Buster had his secretary go back through the files and retrieve reports that concurred with illegal racing at the Otto site or any other in the area, the time of day, and what day of the week was popular. He solved the simple equation by triangulating the three and came up with Friday night starting around 9:30 p.m.

The next morning, there were three squad cars in front of Lucy's. There you could find the sheriff, his deputy, and the two staters going over the blueprint of the plan Buster had unfolded on the table among the coffee and donuts. This time they were being quiet and secretive and were sitting at the table clear in the back, next to the wall. Buster had asked for this arrangement and Lucy had the reserved sign on it when they arrived. The only other customers at the time were a couple of mill rats who were sitting at the coffee bar and a Belkin's driver who was having the daily special.

Anyway, they were hunched over the map Buster had drawn out with a pencil as true to scale as he could. From where Lucy was pouring coffee, it looked like it could have been a chess game the way Buster was moving the spoons around like pawns, symbolizing where the squad cars would be, and part of his donut represented the tree that would be Buddy's forward position. Jones and Smith intently listened as the sheriff plotted out the plan, while Buddy seemed as intent on catching the fly that was harassing them as the others were in finally catching those Little Bastards who had been eluding them for so long. Buster had to keep telling his nephew to pay attention while he was moving the spoons around.

Suddenly, Buddy hit the table with his fist with a loud, "Got 'em!" which made the old sheriff about jump out of his pants. Opening up his hand expecting to find the fly, Buddy seemed let down that he hadn't "got 'em."

Sheriff Cleveland assured the two officers he would have Buddy stationed in the tree by 6:30 p.m. Friday. He explained how his deputy would be camouflaged and equipped with a two-way so he could relay the license plate numbers up to him at his command post. Then when he felt he had the goods on them, he would signal via radio and spring the trap. The staters agreed to be at their respective positions Friday no later than 10:00 p.m. flat.

When Friday rolled around, everything started without a hitch. Buster and Buddy arrived early up at the pit. Buster leaned on the fender of his black and white, smoking a cigar, while Buddy played with a yo-yo Lucy had given him that day at the cafe. At 6:00 p.m. sharp, Otto called his cows in to be milked, and the sheriff knew right away the jig was on, because the cows entered from the highway side pasture, but were exiting out the back. Buster and Buddy hurried down to the tree and uncovered the ladder the road crew left for them behind some brush and got Buddy situated in his forward position while old Otto was busy with his cows.

Buddy was all tickled with his treehouse affair and was rubbernecking around with the binoculars, all excited about how far he could see. This made Buster a little apprehensive about his nephew's qualifications, but Buddy assured him he understood the importance of the operation and would act accordingly. The sheriff then went over the plan again with Buddy, reviewing the steps and checking the equipment and so on.

As Buster stepped off the bottom rung of the ladder, Buddy asked, "Don't you think we ought to synchronize our watches, Uncle Buster?"

"Jesus, Buddy," the sheriff said. "Yeah, okay, but quit calling me Uncle Buster. I'm Sheriff Cleveland to you."

"Okay, Uncle Buster," he said while adjusting his binoculars.

Sheriff Cleveland made one more tour of the layout. When he came back around, he noticed the gate to Otto's front pasture was open. This gave old Buster a little shot of adrenaline as he reached for the mic to do a radio check with the deputy. "Deputy Cleveland, this is Sheriff Cleveland, do you read me?"

"Hi, Uncle Buster," Buddy said with his high voice. The sheriff, upon hearing this, just dropped the mic onto the receptacle and headed up to his command post to wait.

At about this time, early evening on Friday night, every teenage hangout in Willamette was abuzz with activity and anticipation of what was predicted to be the giant of all drag races ever to be held in the region.

Chapter 18

This potential phenomenon had been brewing for some time among the usual crowd, as well as another faction, the spectators. Otto's farm was the best location, because it was close to several surrounding towns, had space with the open fields, and had the security of Otto's collaboration. The biggest spoiler of the event would be the same as all other sites, the intervention of law enforcement agencies. Normally, the law would rather not know about the racing activities, because their record of convictions was nil to none. A complaining neighbor could force the police to respond with a squad car, which would usually be spotted before it could get close enough, and the drag racing would cease, leaving the officer to file another disappointing report. In the case of a large gathering, like the one developing for that Friday, some spotters would be located at strategic locations and would merely flash their lights upon seeing any cops getting close.

Central Market did a thriving business that particular Friday. By 8:30, they had sold out of Oly and were running low on Blitz. You would have thought it was kickoff night for the Indy 500. Unknown to the racing enthusiasts, things were about to change with Sheriff Buster Cleveland's personal vendetta and his elaborate plan to trap and bust, once and for all, this menace that had eluded him for so long.

At exactly 8:46 p.m., the first suspect came around the corner under Buster's hideout with only its parking lights on. It was a summer night with a starlit sky only a country setting could have. The usual little critters were already out chirping and croaking. The sheriff shut the Yankee's game off and picked up the binoculars as the red and white station wagon pulled through the gate into Otto's pasture. The car followed the fence, which paralleled the pavement, to a point about a hundred feet past the starting line. The wagon then swung around and backed up perpendicular to the wire, leaving walking room between the bumper and the fence. The driver, a young man, got out and opened the tailgate for his female companion, who covered it with a blanket as they prepared for an evening at the races. At that time, the sheriff radioed the deputy to see if he was set at the forward position.

"This is Sheriff Cleveland calling Deputy Cleveland; come in if you read me, Deputy." After a moment of static, the deputy came back with, "Hi, Uncle Buster, I'm eating my sandwich now."

The sheriff groaned, "Okay, keep your eyes peeled; we have our first guests back at the pasture."

Buster turned the squelch button a little to the right to silence the static, then placed the mic next to him on the seat and resumed with the ballgame. He was relighting his cigar when more cars began to arrive, quite a few more cars, taking the best spots along the fence. It was a rerun of the arrival of the station wagon with the repetition of preparing for the spectacle.

"This is going to be big," Buster muttered to himself.

In the middle of the whole conglomeration was Otto and his wife, who climbed into the back of his flatbed and sat on an old couch he had dropped in for the occasion. At one end, next to Otto, laid Chester, Otto's hound, with his nose hanging over the armrest. It was getting dark, so the sheriff couldn't make out who was who, just that there was a hell of a lot going on down there with the chattering and boozing. In the pit area, Buster could see shadows of bodies around the headlights and hoods going up and down. There was a hum of communication between the sounds of motors firing up and revving.

By the time Billy and I arrived, the pits were about full and the whole quarter mile was lined with cars and pickups. Billy made the comment that Otto's pasture looked like the parking lot at the state fair. It was huge. Everyone was there, including the Olsen girls and, of course, Eddy, who was in his element. It seemed he was the only one not drinking beer. He was getting high just on the smell of smoke, gasoline, and American ingenuity.

Billy and Joe thought it prudent to send down a single to check out the condition of the asphalt surface.

Eddy volunteered to go down first with the Simca, which caused a laugh.

"Jesus, we don't have all night, Eddy," Gary said as he headed for the Merc.

Meg and Denise Olsen had their noses under the hoods right along with the boys and were genuinely interested in motors. They had spent a lot of time down at Fletcher's and over at Billy's garage and knew how these marvels worked.

Denise was the younger of the two, and God had been good to her; blonde with blue eyes, she was as naturally good-looking as her sister, but didn't get nearly the mileage out of it. Meg had a brooding look about her, with sort of angry lips that were noticeably large, and her breasts were big for her small, shapely body. You could see the sides of them inside her arms when following her down the hall at school. She had tempted, teased, and flirted her way through Willamette High. By the time she was a sophomore, she was being picked up after class by one or another older boy, taking her out of the market for us school boys. It seemed to just add to her aloofness, but it didn't detour her teasing and flirting, and we loved her for it.

While Gary was getting ready for his single pass, the Olsen's decided to walk down to the finish line where they could see the cars fly by. Denise was caring a six pack of Oly missing two bottles at one end, which made the others sort of hang there horizontally. She had one of the missing beers in her other hand. Meg had the other stubby, along with a cigarette that came from the pack in the rear pocket of her Levi's. They both wore jeans with the legs rolled up and light cotton shirts. Everything under their clothes moved as they walked along in front of the headlights as they flashed on to illuminate the area for the race. They knew they looked good and didn't mind being looked at either. Their display resembled opening night at Grauman's Chinese Theatre with two stars making their way past the exploding flashbulbs and admiring fans with envious stares.

When Gary returned from making the pass, he signaled that everything was cool. The races were on.

From his vantage point on high ground, Sheriff Cleveland could see the single car leave the line with the headlights rising each time the driver changed gears. He also noticed the small light on the trunk illuminating its license plate. He grabbed the mic to check with Buddy. It was crucial that his deputy would be able to make out the license numbers or all would be for naught.

"Buddy!" he yelled with his teeth clinched on his cigar. "You get that number?"

Static. "God damn it." *Static.* "Six, eight, dash, three, five, two," Buddy's voice came from speaker.

"Good," said Buster as he slammed his fist on the dash.

"O-R-E ..." came from the speaker.

"What?" Buster yelled again. "We don't need the goddamned state! Just the goddamned number!" The sheriff was getting red and his glasses were popping up and down by then.

About the time the first two racers paired up, Meg and Denise were almost to the finish line. One of the guys in a Chevy had some questions about the rules, delaying the first race. It took a while for Joe, who was the starter, to get it through this guy's head that there weren't any rules.

Meanwhile, Buddy got the binocular strap tangled up with the two-way and failed to get the numbers on the first two racers as they passed his tree. After Buddy explained this to his uncle, old Buster, trying to keep his cool, went over the assignment again, emphasizing that he had to get the numbers off both cars. He reminded Buddy they had to match up or they wouldn't be permissible in court.

The Olsens, upon reaching the finish line, decided to make a dash for the tree on the other side of the highway. Meg was still a little cautious after the time out on South Muddy when she was hit while flagging a race and ended up in the county hospital all bruised and banged up. The tree made a natural barrier in case one of the cars got a little wild at the top end.

Denise was bending over to set down the beers by the tree trunk when she thought she heard noise like static from a two-way radio. *Static*. Then Meg heard it too, followed by, "Buddy are you there? Buddy, come in." *Static*.

Both girls looked up at the same time to see someone sitting up in the tree in a chair. He was bobbing around with his binoculars like he was bird watching or something.

"Hey, what y'all doing up there?" Denise demanded in the southern drawl she liked to use.

This about scared the shit out of Buddy, which got him all flustered, and he started doing a juggling act with his two-way, the binoculars, and his flashlight. He grabbed for the two-way since it was talking to him and let the others go. They plopped, clinked, and finally clanked, as they bounced off the limbs and hit the ground by the girls' feet.

Meg looked up with her hands on her hips and said, "Hey, you didn't say what you're doing up there. What gives?" she asked.

"Nothin'," was Buddy's reply. Then two more cars went roaring by, and Buddy said, "Ah, shit."

Over the two-way came, "Buddy, give me the numbers! Buddy!" *Static.* "Buddy! Buddy, do you read me?"

"Yeah, what gives?" yelled Denise over the sound of the open exhaust pipes. "Why don't you answer him?" she added.

"Sorry, Sheriff, I dropped the binoculars."

"Damn it to hell, Buddy. Those are brand new Bushnell's," Buster said.

"Uncle Buster, I can't call in the numbers to you because these girls got 'em," Buddy explained.

"What girls?" Buster asked.

"These two girls here watching the racing. They got my binoculars and my flashlight and they won't give 'em back," Buddy said.

Denise was gawking around with the binoculars, which she couldn't hold still because of the mouthful of gum she was working on.

"I get it," said Meg, with her hands still on her hips. "You're calling in the license plate numbers off the racecars to the sheriff so he can pop right in here and pinch everyone. Is that it?"

By this time, up at the quarry, old Buster was really getting lathered up.

The words that were coming into Buddy's two-way would make a logger blush. While keeping an eye on Buddy, Meg said to Denise, "Hand me that flashlight and we'll find out who this plant is."

Buddy had his arm over his eyes to keep from being blinded by the light Meg had on him. She recognized him easily and said, "Hell, Buddy, why didn't you tell us that was you?"

They had had their run-ins with Buddy and his uncle before. Meg rotated the light a few degrees to the north and began flashing it on and off towards the starting line. The spectators along the fence caught the signal and began flashing their headlights on and off and honking their horns.

Joe backed the two cars off the line and cleared the road just in time. Sheriff Cleveland's black and white Chevy came screeching up to the starting line with its red light flashing and the siren going. Knowing the whole thing was a failure, Buster stuck his arm out the window, pumping his fist as he yelled to no one in particular, "I'll get you Little Bastards if it's the last thing I do!"

He mashed the throttle clear to the floor and dumped the clutch. His big police motor started to spin the rear tires as the smoke bellowed out from under the fenders and the car started fishtailing to the left. Buster corrected, and then he was gone, leaving two black marks about 30 feet long. At the other end of the track, he backed off and pulled over by the oak tree. By the time he got to the debunked forward position, the girls had gotten the ladder and helped Buddy out of the tree. The poor fella was standing there with the Bushnell's hanging around his neck, holding the two-way and the flashlight when Buster jumped out of his car. He left the door open and the siren was making a little chirp about every fourth revolution of the gumball. Officers Jones and Smith were never seen that night.

Meg told me the last she saw of Sheriff Cleveland, he looked devastated with the breakdown of his scheme and he was beating Buddy over the head with his fedora while pressing him into the car. I didn't know it at the time, but the humiliation of Buster Cleveland would come back to haunt us.

We were pretty sure we had seen the last of the law that night, so we raced and raced until everyone had had their fill of it. I ran my '40 only once that night, which was the last run, and it was for the title of "Top Eliminator." I was kind of representing the home team and this guy from Portland was the challenger. He was kicking everyone's ass with this '57 T-Bird that he towed with a Ford pickup filled with tuning equipment. He had an older fella helping him who wore a shop coat that came down to his knees and made him look like a scientist or something. The Bird was painted an intimidating red, with black wheels, and tires with no hubcaps. No one could get near it, but Eddy said it had a blower and the exhaust smelled like he was using some exotic fuel. I noticed the front of the car was a little higher than stock and it had traction masters and was running cheater slicks.

When it came down to us, I had my motor warmed up and ready to go. I figured the cars were pretty even, so I thought it might come down to strategy. He was several years older than me and was loaded with confidence, so I decided if I was going to get into his head, I would have to pull something extreme. If he would have been a regular guy, I wouldn't have even thought of what I was thinking, but he seemed like a guy who needed to be beat.

I talked to Joe, who was still flagging, during a little break and told him what I was going to do. He kind of rolled his eyes at me, but nodded, so I figured he was in. When Joe called us up, the people who could manage it were standing on their cars, and the others had run up to the fence to watch. Joe had two green flags in his hands when we approached the line. In a normal situation he would stop us and stage us as evenly as possible, and then get a nod from each driver when he pointed one of the flags toward them. One and then the other. He would then slowly lower the flags, giving each contestant time to raise their RPMs. Then, suddenly, he would launch the banners skyward bringing both feet off the ground.

Joe, following my instructions, brought us up to stage, and before he was to signal us to rev, held the T-Bird with the flag in his left hand and gave me a flick with the other flag to release me. I instantly brought the Olds up in RPM, much higher than I would for a normal launch, and dumped it. I got the cheaters churning and held my SW tach at 6500 until my tires caught hold about one third of the way down the track. With brakes I came to a stop. I couldn't see a damn thing because of the smoke off the tires. Taking my time to let the motor settle down, I eased the transmission into reverse. Knowing I was straight with the highway when I stopped, I started backing up, holding the wheel straight and opening the door to let out the smoke.

The crowd was going nuts, whooping and hollering and the like. I wasn't sure what I was doing backing through the fog, but they were loving it and it was exhilarating as hell. Later, when asked, I just said I wanted to get a little heat in the tires for better traction. When I passed over the starting line, I gave it another thirty or forty feet while Joe walked across in front of my car and stood between it and the Bird.

Like me and everyone else there that night, I'm sure the T-Bird driver had never seen what I had just done. He might have been wondering what I was going to pull out of my hat next. That was the idea. I needed to have him wondering and not thinking about the flag dropping. Joe motioned me up and I gave the car a couple of hops to clean the tires, which made the crowd go into a frenzy. The show was over, and when I pulled forward, I let my brain enter the zone.

With one eye on the tach and one on the flag, I staged. It was like slow motion when Joe lowered the flags. He hesitated, and out of the corner of my eye, I could see the flag begin to ascend, a perfect start. When I slowed for Otto's driveway to return to the pits, the T-Bird went by and kept going, leaving his tow truck and his crew chief behind.

Billy and I got a chance to visit with the T-Bird's tow truck driver over a couple of Olys, and he showed us his equipment and how it worked. He asked me if I thought the warming of the tires helped much with the traction. After a moment of silence to give the fella the idea that I was in deep thought, I answered, trying not to look over at Billy, whose eyes were rolling like two marbles in a squirrel cage. I told him that without further testing, I wasn't convinced, but it sure as hell was fun.

Chapter 19

Billy's twenty-first birthday fell on a Friday in early January. He was home from college for Christmas vacation and we decided to throw a party. For us, a traditional bash meant a trip with the guys up to Richardson's Quarry or out to the old mill site with a case of beer in the trunk. We started the night out at Pop's, fooling around, waiting for everyone to show up.

We kept switching to bigger cars as more of us arrived and finally settled into Gary's Merc, which was large and soft with a nice radio and heater. It was still the same gorgeous hardtop we had all spent some time in over the years. He had owned the car for enough time that it became totally Gary. It was a babe magnet, just like Gary. The girls loved Gary and they were always hanging on him. I was a little surprised we were able to tear him away for the evening. Besides Gary, Billy, and me, Joe Harden and Johnny Smith showed up. It was less than half of us who hung out together, as the bunch was starting to dissolve. I think we all knew it, but it was something no one wanted to admit. Miles was gone, and some of the others had drifted one way or another.

Billy, being older by two years, had led the way and included us, and when he entered a new phase, we went right along too. This particular night, he became of legal drinking age, so we all got the benefit of his license to buy, a luxury we hadn't experienced before. We were usually able to get some beer, but it wasn't always cold and it wasn't always our brand, but we always got it. It was usually someone of age who needed a buck or two and was willing to step up to the plate.

As Gary pulled out onto the Boulevard, we rolled the windows down to let out the steam and the smoke. Hardtops look cool with all the windows down, and we liked to look cool but not frozen, so it was a quick fix. Out of habit, we drove around to the back of Central Market, where it was the darkest, and Billy went in with five singles. I had the trunk open by the time he returned with the goods. He handed me one end of the carton and we carefully placed it on the floor next to the spare tire. There was the familiar clinking of glass as the bottles shifted around, finding their place in the case.

The trip out of town was routine, as we had taken the same course many times before. Gary made the left onto Highway 68 after crossing the bridge and headed towards Bridgeport, a town about the same size as Willamette and only twelve miles to the west. I might have been tied and gagged in the trunk and I could have told you we were headed for the quarry. It was a great place to tip some beers or park with a girl, because you could see an intruder coming for miles. I guess it was because it was dark and uninhabited that we stopped short of our destination. Gary just pulled into a deserted-looking driveway a few hundred feet from the entrance of the quarry and shut it off. No one seemed to care, as we kept chattering along and reminiscing about the beer busts of the past.

Joe, who was riding shotgun, naturally had the pleasure of getting the beer. He pulled the keys out of the ignition right in the middle of "The Battle of New Orleans" and headed for the trunk to liberate the twenty-four little maidens. The reception up on that hill was great and we were getting stations all over the place. Gary was pushing the radio buttons like a typewriter, dodging football games and jumping from one good song to the next. Andy Williams got out about two notes of the "Hawaiian Wedding Song" before being cut off with "So Fine" by The Fiestas.

Joe was shivering when he returned with five stubbies cradled in his arm. He distributed them around with his other hand like a soldier passing out ammo. He hit the top of the dash with his fist in a strategic location, which popped the glove box door open. Joe reached in for the church key, pawing around in the dark and came out with a pack of rubbers.

"What're these for?" he asked Gary, flashing it around for everyone to see, garnering some attention.

"You sure as hell wouldn't know," Gary said, reaching for it.

Joe tossed it back in the box and continued searching for the bottle opener, finding it on the bottom, under a pack of Pall Malls and a box of fishing weights.

It was great with all the popping, fizzing, and burping. We were rocking. With each trip back for more ammo, Joe would line the empties up on the top rail of the gate that guarded the entrance to the pasture next to the road.

Every so often someone would cry, "Piss break!" and the doors would fly open. We would all line up side by side and pee in the ditch, and as the night wore on, the row of empties began to look like a platoon of toy soldiers.

Gary had turned the car around, which was a precautionary measure we always took so we would be able to leave at a moment's notice. We had just gotten back in and Gary was reaching for the radio when we noticed a pair of headlights coming from our right on the paved road by the entrance to the gravel driveway we were occupying. Gary retracted his hand without turning on the radio and Joe cracked his window to see if he could hear the sound of the motor coming.

"Damn it, he's turning," said Gary.

No one said a word as the headlights came closer, bobbing up and down as the car slowly worked its way around the ruts and mud puddles in the gravel.

"It's a cop," Joe said between his clenched teeth. "It's got solid lifters."

Some police cars were equipped with high lift cam shafts for performance reasons and they made a distinctive ticking noise when they idled. We were all listening. It was like we were a group of sailors sitting around a radar screen in a sub listening quietly for a ship overhead ready to dump a load of depth charges on us. It was a '58

Chevy two-door post and Joe was right; it was black as the ace of spades and had an aerial sticking out of the top of the rear fender.

The police car came to a stop in the middle of the lane, about twenty-five feet in front of the Merc, blocking our getaway route. In the brief moment before the flash of the spotlight, I could see two people through the windshield. One was an older woman sitting in the passenger side. The spotlight turned on in its downward position and then rotated as if it was looking for bombers in the sky, before it fell on us. We were momentarily blinded as our eyes fought to adjust to the light. The Chevy's window slowly descended, then the door opened and a stout, older-looking fella wearing a tan fedora got out.

"God damn ... shit," said Joe. "It's Buster Cleveland."

You could hear the air rushing out of our lungs.

"We're going to pay for this," said Gary. We were all a little worried after what had happened out at Otto's farm the past summer. We hadn't seen a thing of Buster since the affair and had kind of forgotten about the old lawman.

He pulled the trench coat he was wearing together in front and tied the belt. As he approached our car, he motioned for us to roll down the windows and all four came down simultaneously. He stopped a few steps from Gary's door, flicked on the large flashlight he was carrying, and shined it on the front spinner hubcap and then slowly walked the light rearward, revealing a dropped down, macho kid's car. He then bent down a little and shined the light inside the car, lighting up our faces from one to the other like he was taking a headcount. It was methodical the way he straightened and made the last couple of steps to the window. In the way he moved, so sure of himself, you knew this wasn't his first rodeo. The light reflected off the bottles like they were winking at him as he moved the flashlight along the floor boards, front and back.

He broke the silence by introducing himself as Sheriff Cleveland of Willamette County. At that, he paused and relit the cigar, holding the light under his arm. He kind of twisted his face around and his glasses began to bounce a little as he informed us that he wasn't happy about us loitering on private property. When he asked if we were aware of that fact he was met by five solemn faces wagging back and forth. He reached through the window and pulled Gary's light switch, turning on the headlights that were pointed straight at the stubbies sitting on the top board of the gate. Buster took a draw off his cigar, held it, and then let it out. He had a thoughtful look on his face.

"It looks like you boys have been consuming alcohol while you've been here using *my* private property." He flashed the light back around inside again, taking a careful look at each of us.

"And," he drew out the word, "it doesn't look like y'all are old enough for such behavior."

It hit me like a bolt of lightning. Billy was twenty-one. The look on Billy's face confirmed my concerns. It was bad. He would be charged with contributing to a minor, which was a more serious offense than a minor in possession.

Sheriff Cleveland said, while opening Gary's door, "I think you boys better get out of the car, and we'll look over what we got here."

Chapter 20

Sheriff Cleveland backed us up to thc fence in front of the squad car. It was scripted right out of the movie *Stalag 17*, with all of us lined up under the light, in front of the barbed wire, with our bomber jackets on. The sheriff pulled each of the open containers from the car and set them along the roof. Then, with Gary's keys, he walked around to the back of the car and opened the trunk. He added the three unopened bottles to the ones on top of the Merc and returned to his car. The interior light illuminated the lady in the car for an instant. We assumed it was Buster's wife. He closed the door after entering, without shutting the window, so we could hear some of the conversation.

The words were garbled but we got the drift; it was a conversation about what was to be done with us. We couldn't hear her voice as well, because she was on the far side of the car, but we distinctly heard Buster say he had a score to settle. We, of course, were conversing back and forth among ourselves about the odds and possibilities of our immediate future. Our hope was he would give us a lecture, make us pour the beer out, and send us home. This was a pretty common practice if respect was shown and remorse was obvious. Believe me, we had the routine down with the "yes sir, sorry officer" and so on.

My teeth were chattering a little when Buster returned from the warmth of his car, which he had left running. He marched up as far as the center of our line and faced us. He brought the flashlight from under his arm like General Patton raising his quirt, preparing to give the troops a good ass-chewing. He pointed the light randomly at us as he was making his points during the sermon.

I was thinking things were going pretty well and we would be on our way home shortly, when Johnny Smith let out a fart. It wasn't just a little squeaker either. It was a full-blown, longer-than-average fart, and when it ended, we were stunned. Of course, there was some uncomfortable silence, and then he popped off one more little blast. It was too much for us and we burst out laughing. Buster got red as hell. He did an about face and returned to his car, opened the door and grabbed the mic.

"Base, this is Sheriff Cleveland. I need a backup unit at 412 Forest View Drive."

"Sheriff Cleveland, this is base," came a feminine voice. "That's your address; what's up, Buster?"

Billy bumped my shoulder and said, "I'm going."

He turned and jumped the fence behind us. When Billy pushed down on the barbed wire to swing his leg over, it made a long screeching sound as it stretched through the staples that nailed it to the cedar post. This got the sheriff's attention for a moment, but then the lady in the car said something, and he returned to his conversation on the two-way. I made the split second decision to go with Billy. I hated like hell to leave my buddies behind, but I didn't want him to have to go it alone. Buster hadn't checked our ID's, so he didn't know our identities yet, and I knew he wouldn't be able to pry it out of my friends short of life in Sing Sing.

We were running across a rolling field and our first few hundred yards were downhill. It was so dark I was following footsteps I could only hear. There had been a long rainy spell, so the grass was wet and spongy, and our boots made a sucking sound as we ran, all out, into the night. At the bottom of the first hill was a ditch full of water, which we splashed through without slowing or looking back.

At the top of the next hill, Billy hit a fence at full tilt, making a god-awful sound as he tangled with the two strands of barbed wire at the top and flipped over on his back. I helped him unwrap from the wire and the devilish little barbs that tore into his hands. His leather jacket saved his arms, but his left hand was bleeding. I gave him the red shop rag I had in my pocket so he could wrap it up as a bandage while we were leaning over with our hands on our knees trying to catch our breath.

Once we regained our strength, we began looking around from the hilltop and we could see the glow of lights over Willamette and the same over Bridgeport to our right. We knew that Highway 68 had to be between, so we headed in a southerly direction, intending to intersect the road that would take us home. Every so often, the moon would pop through the clouds and we could map out a route, skating around obstructions we would not have otherwise been able to see. Upon reaching the crest of another hill, we could make out headlights going both east and west of what had to be the highway.

The last fence and ditch that stood in our way of reaching 68 was the highest and deepest. After scouting, we found a hole in the wire and made the ditch crossing with a running broad jump. We could have been a couple of madmen escaping from a mental hospital by the way we looked, which made us concerned if anyone would stop and give us a hitch to town. Our concerns proved relevant as the cars seemed to speed up when they saw us, two vagabond maniacs trying to flag them down. After a few minutes of disappointing attempts at hitchhiking, a couple of headlights came at us that had to be on the front of a hot rod or a Jeep, because they were closer together than on a normal car, and by the way they were vibrating, we guessed the former. We ran to the middle of the highway and began waving and jumping up and down. The headlights dropped from deceleration, and we could hear the car's power plant seesaw up and down in RPMs as the driver downshifted.

It was a fella named Scott, who we knew, driving his '32 Victoria filled with friends from Bridgeport. He said he had a pretty good load already, but he could squeeze one more in the backseat. I insisted that Billy go because of the cuts on his hands, and of course, he wasn't having anything to do with that. Then another car pulled up behind us while we were trying to push each other into Scott's Ford.

It was one of those little Volkswagen Beetles. This was a lime green one we had seen buzzing around town full of high school girls. The windows were steamed up, standard for Volkswagen, because the motor was in the back and it was difficult to transfer the heat to the front. The windshield cleared as the passenger side window came down, revealing a collage of high school sports euphoria. Cheerleaders with big hair, sitting in a pile of pom-poms, wearing lipstick, and blowing bubbles. There was constant motion making the little car wobble and bob like a boat full of drunks. They were all in blue and white, Willamette High School colors, on their way home from the basketball game with rival Bridgeport.

Alice Johnson, the girl in the backseat on the right, had her head stuck out the window over the girl in front, who was ducking out of the way. She was beckoning me in, saying how they had plenty of room and all.

"I guess I got a ride," I said to Billy as I gave him a final push into the Victoria.

The door of the Volkswagen opened and the girl riding shotgun had to lean forward while holding her seat back ahead so I could enter. There were two girls in the back. Along with Alice was Linda Nelson and they had stacked themselves in the left corner, leaving room for me. Willamette had won the game with a last minute Hail Mary shot from half-court, and I'm here to tell you the car was rocking with jubilation. Susan Bell, behind the wheel, churned gravel as she got us back on the highway, banging shifts and chewing bubble gum at the same time.

Everyone was talking at the same time, except the girl in the front passenger seat, who seemed to have a different demeanor about her. I recognized her, as I was trying not to squash her against the glove box door. Her name was Marylyn Swanson, a senior at Willamette and daughter of John R. Swanson, who was the president of the First National Bank. I had seen Miss Swanson at the bank with her dad on occasion and at school, where I couldn't take my eyes off her.

I'd been ogling the girl ever since I'd noticed her for the first time sitting across the desk from her dad at the bank. She was the only female I'd ever seen in that chair, which was all leather and matched his big, intimidating throne. She had this way about her, not only her good looks, but she had it together. I mean, way together. She was in all the right clubs with the intelligent set, but she also had friends in other circles, like the three teenage rockers who were in the little German vessel, wiggling and giggling. I was so close to her I could feel the warmth of her body and see the contour of her neck as it disappeared into her sweater. Her skin was light with kind of an olive tone, and she had a mole almost hidden by her dark hair, which hit her shoulders and then turned up. After hours of physical stress on the basketball floor, I thought she still looked pleasantly perfect.

Alice was also in a cheerleader outfit and was turned toward me, sitting on Linda's lap. She was a senior like the rest of them and had become curious about what the Little

Bastards were like. When girls like these were freshmen, they wouldn't even look at us, and when they became sophomores, they would look at us and then turn away and giggle. It was like we were from a different planet, and now they had one of us captured. With their maturity, they began to kind of like the way we were and tempted themselves to join our ways of freedom-loving independence. I felt as if I was on a table and they were going to dissect me to see what I was made of and what made me tick. Alice reached into her purse for a scalpel and brought out a pink and gold comb and she began combing my hair. I looked pretty bad with my boots full of water; my pants were wet up to the waist, and as they warmed, the steam they generated kept Marylyn busy wiping the windows with her hanky. When Alice was finished, she gave a look of approval as she slid the comb back into her bag.

Then she rubbed her hands together and began the interrogation. "So, Sonny, what were you and Billy doing way out here? That was Billy, wasn't it?"

"We were out for a walk," I said.

"Hey, don't give me that," she said. "Where's that famous car of yours? Why aren't you driving it?"

"I left it at Pop's." I said, not wanting to say more than necessary, because I thought it would be less fuel for the fire.

Susan chimed in with, "Is that car of yours really the fastest car in town?"

"It's fast," I said.

"How fast?" asked Linda, the first words that came from her.

"Fast enough," I said.

Then Susan turned around in the seat and asked, "What's it like to get drunk, Sonny?"

Oh God, I thought, *where is this going?* I told her I'd let her know when I found out. She wouldn't take that answer, but soon her patience wore thin, and she was back at driving and jacking up the volume on the radio.

During all of the fuss of getting me into the car, the passenger side sun visor flipped down against the windshield, revealing a mirror used for makeup and such. I was crammed into the right side corner of the backseat, so my natural line of vision was right over Marylyn's shoulder, with the mirror square in the center. It was at such an angle that it reflected Marylyn's hands engaged in wrapping and unwrapping her handkerchief. She had slim wrists and long, lovely fingers with nails that were manicured but not colored. As the running conversation switched from the ballgame to music to my hair and back, Marylyn showed no facial evidence of anything more than mild interest, but her hands seemed to give a hint of what was behind her facade. When the focus was on the game, her hands were as relaxed as they were when the conversation went to small talk, but when my name or Billy's came up, her hands got busy. I was probably just imagining this, and I admit I was grasping at straws, hoping to identify any slight bit of interest Miss Swanson had in me in any romantic sort of way. As far as I was concerned, I was falling head over heels for Marylyn Swanson.

When they dropped me off at Pop's, the drive-in was lively, being as it was Friday night. I was relieved not to see law enforcement officers waiting by my car. Marylyn opened her door for me while leaning ahead and pulling her seat forward to let me out. I was hoping to see her face up close, but it was hidden behind the seat. I held the door long enough for her to return to the sitting position and continued to hold it there until her eyes rose and met mine, questioning what the pause was for. Looking directly into her eyes, I told her I was glad we had been introduced and that I was happy to know her. It was a bit of a stretch, but I wanted her to know I considered us introduced.

A faint smile and nod appeared on her face, but as far as any encouragement, none was shown. She could play poker.

As I turned to walk away, I felt a rush of air hit the back of my neck when the Beetle's door shut, blowing away the femininity I had been swimming in. It was such a contrast when I opened the door to my '40, which was cold, dark, and smelled like leather. I was enjoying the exhilaration of being a small-time fugitive and meeting Marylyn Swanson in the same night. I flipped the switch, pushed the starter button, and the Ford came to life with a roar of masculinity.

Chapter 21

After turning and churning all night, I jumped out of bed at 6:00 in the morning. I had spent the night thinking of Miss Swanson, wondering what was happening to me, since I had never been influenced by a girl in this way before. I weighed the good and the bad of what a relationship with her would do and how it would affect my life. All other waking moments that night were used worrying about what happened to the buddies I had left under the guard of Sheriff Cleveland.

My engineer boots were still wet, so I pulled on my Red Wings and grabbed my Levi's jacket as I headed out the door for work. I had been working at Dunlap's Sawmill since graduating in June.

My scheme for the future began to develop when I met Fred Peterson between the east and westbound lanes of the Boulevard on a rainy day the year before. Billy and I had rescued Fred and his Chevy pickup when his motor quit in the middle of the busiest intersection in town. Of course, it was during rush hour, if there was such a thing in Willamette, and he was looking a little tense.

We towed him off the street with a rope and got him going again. Well, it was really Billy who got the motor going while I became acquainted with Mr. Peterson. Come to find out, he was the manager at the employment agency downtown. He mentioned he had no understanding of how a motor worked and had trouble from time to time with the pickup. I suggested he bring it down to the station so we could keep it tuned and serviced for him. We drummed up business for Mr. Fletcher, partly in trade for using his station, but mostly because he was a friend.

The problem stumped Billy for a while, so Fred and I had a lengthy conversation, mostly about school and what I had planned after I graduated and so forth. Up until then, I hadn't given it a lot of thought, but he had a way of getting me interested. After we got him running, he told me to drop by the office sometime and we would continue our visit.

He became a steady customer down at Fletcher's Mobil and we got to know Fred pretty well. His wife would bring in the family car weekly for gas and we serviced both rigs routinely. During my senior year, I began to map out my plan, and with Fred's advice, I decided to stay out of school after graduation for a year and earn all the money I could and then enter a state university. My grades were fair, considering I had never invested a lot of time improving them.

That's how I ended up working for Dunlap's Sawmill, pulling on the green chain. The mill paid as well as others, but offered more overtime than was common, and according to Mr. Peterson, was in sound shape and I wouldn't be laid off during the winter.

I'll never forget him saying, "And one other thing, Sonny, you won't fall in love with the place. You're not going to like it. You'll be ready and raring for college to start in September." He was right about that. It was drudgery pulling long, wet lumber off a chain and stacking it in piles according to dimension. The boards were heavy and never quit coming at you.

That particular day was Saturday, and I was working for time and a half until noon, when the place shut down for the weekend. At 12:04, Sage, the foreman, finally blew the whistle and the monotony ceased. He was dedicated to the outfit and always got a couple of free minutes out of us. It was about making lumber for him.

As I was heading for my car, I waved at Randy Parker, who also worked at the mill and who lived in a small town south of Willamette called Reed's Corner. He had a pretty hot '56 Chevy that was lowered down and had a scallop paint job.

Randy was looking up at the sky when he yelled over to me, "Looks like there will be some action tonight."

I nodded back as I reached for the door handle. He was talking drag racing. It was the first day in about a month the sky was clearing and the streets were drying out. Everyone was itching to get at it again, and you can bet there were scores to be settled; there always were. Saturday night in Willamette and Randy was right; there would be action.

I fired up the coupe, sat back, and lit a cigarette, letting the motor warm on its own. There was always fine sawdust around the mill and it crept into the tightest places. I wiped a film of it off my dashboard with the shop rag I had rolled and draped over my steering column. My cleaning job revealed the darnedest example of art ever laid on a car.

A couple of years prior, a California fella who called himself the Duke spent some time with a family in Willamette on his way to who knows where. He was an honest to goodness beatnik, who wore a top hat and a t-shirt that reeked with the smell of paint thinner and wine. He was tall and skinny, like he hadn't a care for food, and he usually had a stoned look about him. You would almost catch yourself feeling sorry for him since he seemed tortured, but then he would let out a spontaneous grinning laugh, only to make you feel foolish.

He worked out of the garage at the house where the family lived and had a gallon wine bottle hanging from a rope, and when passing it, he would take a lug. He liked painting scallops and lettering names on cars. Suddenly, every cool car around was named. Three that come to mind were: *Mary Maker*, *Comes Quickly*, and *Play House Nightly* after the television show.

I dropped Gary off one day after school to pick up his Merc, which had become *Enchanted Lace*, and somehow, I let the Duke talk me into leaving him my '40 to "personalize" for me. I can tell you I was apprehensive on the way over to pick it up the next day. Joe and Johnny were predicting what my car was going to be like as we meandered our way along in the '50. They knew I was a little worried, and they were having some fun with me, and I was trying to take it.

Joe pulled up to the curb in front of the driveway where the Duke had my car with both doors open, and he was whirling around like he was in a ballet, paintbrush in hand. He had some station tuned in on my radio playing weird music from San Francisco, and man, was I sweating until I saw that dashboard.

He had transformed the cold steel object that held my instruments to a canvas, recreating a whole Civil War scene. Confederate troops were firing cannons over the top of the speedometer, marching with their flag, running and shooting over the radio at the Union troops who were marching with the Stars and Stripes and firing back. There was a soldier on a white horse with the troops on the right who I assumed was General Grant and who seemed undaunted by the cannon balls whirring over him from the artillery that was belching out smoke and fire. I about fainted with excitement. I was so impressed and relieved, I was just babbling.

The Duke backed up a couple of steps and took a draw off the jug, wiped his mouth with his arm, and began cleaning his brush with his t-shirt. I could hardly wait to get around town and show off my masterpiece, but he wouldn't let me until the paint hardened up about 7:47 that evening. That's what he said, 7:47 not 7:45.

Back at the sawmill, I finished my cigarette about the time my motor smoothed out and began its uneven but healthy idle. I eased into low and pulled out of the parking lot, and as I reached the pavement, I goosed it a little to blow the sawdust off. I had a little encounter with Randy and raced him until the spot where the street became one lane when it crossed the little bridge over Kane's Creek, but I let him go. I saw the shit-eating grin on his face when he passed me just before the bridge. My mind was somewhere else, and I had a couple of urgent things to do, but first I swung by our house to grab my leather jacket and the boots, which I had left by the fire.

The night before, in the Volkswagen, over all the racket, I heard of the girls' plans to go to the matinee down at the theatre. I figured they would be coming out about 1:30, and I thought I might get a glimpse of Marylyn out in front where they liked to stand around and visit after the show. The other pressing thing I had on my mind was getting down to Fletcher's to see what happened to Joe, Johnny, and Gary.

First things first, I thought as I headed for the Paramount. It was our indoor theater that sat on First Street past the bridge toward the end of the block. It had been there forever and was ornate and old-fashioned. The Little Bastards had spent a lot of time there growing up, and we became known as the "scourge of the balcony." Seeing the crowd out in front, I knew that I had hit it just at the right time. The little, green Volkswagen was sitting at the curb to my right as I went by. I had my right window down like a radar antenna trying to scoop up some chatter from the street, and among the bodies, I picked out Alice Johnson waving at me to stop. Standing beside her was Linda Brown, right in front of a taller, dark-haired beauty, Marylyn Swanson. My heart started jumping around, but I stayed cool while Alice was working me over about how they had been worried about me and were sure I had died of pneumonia. Cars behind me began piling up and honking, so I had to pull out without getting a look a Marylyn.

I was a little high with the encounter, but when I looked in the rearview mirror, my high went right over the top. Everyone had gone back to what they were doing, except Marylyn Swanson, who was standing next to the curb watching me pull away.

Yowee, what a rush! I knew we had made a connection. My heart started beating like hell with the exhilaration I was feeling. It was a little like being ahead a half-car length at the finish line, only different. It was heavy. It was euphoria.

I turned left onto Gleason and then left again on Third, heading for Fletcher's. The sun had come out from behind the clouds and it was turning into a nice day. I was trying to wipe the goofy smile off my face before I got to the station, since I wasn't ready to share news of my love life with my peers. When I rolled in, I was relieved to see Johnny sitting on the Coke machine across from Billy, who was leaning against the Merc with a bandage wrapped around his hand. Joe's '50 was on the hoist and it was like any other day in paradise. I jumped out, slamming the door, with my arms spread out in a "what happened" gesture. Joe came out of the lube bay with Gary, who was wiping his hands on a shop rag, as Johnny slid off the cooler.

We got around close to the Mercury so Billy and I could hear the story. I was leaning up against the car next to Johnny when I decided that it would be nice to have a smoke while enjoying the recall. I reached one out of the pack Johnny was carrying in the side pocket of his bomber jacket.

I was standing there with an unlit weed in my mouth, both hands in my jacket, leaning on the car, when Johnny automatically whipped out his Zippo to give me a light. He carried one of those brass G.I. issue jobs that his dad hauled all across Germany during the war. It had a dent in the side that his dad said saved his ass during a shootout with some "Krauts." Unbeknownst to Johnny, the thing had been leaking in his pocket and was swamped with fluid that erupted in a pretty blue and red ball of flame when he spun the gear against the flint. This was common and didn't hurt a lot, but it looked impressive when fire engulfed your hand like a torch. What does hurt is when you hang on to the lighter as it gets hot and burns the shit out of your fingers, and that, of course, is what Johnny did until he got the wherewithal to drop it and dunk his hand in the car wash bucket.

Joe, seeing my predicament, pulled a book of matches from his pocket and did one of those contortionist things with his fingers bending over the match and lighting it with one hand. When it came to cigarettes and matches, there wasn't much we couldn't do from years of practicing down at the clubhouse in the berries.

Gary was the smoke ring champ with the most and fastest. He leaned back and sent a couple in the air and began to talk.

"This is what happened. When you guys bolted, Buster was on the two-way with the lady at the office who was explaining to him there had been a bad wreck south of town and they were short on cruisers. The conversation was somewhat garbled, but we could get the gist of it from where he had us lined up. From what we figured out later, there was another conversation going on at the same time between Buster and the woman we assumed to be his wife.

They had been on their way home from his retirement party and had planned on a nice evening alone by the fire when our confrontation happened. She was reminding him of this and was suggesting he let us go. Of course, he was getting hot with the deputy on the radio about his seniority and how they should peel a car off and send it right up. About this time, Buster's wife got out of the car and walked up to where we were freezing and introduced herself as Marge and asked us to get in their car where it was warm. We followed her to the car and got into the backseat. After shutting her door, she turned in her seat and looked at each of our faces, one by one. She stopped at Johnny and asked him if he was Gracie Smith's son. Johnny was shivering and his teeth were chattering, but he got out a yes. Marge explained how she and Gracie were in the same bridge club and that she remembered Johnny from being at their house for games."

Gary paused to blow a ring for effect and then continued.

"By this time, Buster had given up on getting a backup anytime soon and was sitting there trying to cool down.

Marge faced Buster again and told him to drive us all up to the house so we could warm up and to give us boys a little time to get over the effect and all. Buster wasn't liking it much, but he gave in and followed orders.

"The Cleveland residence was a ranch house at the top of the hill and at the end of the driveway where we had parked. It was an inviting, cozy place with Buster's hound asleep on the porch, and smoke coming from the chimney. We entered through a large, Spanish door into an inside porch that was used for storing boots and jackets and had bridles hanging on the wall.

"Buster walked on past the saddles and slammed the back door, saying he was going out to check on Marsha. As Marge was ushering us through the kitchen dining area, she explained that Marsha was their milk cow and she was close to calving. Our final destination was the living room, which was a long, rectangular affair with an open beam ceiling, and it had a large stone fireplace at one end with a moose looking down at us. She motioned for us to sit down on the leather couch that was along one wall and asked us if we liked hot chocolate. We all nodded in unison and she left us alone with the moose and all of its hairy friends. There were wild animals all over the walls. At the opposite end from the fireplace was a matching stone wall with an elk's head in the middle, between a deer and an antelope.

"We were back off the couch as soon as Marge went around the corner, looking at the several pictures hanging on the walls of Sheriff Cleveland in all sorts of hunting venues, including one with him and the bear whose skin was lying on the floor in front of the fireplace. Resting in the middle of the mantel was a picture of three soldiers posing in front of a tank wearing their uniforms and doughboy hats that looked as if it was taken in Europe during WWI. On the right bottom, near the corner of the frame, was a purple heart attached by a pin, and it looked like a casual afterthought that wasn't intended to take away from the importance of the photo.

"We replanted ourselves on the couch when Buster entered the house. He carried a log, which he laid in the fireplace, and then rearranged the fire with a poker, causing the burning wood to pop and send sparks flying. Upon completing that chore, he straightened up, still holding the poker, which he pointed at us with the invitation to tour his animal kingdom. You could tell he liked to talk about his hunting and the trophies he displayed. We jumped up and followed the poker from one adventure to the next, which impressed the shit out of us.

"When we arrived at the photo in the middle of the mantel, Johnny asked him if he was a war hero. With a moment of thought, Buster answered no. He said the other two men were the heroes and they were still in France, six feet deep.

"At that point, he walked over to the 21" Sylvania and flipped the switch. We sat down as we were ordered and waited for the tubes to warm up. He said he hoped we liked *Wagon Train*, because that's what we'd be watching. The four of us settled in to watch television as Marge brought in hot chocolate with marshmallows and coffee for Buster. Mickey Rooney was the guest star, portraying a greenhorn who had signed up in Missouri to join the Adam's train to California. Of course, Ward Bond had a hell of a time with Mickey, shaping him up for the task.

"When the show ended, Buster got up and motioned toward the door and we got the hint. As he walked us out, he reached down and picked up what was left of his cigar. Out on the porch he asked us if we needed a ride back to our car, and of course we declined, saying that we liked to walk. Buster relit the cigar and took a long draw, blew out the smoke, and then said, 'I hope those other two Little Bastards liked their walk back to town.'

"We were standing there dumbfounded, our mouths about down to our belts, while Buster reached down and gave his hound a pet on the head as he walked into the house.

"I guess we were a little humbled as we walked down the driveway, until we got to the Mercury and discovered the three full beers were still on the roof, nicely chilled in the January air. I warmed up the car while they gathered up the empties and put them back in the carton.

"Joe and Johnny got in the backseat with the case of empties sitting between them and I got behind the wheel with a beer and opened the other two as I passed them over the seat. We rolled all the windows down as I pulled the Merc out onto the highway. I turned the radio up as loud as we could stand it, and we hauled ass down the road, flinging bottles at mail boxes and highway signs all the way back to town."

Chapter 22

Listening to Gary tell the story about Buster's cozy fireplace and Marge's cocoa reminded me that I hadn't eaten for a while.

"Damn," I said, "I'm starved. Let's go out to Pop's for a burger."

Joe rode with Gary and Johnny in the Merc, and Billy piled in with me in the '40. Pop's Drive-In was a typical drive-in restaurant with outdoor service and an indoor area with booths and a soda bar. It was accessed from the Boulevard by a paved drive that circled the lot, so you could order from the car or go inside to eat. Joe suggested we eat inside, which I had been noticing he seemed to prefer. We parked our cars on the other side, in our favorite space, the gravel lot, and stepped over a pile of bicycles and entered the building.

We were greeted by Angie, who had been waitressing there for a while. She was tall, thin, and good looking, in a jaded sort of way. In high school, she had been involved with a flyboy out at the base who had gotten her pregnant before shipping out, and she became a single mom at a young age. Angie had grown up on our side of town and was only about a year older than us. We considered her a friend and we treated her as our equal. She brightened up when she saw us. The small time she had with us was like a flashback, reminding her of her youth, before she became entangled in responsibility. We sat in our usual booth, which was a red and white vinyl closest to the bar and cash machine. It was a big semicircle and had a remote juke box so we could select and play tunes without getting up. Gary plunked in a quarter, and after punching some buttons, we were in the midst of Buddy Holly and The Crickets.

When we had plopped down and slid around, I noticed three juveniles sitting in the next booth who I guessed were the bike jockeys. I'd seen these kids around the neighborhood close to Lincoln Grade School. They were around twelve or thirteen, guessing by their looks, and you could tell they didn't have much. The one in the middle was stout and a little shorter than the other two, and to his right was a small, redheaded kid with large ears and freckles. They were all in the need of haircuts, including the one on the right who combed his in a ducktail and had Coke-bottle glasses. They were making a lot of commotion and messing up their table with catsup-flavored water full of sugar. They had gotten their hands on some straws and were blowing ice at Angie and whoever else got close.

When she delivered our water, Joe arched his head in their direction in a questioning way. Angie described the torment they laid on her on the occasions of their presence. She went on saying how the little turds would come in and order water and catsup and make their little cocktails, which wasn't so bad, but they were real mouthy and called her names. She said they were poor and she sort of felt sorry for them, but they had an attitude and she was getting sick of it. One of the little shits interrupted her then, demanding more water, and as she poured it, we heard one of them call Angie a bitch. About this time, they got this look from Gary. They knew they were in deep shit and they made a lunge for the door.

Joe, who seemed to be taking this personally and was sitting with his back to them, also heard the demeaning slur. Rising, he cut off the escape route of the punk on the outside. He looked like an Olympic athlete throwing a discus as he came around, securing the first escapee by the neck and going for the other with his right hand.

He drug the two out of the booth and yelled at the third who was making for the door, "Don't leave your buddies behind, you little shithead."

As Joe was ushering his captives to the door, he looked over at Billy and me with a grin, which made me cover my head in shame for leaving my buddies the night before. We were all having some fun as Joe was righting a wrong, and we got to watch the glow of Angie's face as it happened.

"Hold the door open for these two scums I got here," Joe said to number three as he crammed his and the other two bodies through the door at the same time. The whole building shook a little as the little shits were rattling against the jamb. Joe was intimidating as hell, being a foot taller, wearing a leather jacket, and with his blue eyes gleaming. Outside, he slammed the two against my coupe. Then, with one hand, he placed number three in line and began to straighten the bunch like he was shuffling cards. They kept looking down at the ground while Joe was lecturing, and from time to time, he would bop one on the chin and make him look up. We were enjoying the whole affair through the window while admiring the way he went from one to the other, thumping and rapping on them to get their attention.

Pop, who began to wonder why the burgers were getting cold, came out of the kitchen wiping his hands on his apron and followed our eyes out the window to take in the spectacle. All three of the boys began to nod at the same time as Joe was reaching into his pocket. He handed each an object and then marched them back into the restaurant and lined them up in front of Angie, who was standing behind the cash register wringing her hands in her bar towel.

Joe gave the one next to him a little shove to remind him of his duty. They all came out together with the apology, saying they had become aware of their misdoings and wouldn't act like that again. After Angie, bless her heart, accepted their apology, they asked if they could sit down and each buy a Coke since they had come into some money and all.

Angie came out from behind the counter, slipping off her apron, and caught Joe before he could sit down. She wrapped her arms around him with more than a motherly hug. At first Joe, surprised and a little embarrassed, just stood and took it, then he gradually put his long arms around her little body and squeezed.

Of course, we were just sitting there gawking until, finally, Gary, who understood such things, began to clap, which turned into applause from our section and whoever else was around to witness. It came to me then why we had been spending more and more time inside Pop's than out. Joe was in love.

Chapter 23

While we were eating hamburgers and discussing the evening prospects, I noticed the lime green Volkswagen enter Pop's from the east. You could see cars coming in and leaving because the whole front of the building was windows, while the back lot was hidden because of the kitchen and bathrooms. I stopped chewing and my heart rate increased as I waited for the VW Bug to appear in the peripheral vision of my left eye. The other fellas didn't seem to notice, which was okay with me, since I still wasn't ready to reveal my predicament with Marylyn Swanson. Sure enough, the little car chugged by the window, stopped at the stop sign, and then buzzed out, going north towards Billie's Big Burger. The way the VW's windows were fogged, I couldn't tell who was aboard, but as usual, it looked full.

Another car, owned by Morton Johnson, came rolling past. I assumed he was driving, and the guy riding shotgun was wearing a Willamette High letterman jacket. Morton had graduated the previous June with me, but we ran in different circles, and I really didn't know him. He was a football star like Willamette had never seen. On offense, he was a receiver who knew no fear. He never heard footsteps and would run headlong into a cement watering trough if it meant a reception. He held the state record for the most catches, among other achievements. Upon graduation, it became difficult for him to enter a world without a football. He had gotten on at the fire department because of connections, but it seemed he needed greater challenges, which he created by making up speed games he would attempt to win.

Morton bought a new Plymouth Fury that had a big motor with lots of horsepower, and he used it hard. He would time himself on how long it would take him to get from Willamette to Bridgeport and back, and he would keep at it until he was satisfied with himself. Another one of his pastimes was roaring down the Boulevard with his throttle clear to the floor, weaving through traffic trying not to let up. He talked often about his greatest challenge: to leave Pop's a minute or two before 11:00 p.m., holding his foot to the floor, and beating the 11:00 train that crossed the Boulevard in South Town. To increase his nerve and relax his fears, he began drinking before and during his personal contests.

Morton never reappeared. He was either still in the back lot or he turned left on the side street and went downtown. As I pushed my empty plate away, I saw the Bug reappear, back already from Billie's, I guessed.

Billy and I were getting into the '40 to head back to the station where I was going to set the timing and run the valves on the Olds, when I noticed the V-Dub and the Plymouth were side by side with the drivers in conversation. By pulling forward in the gravel lot, I was able to get by both cars without interrupting their visit, and while doing so, I thought I saw Marylyn's silhouette through the car's window. Billy commented that he had heard Morton and Susan Bell were an item, starting back in their days together on the football field, with him the star and her the cheerleader.

We spent a couple of hours working on the '40 in the lube bay at the station, adjusting this and that, getting ready for a night of defending my title. I had my street tires on for the winter, as well as the high gears, but everything else was in race mode. I pumped in a quarter-tank of ethyl to keep the weight of the car to a minimum for performance, while Billy lowered the tire pressure to twenty-six pounds in the rear tires for traction.

It was a little early to hit the Boulevard, so we decided to head out to the new freeway project coming through Willamette. It wasn't finished and not used yet by motorized traffic. It was an extension of the same new highway that we had taken to Tijuana for the upholstery job. The part that went through Willamette and south for miles was straight as an arrow and called the gun barrel. We called it something else, the Drag Strip.

It was perfect since it was totally uninhabited on the weekends, when the work ceased. We would just go out and make ourselves at home on lonely stretches of brand new, tire-biting asphalt. Billy and I found the entrance the freeway workers always left for us and took a shot down about five miles to the first intersection, then got back on the other side for the return. I wound it up to about a 100 mph for four miles, and the Olds motor hummed under the Ford hood, cutting wind.

Billy was to have dinner with his family, so I dropped him back at the station. Frank was there doing the books and smiled when he looked up. I waved to him with the red shop towel as I entered the lube bay. There was an empty 15-gallon grease barrel in the corner where I threw the rag on top of a pile of dirty ones. I grabbed a clean one out of the box and returned to the '40, rolling and folding the cloth. While waiting for traffic so I could get back onto the street, I slid the cloth around the steering column. I was ready for the night.

I made for the Boulevard and the exit into Pop's parking lot without seeing a soul I knew, but that changed at the drive-in area where the evening was brewing with weekend excitement. Glancing around and hoping to see the green Bug, I noticed the acknowledgement my '40 received as its motor idled by the masses of teenagers.

Back on the side street, I goosed it a little, chirping the tires, while scanning the side lot, to no avail. *Maybe she's out at Billie's Big Boy*, I told myself. I turned left on the Boulevard and headed north.

About halfway out, I met Randy in his '56 going the opposite way, and we waved. There is a lot in the way people wave. When I was little I noticed how my dad would wave at someone on the street, and how they would wave back. Of course, it's just an acknowledgement of your mutual friendship or just that you know each other.

You can tell a little about someone by the way they do it, kind of like what they wear or what they drive. Now the way my mom would wave to a lady across the church parking lot would not be like John Wayne waving to Marlon Brando. I think it's like your signature or personal stamp. A guy who is eighteen, wearing a leather jacket, and driving a hot car should make it obvious enough so the person knows of the acknowledgment, but it should also be crisp and masculine.

The Big Boy, like Pop's, was beginning to vibrate with activity. I pulled into the lot and entered the never-ending rotation of cars that circled the joint. Eddy, from out of nowhere, jumped on my running board, talking a mile a minute.

"The Pharaoh is looking for you," he said.

"Who's The Pharaoh?" I asked as I rolled the window the rest of the way down.

"He's that new guy from up in Washington that drives the '59 Corvette," he said.

I'd heard about the guy, but I thought Eddy might as well tell me about him, since that's how he got off. We cruised on around the drive like that, with Eddy on the running board and me listening until a parking spot emptied for us. Eddy jumped off in time to miss the ordering phone and ran around to get in the passenger side. Not stopping to take a breath for a full two minutes, he continued to fill me in about this stranger in town with the red corvette. According to Eddy, this Pharaoh guy came to Willamette from up around Seattle to work at the new metals plant. His dad was an engineer who worked for Boeing, and upon taking delivery of the new car, they totally disassembled the motor to balance and blueprint it, among other things. "Why would he be looking for me, Eddy?" I asked.

Eddy rolled his eyes, and playing the game, he replied, "He wants to kick your ass out on the freeway. Why do you think he's looking for you?"

I ordered us a couple of Cokes over the phone, and while we were waiting, Eddy went on with the results of his investigation of the stranger and his machine.

"This Pharaoh guy has an older fella riding with him on occasion who wears headsets under his fedora that are wired to a box that has these switches and gauges. It's like he's tuning as they go."

"I wonder what that's all about," I said.

"I wish Billy was here; he might know."

"Maybe he's adjusting the timing on the go," I thought out loud.

"Yeah, whatever it is, it's scary," Eddy said.

When we finished, I set the empty Coke glasses on the tray by the phone and fired up the '40. The place was busy with the hubbub of cars circling, looking for places to land, and the constant chatter of the crowd. While backing out with my arm over the seat, I saw Morton's Plymouth through my back window. It entered the lot and made its way to the gravel lot on the west side of the restaurant. The west side lot was the common place where truckers would leave their freighters while they took on coffee and something fried inside the restaurant. It was also a popular place for kids to park their cars among the big rigs to drink and raise hell. I just saw the back of his car disappear into the shadows of the big trailers when I was pulling out into the rotating traffic.

Suddenly, the red Corvette appeared. It had entered the lot but turned left against the flow and was approaching us on the right. It stopped alongside my car, and the passenger window came down, revealing a hot girl wearing a cowboy hat. She had blond hair long enough to hit the top of her denim jacket, ending about at the pockets. She had lips that were painted red and it drew your eyes to them. Leaning way back in the seat with one knee up made her look confident and sure of herself.

"Are you Sonny Mitchell?" she asked.

"Who wants to know?" I answered, getting the game started.

"This here is The Pharaoh," she said, motioning with her thumb in the driver's direction. "He wants to know if you can drive that old wreck you're sitting in."

I came back with, "Why don't you tell him to take that little sports car home and come back with a real car and we'll find out."

Of course, Eddy was really getting into it as the bantering went back and forth. Every time he would try to get a word in, she would interrupt him and cut him off, which was the first time I had ever seen anyone get the best of Eddy in a talking contest. Under her left knee, which was not far from her chest, I could see the driver's hand on the gearshift lever. His fingers were pounding the front of it like he was punching buttons on a saxophone.

Could he be nervous? I wondered. Occasionally, the girl would glance over at The Pharaoh to receive instructions for the oncoming moves in our little mind game. Above her collar, on her neck, you could see the top of a spider tattoo about the size of a half-dollar crawling north, which made me wonder about the night she had the needle. The only tattoos I'd seen up until then were on old sailors who worked at the mills and hung out in the taverns downtown.

After a couple more rounds of offensive remarks, we agreed on a time and place for a speed contest. We were to meet right there on the Big Boy lot at exactly 10:00 that night, which was about two hours away. I wondered why the guy needed the two hours and several thoughts flooded my brain, including the red lips.

Eddy was getting hungry, so we decided to head to Pop's so he could have a burger and some fries. Circling around to the other entrance, I passed in front of Morton's Plymouth and noticed a reflection off a bottle being lowered from the lips of the person in the middle of the car. It was dark between the trucks, so I couldn't make out the occupants, but it looked as if the front seat was full.

We took the east route back to Pop's to ease the monotony of driving the same old gut night after night. There were a couple of other hangouts that deserved a casual glimpse on passing but never really yielded anything interesting. I turned on Highway 46, which cut through the mountains to Eastern Oregon, but by going right, it returned us to the Boulevard. The usual bunch loitered around in the gravel at Pop's, and after a visit to bring us up to date on the night's events, we pulled into a stall for Eddy's burger.

Louise Henderson, a Pop's waitress and sometimes carhop, came up to the window and took our order in a way that you knew she wanted to be somewhere else. She had started waiting tables in June for summer vacation then just never got around to going back to school. She perked up a little when she saw Eddy, because he always talked to her when it wasn't busy and it was just the two of them. Most people ignored Louise.

We had a good spot where we could observe the cars coming off the highway, seeing who was with whom and who was doing what. I was sitting there with the radio playing, munching on some of Eddy's fries, listening to him talk between bites about his new job out at the metals plant. He had gotten on this school-work program where he was part-time after school and then worked the graveyard shift Saturday nights. He was still on a probation period, but hoped to get on full-time as soon as he graduated, come June. We had a couple of hours to burn before our rendezvous with The Pharaoh, and I made sure Eddy knew not to get us in any other races in the meantime.

About halfway through the fries, Morton's Plymouth appeared from the left, and my eyes followed it as he goosed it, playing like he was going to run over the guys in the gravel. I had gotten pretty jumpy about those kinds of antics over time, especially when it involved a 3,500 pound car and a bottle of booze. After a few moments in the gravel lot, the car backed out under the light to leave, revealing the passenger on the right. It was Marylyn Swanson.

It took me a few moments to recover from the shock, but then it started to come together. Morton's girlfriend, Susan Bell, was sitting in the middle next to Morton. And Marylyn, Susan's best friend, was sitting next to Susan. I was not liking what I was seeing, knowing Morton's reputation of wild-ass drinking and crazy driving. As soon as they pulled around and left in the direction of Billie's Big Burger, I got out of my car and walked over to the gravel to interrogate my friends and find out what danger Marylyn was in, if any.

Gary was in his Merc with a cute little gal from Bridgeport crawling all over him and Joe was leaning in the window shooting the breeze. I probably seemed a little more urgent than usual when I asked about Morton and the two girls. They told me Morton and Susan were getting pretty soused, but they didn't think the Swanson girl was drinking and she seemed a little worried.

Apparently, Morton was talking about beating the train again, which he claimed to have done once before, but no one believed him. He had been bragging about it, saying that he had the timing worked out, and he knew exactly where he had to be on the highway when the warning lights began to flash for a serious train that intersected the highway at the edge of the city full speed every night at 11:00.

I was getting concerned and decided to return to my car to head back out to Billie's and sort of bird dog them and see if I needed to intervene. Upon hitting Billie's,

I wheeled around to the other island for a slot where I could keep an eye on the Plymouth if it was parked between the trucks. Sure enough, it was sitting between a Ford wagon that looked like a jock's car and a cabover Freightliner pulling a bull wagon. Eddy and I were so full of Cokes we could hardly wiggle, but I ordered a couple more as a sort of rent for using the space.

I learned a good lesson watching Morton that night. I saw him get out of his car and take a piss on the trailer tire of the Freightliner, thinking no one was looking. It was a repugnant thing to do with two ladies in the car. He was swaying back and forth as he was trying to zip up his pants while walking back to the car. I considered swooping by and saving Marylyn from this crazy daredevil, but if she didn't want to leave them, I would look like an idiot and be banished from her for life. I was in a tight spot.

At exactly 10:00, the Corvette pulled into Billie's coming from the opposite direction it had left. It came around my left and stopped broadside in front of our slot, showing only the girl's side again. She motioned us to follow with a jerk of her head and rolled up her window as they departed the drive-in. I set the Cokes on the tray and backed out, glancing once more over at the truck lot, making sure Morton was still there. We headed out, following the Corvette's taillights down what was going to be frontage road on completion of the new freeway.

About two miles south, The Pharaoh left the highway, going through a construction site filled with cats and scrapers shutdown for the weekend. He had done his scouting well, since the place he had chosen to race was smooth and unnoticed. As we were shooting down the mass of cement, I told Eddy to insist that we were not going to do a standing start, because I had my street tires on and my high gears in for the winter.

Upon leaving Billie's, I had noticed the Corvette had traction bars and cheater slicks, like it was the middle of racing season. I also noticed, by following him, he had really low gears, and he was shifting a four-speed. The Pharaoh slowed and pulled to the right side of the highway. As I rolled up to his left, Eddy started in on him about how we would roll with him, but no standing starts. The guy began to bitch like hell, but Eddy kept to his guns while I thumped the throttle a couple of times. I could barely hear them yelling over the sound of the exhaust belching from the 16 cylinders. Eddy reached his arm out the window and yelled that we were going on three.

The Pharaoh and I synchronized our speed so we were both doing about 20 mph when Eddy dropped his arm.

"One," then, "two," and then, "three!"

And we were gone.

The Corvette went to second almost immediately, reaching ten grand, at least by the sound of his pipes. He had gotten the jump on us, but we gained a little in the top end of first while he was in the middle of second. I reached for the Hurst-Campbell shifter and slammed it into second without letting up, and by then, he still had us by a half-car length. He gained again, as my '40 was struggling through the lower part of second gear, while he had speed shifted into third.

This was the longest I'd ever looked at another car while racing one, and I wasn't taking it well. At the top end of second, we were gaining again as he was in the low end of fourth. When we were in the final phase, I knew I would win, because I had the big cubic inches that come on at the end. I passed him, and by looking at my tach, I knew we weren't to the end yet. Victory was mine, but I knew that scenario was coming to an end. The next one, or the one after him, was going to get me, and I wasn't willing to keep spending the money and working to be the fastest in town. It was over. I had bigger fish to fry.

I found a turn-around a couple of miles to the south, which put us on the northbound side, returning toward the lights of Willamette. Eddy seemed alright with that since he needed to get out to the metals plant in time for the graveyard shift. When the Corvette passed us, the chick with the hat was looking straight ahead and holding her middle finger against the window. It was long and straight with a red fingernail at the top, making it look like a used stiletto, but The Pharaoh gave us a little wave over the top of his car. It made me think he was probably worth knowing.

Chapter 24

Upon our return to Billie's, I saw headlights in the gravel lot doing a circling pattern next to the drive-in, like they were on the end of a tether ball, going round and round. I dumped Eddy off at his Simca and then looped the place with a fearful premonition of what I was going to find. It was Morton and his Plymouth doing cookies, throwing gravel and spinning one way and then the other. It was like my dreaded memory of Miles going round and round with his cousin at the wheel.

I had just made the decision to jump in and intercede the moment the car stopped when my right door opened. It was Eddy in a panic.

"My car won't start," he said out of breath from the run across the parking lot. "I need a ride out to the plant or I'll lose my job for sure."

He sounded desperate, and I knew I needed to help him, but I was kind of busy at the time.

"Get in and hang on," I said as I dumped the clutch and hit the throttle.

The metals plant laid about four miles to the north on a two-lane highway that was pretty straight except for the S corner about a mile from the plant's front gate. When I reached the road, I went through the gears just as I had done a few minutes before beside the Corvette. Eddy was hanging on the armrest with his right hand and had his lunch pail under his left arm like it was a football. He had no idea what the hurry was, but I'm sure he surmised it had something to do with the circling Plymouth back at Billie's.

We came into the S corner on compression of the downshift to second, and I barely hit the brakes, accelerating on through the corner with my bumper scraping pavement on the right side and my left rear fender peeling the white off the side of my rear tire. I had just gotten into high when I put the coupe on its nose and pulled into the entryway of the place. Barely stopping, I told Eddy to get out, and a moment later, I was going south through the gears.

It was déjà vu when I hit the corner, my bumper skidded and the tires squealed, but I came out of it right side up with my foot planted on the gas. Like I was afraid of, the Plymouth was gone when I got back to Billie's. The people who had been watching the spectacle told me he kept saying he was going to beat the train, leaving like a madman about a minute before I arrived.

As I exited the lot, I looked at my watch and scanned the gauges, none offered good news. My heat gauge said 230 and was climbing, while my gas gauge was on empty, and my watch said 10:54. I was accelerating towards

South Town and praying I wouldn't run out of gas before I got a chance to do whatever I was going to do. I hadn't put that part of the plan together yet, hoping it would come to me later.

I was weaving in and out of traffic, using both lanes and sometimes the oncoming one if needed. I saw the Plymouth up ahead, pulling out of Pop's and heading south on the wrong side of the road.

At the same time, I saw three kids on bikes appear on the left up ahead, and they looked as if they were going to cross the highway for Pop's.

"Don't do it," I was saying and praying at the same time.

There was no way I could stop.

Thank God, Morton had toured through the drive-in on his way to rendezvous with the eleven o'clock train. He was pouring the coal into the Plymouth, and I wasn't sure if I could catch him, but if I didn't, it wouldn't be from lack of trying.

I had to be going close to 100 mph when I went by Pop's. The bike pilots held their ground and braced themselves for the blast of wind they knew was coming. On the other side of the street, a throng of people were watching the Plymouth leave and me racing after it. I didn't dare look down at my watch, but I knew I was running out of time as I was changing lanes and pushing the throttle through the floor board.

The moment I realized I was gaining on him, I saw red lights in my mirror, which told me I had company. I wasn't slowing for anything, including a cop. I was within a couple of car lengths behind the Plymouth when I saw another cop coming off a side street with its lights and siren going with no chance of ever catching us before this thing was over.

It seemed like slow motion as I crept by them on the right, where I could see Marylyn pushing back in the seat with a look of terror in her eyes. With less than a quarter of a mile between us and the tracks, the warning lights began to flash on each side of the highway.

As soon as I was clear of his bumper, I reefed on the wheel, turning left in front of the car, careful not to go into a spin, then I righted and put on the brakes, preparing for the impact that was coming when he hit the back of my car.

I wasn't disappointed. He crashed into my rear bumper like I was standing still, but I recovered quickly, and lay on the brake pedal as hard as I could push. I could smell the asbestos burning off the brakes in the smoke coming through the floor, but I wasn't slowing him down much. Morton, in his drunken stupor, still had his foot on the throttle and was going to push me into the train that had just appeared to my left.

I could tell he had miscalculated with his timing or speed, because he would have been too late and would have hit the train, killing them all. The bad news was, they were still going to get killed, and so was I.

About the time I was certain of doom, we began to slow, and I assumed it was because Morton finally got his fat-ass foot off the pedal. I could see the eyes of the train passengers getting bigger from us getting closer and with growing astonishment as the spectacle developed.

I had both hands gripping the wheel and both feet on the brake pedal when we finally came to a stop inches from the track as the caboose came flying by. My whole car was engulfed in smoke, and I could see my hands locked on my steering wheel, but I couldn't release them.

Once I remembered to breathe, I started coughing and it brought me back. I opened the door and stepped out into a scene of chaos and destruction, with two sets of blinking lights coming through the smoke and the sound of sirens. Morton was out of his car, hanging over the door puking green and yellow slime, looking too scared to be remorseful yet. Susan was frozen in place, in the middle of the front seat, with her hands over her eyes like she was still waiting to leave this world.

I stepped through the opening between the cars, walking through steaming radiator coolant with its distinctive smell on my way to where Marylyn was exiting the car. When she looked up and saw me, her legs buckled as she collapsed into my arms. I almost carried her to my car, and then I held her there, with one arm around her, while I opened the door. She shook her head like she didn't ever want to get into another car, but I assured her she would be okay now.

Shutting the door gently, I returned through the opening and stepped over the fluids as I assessed the damage to the back of my coupe, wondering if it was still drivable. A cop was coming up to Morton as I was turning for the door, and our eyes met. In the cop's eyes was a look of pure disbelief that soon disappeared as he prepared to do business with Morton.

As I entered the car, I reached down for my red shop rag and put it into Marylyn's hands. She fell into me, laying her head on my shoulder, and I could feel her tears as I reached for the starter button.

The Olds groaned as the starter slowly rolled it over, like it was asking what more I wanted from it. It roared as it fired, and I pulled the shifter into first and drove.

The End

Acknowedgements

My editor, Addie Maguire, a dynamo who came to me after I had written and rewritten the book once. She was relentless in her pursuit of quality concerning my novel.

We hit it off, since we both seem to be in a hurry. She graduated from Oregon State University in 2011, at the age of nineteen. I finished faster, but I skipped the last three years. She never got sidetracked, deviated, or lost hope. It was always full-bore ahead. I will forever cherish the memory of our many meetings when I pleaded my case over a Coors Light and she would banter back over her herbal tea.

Thank you, Addie

My girlfriend and the love of my life, Kathie Whitmire, was such a help in so many ways. She is a librarian and knows books. She supported me from the very start with enthusiasm and patience.

Thank you, Kathie

And thanks to:
William Gedney for taking the picture (cover photo) in Leatherwood, Kentucky, in 1964. The Cornett family for hosting him for the eleven days in which he photographed the parents and the twelve children. The Duke University's David M. Rubenstein Rare Book & Manuscript Library for the safekeeping of the image. Elizabeth Dunn, research librarian, for helping me get their permission to use it.

About the Author

Jim Lindsay was born in Corvallis, Oregon, on February 18, 1947. He was raised on a farm that sustained him, his parents, and brother, Bob, near Shedd, Oregon. After eight years of education in a two-room grade school, he attended and graduated from Albany Union High School. A stint in the Navy Reserve and a year and half of college was followed by 42 years of farming. He has two children, Caralee and Jake, and a girlfriend, Kathie. Jim lives on the same farm where he was raised, with his dog, Ruby. He is a hot rodder, drag racer, and pilot of a land speed racecar.

email: jimlindsay@peak.org
website: jimlindsayauthor.com